**She knew he was innocent, now she just had to prove it...**

Dita felt her insides turn to mush, but she managed to stand firm. "Why do I get the feeling you don't really think you're arresting the right person, Detective Milton. If you have the right person in Dan, then how could it be unsafe?"

"Dita!" Dan snapped.

"No, let me say it. Having Dan in custody will temporarily take the heat off you. But I'll be on your case should you stop looking for Arlen's killer. And after you have thoroughly dragged us through the mud, caused us to shoulder extraordinary expense, I will still be on your case."

"I'm not going to respond to that," Milton said.

Duffy put his hand on Dita's arm, but she wanted to have the last word. She was desperate. "You need to investigate his board. I think they were in total disarray at the end. One of them knows something. Promise me you'll investigate every last one of them."

Duffy placed his hand on Dan's shoulder and squeezed. Then Dan was led away to a holding cell.

"Those are artist's hands. They are meant to express. Those are not murdering hands," Dita said, watching in horror.

Ballerina Dita Marx and her composer husband, Dan Di Bello, have a two o'clock appointment at the now-boarded-up Harlem Center for the Arts with board president, Arlen Van Aiken, whose board voted to close down the center, which was very painful for the community, as well as Dita and Dan. They want to retrieve *The Phoenix*, a statue created in memorial to three board members lost when the World Trade Center collapsed September 11, 2001. But Dita is late, and Dan goes into the center looking for Arlen, whom he finds murdered in the basement, bludgeoned with the very statue Dan has come to collect. When the bodies begin to pile up and Dan is later arrested for murder, Dita is outraged and determined to prove his innocence—even if it means risking her own life...

## KUDOS for *Locked Out*

In *Locked Out* by Sarah Levine Simon, Dita Di Bello and her husband Dan have been working for the Harlem Arts Center, but now it's closed by the board of directors. The community is understandably upset, since the center held dance and music lessons for the children. In addition, many people lost their jobs. When Dan and Dita come to the center to meet with the president of the board, they discover the man has been murdered. And Dan is the prime suspect...Full of marvelous characters, intrigue, and suspense, this is a mystery you won't want to miss. ~ *Taylor Jones, The Review Team of Taylor Jones & Regan Murphy*

*Locked Out* by Sarah Levine Simon is a story of greed, corruption, and murder. When the board of directors for the Harlem Arts Center closes the center without notice, the people who work there are outraged, especially Dita and Dan Di Bello. But when they arrive at the center to confront the board president, he has been murdered. Since Dan discovered the body, he becomes the main suspect. Dan is arrested, and Dita, four months pregnant, is determined to prove he didn't do it, but as she digs for the truth, she uncovers more than she bargained for. The author's character development is superb, her plot solid, and the mystery intriguing, making *Locked Out* one you will really enjoy. ~ *Taylor Jones, The Review Team of Taylor Jones & Regan Murphy*

# LOCKED OUT

Sarah Levine Simon

*A Black Opal Books Publication*

GENRE: MYSTERY-DETECTIVE/WOMEN SLEUTHS/AMATEUR
SLEUTHS

First Publication: MARCH 2019

Published by Black Opal Books **http://www.blackopalbooks.com**

# LOCKED OUT

# CHAPTER 1

Dan Di Bello pulled the Jeep up to the front of the arts center and double-parked. He didn't want to get out. He'd been dreading this all day. Strange word "dread." It also described a momentary emptiness he'd felt from time to time in contemplation of his own mortality. Dan let a long moment pass before finally getting out of the car. It was a fine August day, and he would have preferred a stroll in Central Park. However, a work of art remained in this boarded-up building formerly called the Harlem Center for the Arts, and he needed to get it out of there. His wife, ballerina Dita Marx, had founded and directed the center until its board deemed it fiscally unviable and closed its doors forever. If the rumors of drug dealers now infesting the property were to be believed, it could be dangerous to go in there. Dita was supposed to meet Dan here one last time. But dammit, she was late.

Dita hadn't taken ballet class in several months and had asked Dan if he would mind if she went to an eleven-thirty class at Steps on Broadway, before meeting up with him at the center. Dan had been fine with it. It would probably relax her. His sylph-like wife still turned heads in a ballet studio. He savored the image—curly brown hair frizzing out of a makeshift bun and a sheen of sweat beaded across the freckled bridge of her straight nose, almond shaped hazel eyes beaming out of a heart-shaped face, and those long elegant arms that were her trademark as a dancer. She was four months pregnant and just beginning to show. The belly poking out of her leotard would cut a different profile.

❧❧❧

Dita's ballet class ended at one p.m. She did "barre," some of "center," and then she wistfully watched the new crop of ballet dancers leap, jump, and pirouette across the mirrored studio, cannily avoiding the room's pillars. It was too early to head uptown so Dita took time for a bowl of chicken soup at the Fairway Café next door to Steps. The café was jammed and she ended up taking the soup outside where she sat on a bench on an island in the middle of Broadway and Seventy-Fifth Street with its sliver of greenery behind her, traffic racing both up and downtown on either side. Her feet rested on the grate over the subway fifty feet below. It felt good to be part of the pulse of this part of the city. The air, clean by New York City standards, was enlivened by the scent of greenery.

At one-thirty p.m., she headed into the Seventy-Second Street subway station for the uptown number three-train. The train arrived after ten minutes. It was crowded but Dita got into it anyway, grasping at a pole with a cluster of other passengers their bodies pressing uncomfortably into hers. The doors closed and the train departed for the Ninety-Sixth Street stop, but then it slowed down, lights flickering, and stopped in the tunnel between stations. The alarming smell of something electric overheating filled her nostrils. Barely discernable through the static, a voice over a loud speaker informed the passengers that due to a track fire there would be a slight delay. Dita suddenly had to pee. She had swigged from a bottle of water while she ate the soup. She was beginning to regret the accumulation of liquid. Now she was so late Dan would undoubtedly enter the center and confront Arlen Van Aiken alone.

The subway car remained in the tunnel. An elderly woman hugged the same pole as Dita and began to spew vile invectives about the Metropolitan Transportation Authority. Dita sought to distance herself but she was captive. "They do it deliberately," the woman ranted on. "I've lived here all my life and don't believe any crap about things getting better. They just make sure Grand Central and Lincoln Center look good and the rest of the city can go to hell. I'd like to see Hizzoner down here among us. I'd fart on him. No, I'd shit in his face." A few people laughed. Most tried to look away. Dita didn't dare laugh. Her bladder was now painfully full and she squeezed to hold back a stream of urine. Pregnancy certainly brings on new inconveniences, she thought. The train started up with a jolt. *Finally!*

At Ninety-Sixth Street, she got out and ran upstairs to a McDonalds to pee. She tried Dan's cell and got no answer. Afraid to go back down into the subway, she hailed a cab. Everyone had the same idea and there were no cabs available. She started to walk up Broadway, thinking to catch a bus across town at 125th. A glance at her watch told her she couldn't possibly make the two o'clock appointment. Dan would be angry with her but the circumstances were beyond her control. Everything in her life seemed beyond her control lately. She hoped to find Dan fuming in the Jeep with the statue and the encounter with Arlen Van Aiken over without her.

യൗ

In a community garden adjoining the center, a team of elderly gardeners worked diligently and waved when they saw Dan approach. They were the eyes and ears of the neighborhood. Their garden was lush and verdant, a series of tiny raised plots. They gardened above ground. It meant more watering but the soil was organic and they could eat what they grew without worry about what had been dumped in the Harlem soil over the years.

Staked cucumber vines and spicy pepper plants flowered. Morning glory vines fastened their tendrils firmly to the bars of the fence and had climbed until they hung over the top. A variety of cutting flowers bloomed graciously in abundant clusters of color—dahlias, zinnias, cosmos, daisies and fleshy cockscombs. The sunflowers had grown to the height of ten feet. The productivity and bountifulness of the garden stood in stark contrast with the boarded up arts center. Dan's soft brown eyes misted over remembering the rich cultural community Dita had created with her hard toil.

Oliver Outlaw, otherwise known as "Tomato Man," came to the wrought iron fence, and put his hand out to shake Dan's. Dan wasn't a tall man but he towered over Oliver. He was famous for growing huge yellow and red heirlooms he fertilized with a mixture of fish scraps from R&B fish, and compost he collected from his friends and neighbors. As usual he wore a Yankee cap over his bald-head.

"How you been. How is the missus?" Stout Earline Wilson remained on her knees weeding but waved to Dan. Getting up and down was a problem for her. Two women were gabbing and shading themselves on a bench in a far corner. They waved to Dan then quickly returned

to their chat, leaving Dan to make conversation with Tomato Man.

"We're surviving, Olie." Dan pushed a lock of wavy
hair off his face. Since the closing of the center the dark
brown was more threaded with gray.

"We miss you all. How 'bout some tomatoes?"

"Can't say no to that."

"You better not. Heirlooms. Only kind I grow."

"I have a meeting in there with Arlen, I'll come and
chat with you on my way out. I came to get the Phoenix
statue. It's going to have a new home in the Schomburg
Center."

"That's good," Tomato Man said, shaking his head
and indicating the boarded-up building next door. "That
statue is sacred."

"Yes, it is," said Dan, whose thoughts turned to Ricardo Montero, a local sculptor, who had created the statue of the *Phoenix*, a flaming bird representing rebirth, in
memory of center family members lost September 11,
2001, when the World Trade Center collapsed. The statue
was created out of lively colored enamel over metal, and
had stood in a wall niche in the center parlor floor. Dita
and Dan had come to think of the *Phoenix* as a protector.
Indelible in their memory were those lost—Ferdie Forbush who traded stocks by day and spent every evening
he could at the opera. He loved the arts and freely gave of
advice and funding; Josh Grogan, who was having a
powwow breakfast at Windows On the World that fateful
morning; Jesus Avila, a waiter at Window's on the
World, who was so proud that his children learned to play
and sing at the center. He helped out in many small and
large ways with mechanical, gardening, and painting
skills and served on the arts center's board as its neighborhood representative.

When Dita had told Ricardo that the center had

closed, he told her emphatically he wanted his work back. "I don't trust those bastards," he said, referring to the board members. Now that Ricardo had a following and exhibited in prominent galleries, Dan felt his request was reasonable. The board members would probably argue that the sculpture was commissioned and therefore the property of the center. If Dan remembered correctly the commission amounted to five hundred dollars paid in two installments—really a joke.

Tomato Man interrupted Dan's thoughts. "Let me know if you need help. But you be careful in there. Before they boarded the windows there was a drug dealer sneaking in there. Then a coupla homeless guys. Don't know if anyone's in there now. Best be on the alert."

"Hopefully the only person in there is Arlen."

"I ain't seen him come out."

"Well then the meeting is on."

Dan felt clammy apprehension. But if Arlen was in there, he thought it would be all right. "Thanks, Olie," Dan said. "I will be very careful."

He crossed the center's paved front yard. The building was a brownstone located in a block-long row of brownstones in varying degrees of repair. Some were mere shells. Dan saw that the ground floor entry door of the center stood partially open. He waded through a heap of take-out menus and other debris into the doorway and pushed the door open even further.

The interior was totally dark. He felt for a light switch. He found one near the doorframe and tried to flip it on. The electricity was turned off. With the windows boarded up, no light could enter. "Arlen," he called out. Then Dan repeated the name. He heard his own voice echoing in the empty building. He could barely make out the staircase leading to the parlor level and was hesitant to wander in the dark. He heard a whirring. A sound a bat would make. But didn't bats sleep during the daytime? What could he possibly find? *I'm a grown man. Why am I freaking out over neighborhood rumors? Even drug dealers need light.* Dan returned to the Jeep where he found a powerful flashlight in the glove compartment.

As he returned to the center, Tomato man came once again to the fence. "When I seen him go in there about twenty minutes ago, I pretended I didn't know who he was."

The image of the wizened old man ignoring the Armani-clad fop made Dan laugh. "Did he come by car again?"

"Wouldn't dare bring that fancy car up here."

"Guess not!"

Dan anxiously consulted his watch again. He looked at his cell phone to double-check the time. "One of us will probably have to stay with the Jeep if we can't park in front of the center," he had told Dita.

Parking spaces were a rare commodity on the art center block. He worried about getting a parking ticket. They couldn't afford the fifty dollars right now.

Dita was probably avoiding this encounter, Dan thought. She'd had an attack of nerves just thinking about seeing Arlen. They'd had practically no contact with him since he, as board president, had closed the center.

Flashlight in hand, Dan returned to the boarded up building and stepped inside. He mounted the staircase. His light beam fell on balls of dust that had accumulated in the corners of the stairs. No one had swept in months. The center was sadly abandoned, which Dan didn't want Dita to see. She was taking the center's closing very hard. His very spirited wife had become dispirited and unmoored with nowhere to channel her energy. Their baby was coming, and because of the loss of Dita's job, they found themselves in dire financial straits. Dita believed in

Dan's compositions and didn't want him to stop composing in order to take a day job. He wanted Dita to fulfill
her dream of making dances. They wanted to collabo-
rate—his compositions, her choreography. The center had
provided Dita with a weekly albeit not very lucrative salary they both depended on.

Dan felt a surge of new anger. When he reached the
parlor floor, it too felt closed in by the boarded up windows. From above he heard the whirring sound again.
Maybe Arlen was doing something up there. It was difficult to illuminate the entire space and he began to inspect
the parlor in segments. The front parlor windows had had
a leaded glass border that would allow prisms of daylight
to flood the parquet floor on a sunny day. This was where
they had held concerts. It had served as a dance studio as
well. Where were those beautiful windows? The bastards
sold off salvage after they closed the center. They had
turned the center into another Harlem shell.

Today the room was lifeless and still. The portable
ballet bars and the roll of Marley flooring brought out for
dance classes were gone. The grand piano was gone as
well—ten feet of polished ebony and a mellifluous, rich
sound, a joy to play on. The instrument was worth upward of one hundred thousand dollars. They'd have to
ask Arlen about the pianos. There were other fine pianos
as well in the center's classrooms. Then Dan saw the wall
niche where the Phoenix had stood. It was empty. So Arlen must have already had the sculpture removed. He
steeled himself to search the two upper floors.

All he found were more empty dank rooms with
windows boarded up. The other pianos were missing as
well. Antique glass was missing throughout the building.
Wires hung from the ceilings where chandeliers had provided kaleidoscopic, dancing light that made the rooms
sparkle. Arlen couldn't have intended for him to see this.

But where was Arlen anyway? The only place he had not searched for Arlen was the ground floor and the basement, but there was no reason Arlen would be there—the only things in the area were the mechanicals, a workbench, and some storage.

ల౧ల౧

As Dita continued walking uptown on Broadway, the day of the lock out replayed in her mind. It was May first. Just conjuring up the shock of it sent frissons of anger throughout her body. Fifteen years of her hard toil had gone for naught. In the years of running the center, she had developed an urge to create dances. On the center youth, she honed her skills and grew into a choreographer. As her dance students matured and some of them became advanced enough for professional training, she dreamed of starting a troupe. Teaching and making dances came to her more naturally than being a ballet dancer alone. Maybe that was part of the reason a different path was chosen for her, she reasoned. At breakfast that morning in early May, she found herself toying with the rims of mason jars. She stood the circles up by laying a spatula over the bottoms. A dance using circular objects began to form in her mind. The jar rims jangled in her pocket book as she walked. She intended to begin work on her dance that afternoon.

Instead, when she came to work that fateful morning, she found a crowd milling outside of the Center. Among them four music students from the Juilliard school she had booked to talk about chamber music. The talk about chamber music would touch on cooperation and teamwork. Part of what Dita loved about running the center was that it gave her the ability to send messages to her students. The arts could convey these concepts so well.

Dita remembered wondering why a fire drill would be scheduled first thing in the morning when the kids were just arriving. In addition to her overstuffed pocket book with its jangling mason lids, Dita's arms had been full of books and music in a torn shopping bag.

A line of school buses filled with children waited at the curb. She had recognized the angry faces of two of the teachers who were miffed that the center was apparently closed.

As she drew closer, she saw the gray blue cap and folded arms of an enormous red headed security guard. Dita quickened her pace, but the shopping bag gave way and books plunged onto the pavement. Dita's assistant, Marge Bliss, an older African American woman, shook her head and rushed over to help. Marge had tears in her eyes.

"Something tells me this morning is totally out of control," Dita had said.

"No, it's very much under control. We're locked out!" Marge gathered the books to her ample bosom as Dita slipped the remaining few under her arms and rushed toward the guard. The Center and an adjacent community garden had been padlocked with massive chains. The neighborhood gardeners groused as they waited with pails and shovels.

"They won't even let us in to water the plants. Everything's going to die if we can't get in there," Tomato Man said.

Dita handed the rest of the books to Marge and the crowd parted enough to let her through. She'd found herself looking from the hooded eyes and doughy face of the security guard to the badge. It read Dirk. Dirk the Jerk, she had thought. "What is going on here, Dirk?"

"Place is closed down is all I know."

The center cat, a little black tuxedo kitty with a white

bowtie and three white paws, mewed incessantly from behind the barred window of the front office. Then he appeared on the building roof as if contemplating a jump. "Someone must have left the skylight open. My beautiful cat almost leapt to his death. I work here. I'm the director. I need to go in there," Dita said, as she drew herself up as far as her five-foot-four-inch frame would allow.

"'Fraid that's not possible," the security guard said.

"That animal is hungry. It's inhumane to lock him in there like that."

"Cat's been crying for the past twelve hours since they come with the locks," a bystander screamed.

"Got my orders."

"From who?"

"Mr. Van."

"Van Aiken?"

"He ordered this place closed, Miss."

"We'll see about that."

Dita reached into her pocket book and flipped open her cell phone. The number was readily available but Arlen wasn't picking up. She waited an eternity for the outgoing message. "I think I'm entitled to an explanation and so are the people standing out here on the sidewalk with me. There is an animal starving to death inside, and I'm going to call the ASPCA if you don't let him out immediately."

A hired car had parked in front of a fire hydrant and the driver went around to the back passenger door to help Violet Peters, an elderly African American woman, get out. Help, she didn't need. She had stood rock solid, her arms crossed in mimicry of the security guard. Violet was buxom with a full round face, dark eyes that usually twinkled humorously, but not today. Dita thought she'd never seen Violet wear the same outfit twice. Today she wore a mint-colored light spring wool suit that made her coffee colored face glow under her wide-brimmed hat. The hat had matching trim. White patent pumps completed the outfit. Violet had been an esteemed mezzo soprano at the Metropolitan opera; and her connections with boards at Carnegie Hall, and Lincoln Center helped to open and sustain the center as a place where neighborhood children could learn to dance or play an instrument, where the ability to pay for lessons did not matter. The center was Dita's brainchild and Violet was a staunch supporter early on.

Violet had hugged Dita tightly. "I was out-voted. I wasn't supposed to tell you but I tried to call you last night."

Dita choked back tears. "I heard your name in the messages but it was midnight and I thought it was too late to return the call, and I didn't want to call too early."

"For what it's worth, Dita, I'm sorry. The board changed. No one really kept me informed. Everything was discussed before the meetings. They voted to close up the center. Lord only knows why."

The guard's phone had rung and everybody watched as he nodded in response to what he was being told. He closed the phone nervously and addressed Dita and Violet. "That was the boss man." His pale face grew so red with fear, Dita almost felt sorry for him.

"You mean the board president Arlen Van Aiken?"

"If you say so. He said to tell you at ten a.m. the doors will be open for an hour so you can get your personal items."

"For one hour to collect half-a-life time of stuff," Marge demanded. She looked haggard. Her creamy brown skin had taken on a grayish twinge, making Dita worry for her. "And what about our pay checks?" Marge continued.

"Didn't tell me nothing about no paychecks."

"What should we do with the kids?" demanded a teacher. The buses weren't supposed to come back for them until after lunch. "This is a mess. A lot of these kids have to pee now. They've been sitting on this bus since early morning."

"Can I make a suggestion?" Dita took charge, despite the shock of the situation. "Let's walk them over to the library. I'm so sorry this was handled in this way."

As Dita continued to walk up Broadway, she frowned as she remembered Arlen Van Aiken, driving up the day of the closing in his BMW, top down. Showing his usual arrogance, he'd acted like the closing of the center was business as usual. Never mind the lives of students and teachers affected by his actions. All business, Van Aiken had gotten out of his car, straightened his tie, and smoothed his Armani jacket. Rex Turner, Arlen's maintenance man had arrived with a key to the padlock. He looked so uncomfortable, caught between their opposing forces. Rex personified "workman." He wore a well-worn leather tool belt crammed with carpenter's tools around his waist. A pair of work gloves had been clipped onto a loop on his overalls. He was tall and well muscled. He spoke in a gravelly voice with a hint of the south. "I'm bricking windows down on that shell on One Hundred Ninety-Ninth Street like you asked. The cement's going to dry up." He impatiently ran his hand through his short Afro as he looked from Dita with her folded arms to Arlen with his superior smug grin.

"Good," Arlen had said, "but get back here in an hour to close up." Rex meekly agreed with a slight head nod. Dita knew that Arlen had humiliated Rex by making him his gofer. His discomfort was obvious. What she thought was a sympathetic look passed from Rex's eyes to Dita. *Rex was a strange one. Hard to read!*

When Rex had gone, Dita had turned to Arlen. "So? You had to close up the community garden, too?"

"There was no choice. It was all part-and-parcel of the center's assets," Arlen had said, sounding like William F. Buckley. "It's business, Dita. You had your hand in it, too."

"Don't start making accusations here," Dita snapped.

"You ignored our budgetary concerns," he said. She had let him get to her and winced, embarrassed by her choreography daydreams. Arlen crossed over to the security guard, and Dita could hear his strict instructions. "They can have one hour, and that's it!"

Dita noticed Violet eying the drooping shoots of the plants with a self-satisfied air about her. Violet was one of the most stubborn human beings Dita had ever dealt with and, fortunately, her dear friend. Violet pursed her lush lips and a long guttural sigh issued from her throat. The gardening folks had just that very week done their spring planting. The little plants wouldn't survive without a daily watering. *More effort gone to naught!*

"I think somebody ought to go get a wrench and open the fire hydrant. I think the bus driver might have one," Violet said and turned to one of the teachers with the smuggest of grins. "Why don't you go see, and bring some of those kids out to help us send the water in there?"

Dita had seen this look on Violet's face many times before. "I'm afraid to find out what you have in mind."

The teacher had returned with a driver who opened the hydrant. The water spurted out with force. The kids streamed out of the bus. Violet gathered them around and spoke to them in a low voice. "Everything is going to get watered." Little hands converged on the spigot and water jetted in a huge arc right to where Arlen Van Aiken was still giving instructions to Dirk. Both of them jumped back. Arlen's drenched Armani suit clung to his body.

"What did you make those kids do?" Furious, he charged toward Violet, who whispered to the kids again.

Next the kids aimed the spray on the interior of the BMW.

"You're going to pay for the damages, Violet."

"What? Armani melts like the wicked witch of the west?" Violet said to an operatic chorus of laughter. "Anyone riding top down in this neighborhood is askin' for it. You, of all people, should know better, Arlen, Just open the goddamned garden. Otherwise, you're going to be in fear of your life!"

"You'd better do it," Dita said.

"Okay! Okay! I'll let the garden stay open."

The crowd had cheered and jeered at the drenched duo of Van Aiken and his security guard.

෴

Latter on that day when the last of the buses had pulled away from the curb bringing the children back to their various schools, Dita had been able to convince a drenched Arlen Van Aiken, to give them a few more hours to pack up their personal belongings. Then Arlen had driven off in his sopping vehicle, the butt of relentless laughter. Dita imagined him entering his Fifth Avenue residence to get himself changed as she watched the silver beamer weave through the congested street and disappear in front of a city bus. Back at the center, the gardeners continued to laugh as they tended to their tiny plots of earth. Chattering old women sunned themselves on the benches and talked with great satisfaction about "the hosing."

Violet, Dita, and Marge were alone in the center for

the last time. With all of its windows closed, it felt stale and dank—a shabby building, devoid of life, its paint peeling, linoleum scuffed. Someone would pull down the bulletin boards covered with concert ticket information, sell off the scored chalkboards milky with chalk dust where little hands wrote out scales and triads. Dita supposed the murals painted by local artists and their art students would be painted over to give the building a generic life.

Rex Turner hovered nearby listening to Dita's interchange with Marge and Violet. He was taking measurements of the window frames and jotting numbers down on a pad.

"Since you have your tools, do you think you could help us remove the *Phoenix*?" Dita had asked Rex.

Rex scowled. "That's got to go through Van Aiken. And he won't be back today. I don't want no trouble from him."

"You know, you don't have to be Arlen's stooge," Dita said.

"It's work, Ms. Marx, with all due respect. I need to hurry, so if you ladies can finish up in here, then I can lock up." He moved onto another floor with his notebook and tape measure. When he was out of earshot, Violet said, "Part of me can't fault Rex for being a stooge. He has a wife with some sort of horrible degenerative disease. She keeps getting worse and needs more and more care."

"Arlen hates that statue. He calls it Hispanic kitsch. It would be so simple to take it with us."

Dita tried Arlen's cell to no avail. She left a message asking him to set a time for the sculptor Ricardo Montero to get his work. Her calls were not returned. The sculptor also tried to call. Three months had gone by, and he had finally threatened Arlen with a lawsuit. That did the trick.

But Ricardo was in Puerto Rico. He told Dita that the Schomburg Center wanted to exhibit the work and had asked if she and Dan could get the statue and take it there.

Dita had called Arlen once again.

This time he answered. "What can I do for you?" Arlen had asked with the usual noblesse oblige. *The vain bastard still has all of his hair, albeit silver to match the spoon in his mouth. This is as casual as the man can get.*

Dita dispensed with greetings and salutations and came to the point. "Dan and I can be at the center on August ninth, that's tomorrow. We promised Ricardo we'd pick up the Phoenix sculpture. It's going to have a new home in the Schomburg Center."

"How about two o'clock?"

"Works well. We need to get it to The Schomburg Center before five o'clock.

❧❧❧

Arlen had put down the phone, aware his wife Mindy was watching him.

"The artist, again?" Mindy asked. "You seem so nervous."

*The woman is a bother*, Arlen thought. *If she thinks the designer shoes make her look taller or the bobbed nose makes her look less Jewish she is much mistaken.* His daughter was beginning to look just like Mindy. He wouldn't say these things. He knew his unkindness would tip her towards a messy divorce he could ill afford. He also knew he could never live on his own trust fund alone. That was the problem with old conservative money, set up in an unbreakable trust in another era.

Rex Turner had called to ask if he could pick up his check and Arlen reluctantly wrote out a check for him from his personal account. These payments couldn't continue. He needed desperately to raise cash.

❧❧❧

There was still no sign of Arlen Van Aiken. Flashlight in hand, Dan descended to the ground floor. He shined it into the little front office that had been Dita's. More debris. It felt like a dungeon and he backed out, turned, and walked toward the rear of the building. The room leading out to the garden was the building's original kitchen. It had been stripped of its modest appliances and fixtures. He located the entrance to the cellar under the staircase. He found the door ajar and called Arlen's name once again. He consulted his watch. It was now two-fifteen. Where the hell was Dita? He wondered if the basement was rat-infested. If the garden floor felt dungeon-like, he could only imagine the basement. Dan descended the stairs. He shined his flashlight—no sign of vermin. The light landed on a workbench, and on the workbench the Phoenix sculpture was laying akimbo.

Thinking he would retrieve it whether or not Arlen showed up, Dan went to pick up the statue barely managing to hold onto the flashlight at the same time. As he grasped the cumbersome statue, he felt something wet and sticky. Letting the statue rest in the crux of his elbow, he shined the flashlight on the sticky substance on his hand. It had the unmistakable look and metallic smell of blood. He looked for something to wipe his hands on and the statue slipped from his grasp spraying him with its sticky gore as it clattered to the cement floor. Beyond the workbench sprawled a body. Arlen—the back of his head cruelly bashed in, was dead.

Dan backed out of the basement and up the staircase with the flashlight trembling in his shaking hand. When he got outside, he fumbled for his cell phone and punched in 9-1-1. Tomato Man, seeing the look of utter fear on Dan's face, came through the gate. "Mr. Dan, you look like you saw a ghost. What's that all over you?"

"I called the police. I found Arlen Van Aiken in the basement. I think he's dead."

The sirens began to blare. Soon six police cars, a fire truck, and an ambulance blocked the street and a crowd gathered.

"Who called about a body in the basement?" asked an officer named Mulroney.

Dan blurted out that he had had an appointment, and found the body while looking for the sculpture.

"Your appointment was with the deceased? Where is he?"

"In the basement."

"Wait here with officer Clemmons." Mulroney indicated a short, light-skinned black female officer. Detectives emerged from an unmarked car.

"I need to sit down. I need to wash my hands. My clothes are a mess."

"You're not going to be able to wash right away."

"They're covered in blood."

"How did they get that way?" she stared wide-eyed at him, her right hand resting on the gun in her holster.

"From the statue that was supposed to go to the Schomburg Center." Thoughts began to tumble through Dan's brain. He should have washed his hands before calling the police. He realized that he was covered in Arlen's blood. Presumably someone had used the *Phoenix* to murder Arlen and he had touched the weapon. The sculpted flames of the *Phoenix* had caused the horrible bloody striations he'd seen on the back of Arlen's head. The sight of the terrible wound was engraved in his memory. His stomach began to churn. His limbs weakened. He heaved his breakfast and lunch onto the pavement between his legs. Tomato Man could vouch for him. He must have heard Dan calling for Arlen.

# CHAPTER 2

Detective John Milton, otherwise known as The Poet, arrived with his partner, Detective Sheila Nadler. Milton had ramrod straight posture, his thin hair now streaked with gray was cut military short, and he had the kind of skin that wouldn't tan. His eyes were steely blue. When he was thinking, his eyes got a faraway look and he'd have to bring them back into focus. "What do we have here?" he asked.

"I had an appointment in there," Dan said. "With Arlen Van Aiken. I think he's dead."

"You're covered in blood. What happened?" Detective Nadler asked. She had the blush of youth, of a newly minted officer—tall and athletic looking. She was three or four inches taller than Milton in flat shoes. Her irregular features—a bump on her nose, made her seem attractive in an unconventional way. Her blond hair was held back with a tortoise shell headband. She wore a navy pants suit, white silk shirt. Her shoulder holster protruded from the unbuttoned jacket.

"I tried to pick up our statue to carry it out of the center. It was so dark in there except for my flashlight. I didn't expect to find anything like that. I was so frightened it slipped from my hands. That's when I saw him laying there on the floor."

"We're going to need a sample from your hand and I'm going to need your clothes."

"My clothes?"

"At the station house. I'll send a tech as soon as the ME arrives. Stay with the officer and don't go anywhere." The detectives rushed into the building.

"This is very unpleasant. The blood is drying on—" Dan said to the officer. His cell phone kept ringing but blood covering the screen obscured the phone number.

"Just hold on. What did you say your name was?"

"Di Bello. Dan Di Bello."

*ᗕᏇᗕᏇ*

Dita reached 110th Street on foot without seeing a Broadway bus. Why wasn't Dan answering his cell phone? Had something happened to him? She too had heard the rumors about drug dealers and criminals squatting in the center and pressed on as fast as her feet would take her. When she saw a black Lincoln with a livery license, she hailed the driver to take her to the center. The street was impassable and he let her out at the nearest corner. She was told to stay to the other side of the street by a patrolman. Then she saw Dan sitting on the stoop with the policewoman. "That's my husband," she screamed and ran to him. Seeing the blood on his hands, Dita panicked. Her mouth went dry with fear.

"Your hand? What happened?"

"Arlen is dead. I found him."

"How? What? You're covered in blood are you hurt?"

"No!

"I have wipes."

"They don't want me to clean my hand yet."

"What do you mean?"

"I found him, but first I found the Phoenix and I picked it up to take it. It was covered with a sticky substance, then I saw Arlen lying there. Someone smashed him over the head with our statue. I got out of there fast, but I know what I saw."

"Surely they can't think you had anything to do with it. Arlen made a career out of pissing people off." She moved closer to offer him comfort.

"Don't touch me, Dita, you'll get blood all over you. I don't know what they think."

"Oh, my God!" She felt her insides churn and she wanted to heave. It wasn't the morning sickness causing the nausea, but the utter raw fear now consuming her.

こくらこ

Police officers taped off the tiny courtyard entrance with yellow crime scene tape, warning members of the public to keep out. Only police personnel could enter. The medical examiner arrived in a Ford Escape SUV followed by his team in a second SUV. They unloaded equipment and hurried into the building. A reporter kept on the sidelines by police called out questions. "Do they know who the victim is?" Another enterprising reporter entered the community garden to get closer to the sidewalk in front of the center.

こくらこ

In the basement of the arts center, Detective Milton directed the crime scene photographer, and delegated jobs to his squad. Lately he had had a bad run of cases that remained unsolved, including the gang style assassination of one of his officers. There were no new leads to follow. He was at a dead end and he felt the pressure.

He rued the name John Milton because everyone at the precinct called him "The Poet" which was okay when he was on a roll. But now that his solve rate was way down, the nickname took on a different connotation. *Have I gotten to be too sissy a poet to solve a real murder?*

His new partner, Detective Sheila Nadler, had a run of early luck in solving a rash of ATM robberies. She was now assigned to homicide and to him. He liked her. He might even like to get into her pants but he knew that would never happen. He smelled ambition on her—or was he recognizing the burnout in himself? "Sheila, talk to the guy who found him and ask if he moved the body. Also, get a tech for a blood sample off Di Bello's hands." He noticed a flashlight that had rolled into a far corner. "Someone get prints off of the flashlight as well. It looks like it might have fallen from the decedent's hand when he was struck." It would be easy for an experienced detective to roll the guy who claimed he only found the victim. John Milton wouldn't let himself be corrupted. Or would he just let the circumstantial evidence speak for itself. Even if Di Bello was innocent, he sure as hell messed up the evidence. It was going to be very difficult to reconstruct the scene using blood spatter and finger printing techniques. And if the perpetrator wore gloves, all they would find would be Di Bello's prints.

The medical examiner rolled the body over, and gently lifted Arlen's limbs. "Rigor Mortis has just begun. I'm gambling that this guy died within the hour."

ശ്രേഷ

Dita and Dan saw a female detective approach holding out her shield for them to see. She was followed by a crime scene tech. "I'm Detective Sheila Nadler and you are?"

"Dan Di Bello. And this is my wife Dita Marx. She was the director of this place."

"We're going to hear the whole story but we need to know if you moved the deceased?"

"No, I called you immediately."

"Okay, Lou is going to get a blood sample from your hand."

"Finally!"

"And finger print him as well," she said. "We'd like to get as large a sample of the blood on your hand as possible."

The tech produced a paper evidence bag. Dan was asked to place his hand on a large square of tape. He winced as the tech applied pressure to the backing of the tape with a flat tongue depressor then pulled off the tape. A bloody image of Dan's hand was transferred to the wide piece of tape. The tech put the sample into the evidence envelope.

"Can he wash his hands now," Dita asked. The tech handed Dan some pre-moistened hand towels in foil packets to cleanse off the blood. He ripped them open, but the thin little paper hand towels quickly became thoroughly soaked in blood.

"Can I please have a few more?"

The tech handed Dan a bunch of packets and Dita helped to open them. "What he really needs is soap and water." She thought about the garden hose. "Can I get the hose over too him?"

"No!" the tech said.

Dan began to try to clean his clothes as well.

"Not yet, buddy. They're going to need your clothes just like they are." The tech handed Dan some more towel packets. This time, his hands were fairly clean. Some stubborn bloodstain remained around his nail beds but still he felt some relief.

The tech now produced a fingerprint kit and Dan acquiesced.

દ્∂લ∂

Detective Sheila Nadler returned to the crime scene. "He says he didn't touch the body. Called us right away. What do you think, John? Did he touch him hard with that sculpture thing?"

"It's almost too pat to find a guy who handled the murder weapon."

"Unless he wanted to get caught."

"Doesn't seem like the type."

"What type is that?"

"He's genuinely riled. He could have just walked out of here closed the door, and nobody would've found the body but the rats."

"Perpetrators usually turn out to be dumb, Sheila." *But she knows this,* he chided himself. He tried not to underscore her inexperience. She learned fast and he admired that. "We need to question the folks working in the garden," he said. "Find out if anybody else came and went."

"I'll put an officer in there," Sheila said, "and tell people not to leave. I think I noticed four people in the garden when we arrived. There was a pesky journalist as well but he was probably monitoring us and rushed over here. I'll ask them what they saw. If anyone else was working with them in there."

Stepping out into the garden, Detective Nadler commandeered a folding table and two chairs. She stationed herself as far away as possible from the gardeners, and interviewed them one at a time. Tomato Man volunteered first.

"Can you state your name for me?"

"Oliver Outlaw."

She raised her eyebrows.

"But everyone call me Tomato Man in here. I grow the best heirlooms you'll ever taste."

She let him ramble a bit more. He seemed shaken, too, the way he kept wringing his hands then removing his Yankee cap and scratching his baldhead. "Were you here in the garden when Mr. Di Bello entered the building?"

"I was."

"Did you talk to him?"

"Little bit. He said he'd catch up with me after he seen Mr. Van Aiken."

"So explain to me who Mr. Van Aiken was."

"He was board head. Shut the center down and tried to lock us outta the garden, too."

"So nobody liked Mr. Van Aiken?"

"He had his team of 'snooties.' Paid us no mind. Thought he was Harlem's greatest gift the way he'd strut through here. Offered him tomatoes and he said he was allergic. Didn't believe that. He just didn't want to put anything into his mouth from Harlem soil."

"What was Mr. Van Aiken's relationship with Mr. Di Bello?"

"Mr. Di Bello married to Ms. Marx, that's Dita. She runs the center. Did great for the kids around here. They got music lessons and dance lessons for free because of her and Violet Peters, you know the opera singer."

"I've heard of her. So how was Mr. Di Bello involved?"

"He helped out. Teached kids how to harmonize. He's a composer."

"Do you know why Mr. Di Bello was here today?"

"To get our memorial statue. Call it the *Phoenix*. We lost three people in the World Trade and someone made a memorial sculpture to them. Not righteous for it to sit around in a closed up building. It means life after dying. Moves people."

"Did you follow Mr. Di Bello into the building?"

"I did not. I was tending my tomato plants. He said we'd talk after he met Mr. Van Aiken. Wish now I'd gone in with him. Bad that! Poor Mr. Di Bello havin' to find a body."

"Mr. Outlaw, did you know Mr. Di Bello would find Arlen Van Aiken dead?"

"No, I did not, but I can't say I'm saddened by his passing."

"Thank you, Mr. Outlaw." She nodded to Earline Wilson to join her at the table.

"I've been down on my knees too long. Can you help me up?"

Detective Nadler crossed the garden and helped her stand. When Earline was seated at the table, she just kept nodding her head. "Something terrible happened? Something terrible?"

"Yes, something terrible. A man was murdered. Did you know him?"

"Tomato Man said it was Mr. Van Aiken."

"Did you see Mr. Van Aiken enter the center?"

"I wasn't looking that way. But Tomato Man saw him go in there."

"Can you tell me when Mr. Di Bello arrived?"

"I wasn't looking at no watch, but I waved to him and I heard him tell Ollie, that's Tomato Man, that he'd visit the garden after he did some business about the statue with Mr. Van Aiken."

The other witnesses confirmed what Tomato Man

and Earline told Det. Nadler. They were too engrossed in gossiping and watching others garden to have noticed anything. Det. Nadler sighed. None of their statements helped Di Bello.

ब्रुङ्क

Dita and Dan stared at each other and shuddered as Arlen's body was removed in a zippered body bag. She grabbed for his hand. It was as cold and clammy as was hers. Detective Milton now joined them. "Can we go to the precinct to talk?"

"Am I under arrest?" Dan asked, sending a frisson of fear through Dita. "I mean it looks bad, doesn't it?"

"There are many unanswered questions. Many need to be answered by the medical examiner. I'm hoping you will come along with me voluntarily."

"But you're not offering me a choice!"

"Right now, you're covered in evidence of some sort. It needs to be interpreted."

"That's CJ's jeep, isn't it?" Dita asked, indicating the double-parked car in front of the center."

"Did you drive that here?" Detective Milton asked.

"I borrowed it to pick up the statue and transport it to the Schomburg center."

"We're going to have to go over that car." He gave instructions to an officer to have the vehicle impounded.

"I'm going to call CJ," Dita said.

CJ Kroneberg had always figured in the drama of Dita's life, both as a dancer and in what followed. She looked up and down the street and beyond the crowds that had gathered.

Someone had watched from a roof four doors from the center—a lone figure, possibly. Her mind barely recorded his or her presence.

ℰℐℰℐ

The newspapers subsequently gave the closing intense coverage as more details became known. Zealous reporters had interviewed parents outraged at the paternalistic decision made by a few rich, mostly white, people—the board—who in turn blamed Dita for mismanagement. In one interview Arlen stated that Dita had overspent and was not capable of directing an arts organization. She knew she had made her share of mistakes over the years—running courses that strained the center resources and creating a small troupe, a pilot program to send her young dancers into good schools. These mistakes had caused her to go for emergency funding which had usually arrived at the eleventh hour to a communal sigh of relief.

The opening of the center fifteen years ago had almost felt like a lark. Dita conjured an image of herself and CJ with their dancer legs sprawled 180 degrees wide on CJ's living room floor, trying to make sense of the not-for-profit requirements. They were Columbia students and novices, but they didn't lack resources. Dita was teaching dance classes and going to the School of General studies. CJ had family money behind him. Both of them had been repeatedly injured and had moved from the ballet company onward into academic school.

CJ and Dita had been no ordinary undergraduates. They had twenty years of professional dance experience between them if you counted the children's roles both had performed in the Nutcracker and a long list of other ballets. They had come up through the rigors of a professional ballet school together. They were used to the language of funding in the not-for-profit arts. It seemed natural to try to create something. What neither of them realized at the time was that they were launching themselves into the great and eternal struggle for money—pitting them, the Davids, against the Goliath of venerable arts institutions. Money from CJ's parents seeded the endeavor. Violet Peters deeded a brownstone that had belonged to her mother, giving the center a permanent home. After those connections more followed—the center flourished in its early years. Dita and CJ learned to write grants and proposals.

In Dita's mind, the original center was founded in a circle of friendship. To everyone's surprise, it had flourished for ten years until CJ acquired HIV. When the World Trade Center was attacked and three beloved board members were lost in the collapse of the tower, the center's climate changed forever.

Now as she dialed CJ, Dita remembered the weeks after the closing. May passed into June. Dita was consumed by lethargy and could hardly hold her head up. How could she possibly apply for a job, any kind of job? The facts about the center's failure had become known and disseminated by the eternal gossip mill. The passing of blame would be her reality for a long time to come. You could take a little pride when everything ran smoothly but you were always on edge, waiting for small disasters—an overflowing toilet (her resume would read from now on—handy with a plunger), a jammed copier, a bloody nose, scores ordered, paid for and not received; and always this lack of money, lack of man power underlying it all.

CJ brought Dita back from her reverie to the reality Dan's situation. They were to be taken to the Twenty-Fifth Precinct. "Dita, are you there? Are you okay?" he shouted through the phone. She realized that she had left him dangling on the other end of the line.

"I'm here. I just don't know what to think or what to do."

"Dan's going to need a lawyer, Dita," CJ said. "Wrong place at the wrong time."

"You know Dan would never have lost it like that. They are insisting that he come to the police precinct."

"Tell him not to say a goddamned thing until I find someone. I'm on my way uptown."

"Won't it make him look guilty, if he refuses to say anything?"

"Don't let him, Dita. Don't let him say a word!"

She informed Detective Milton that a lawyer was on his way and told Dan that CJ advised he not discuss anything with the police until a lawyer arrived.

Dita and Dan were put into the back of a cruiser gated off from the officer that drove and his partner. Dita remembered with horror her last confrontation with Mitchell Shepherd and then Arlen. It would come out and help finger Dan.

At one point shortly after the center closed Dita confronted Mitchell Shepherd in his law offices. Through Arlen Van Aiken, Shepherd had come to serve as a board member and as a pro bono lawyer to the center. She thought she might learn more of the financial details from him.

She didn't want to confront Arlen until she understood what had transpired to make closing the center at the end of April the only option. Dita suspected there had been some kind of manipulation of the properties.

Mitchell Shepherd's office was in the garment center. It was an incubator law firm—offices shared by ten lawyers in a loose association. Most came and went as tenants. Mitchell was the primary on the lease. The furniture was generic, probably rented. Today, no one manned the front desk, and Dita strode back. Mitch's door was open and he was on the phone. He covered the receiver with his hand.

"You shouldn't be here, Dita," he said. "I don't see anyone without an appointment."

"You refused to return my phone calls. Well, I'm here, and we need to talk."

"We don't need to talk." And into the receiver he said, "I've gotta go."

"Is that who I think it is?" she heard the smarmy voice of Ted Callahan on the other end. She conjured an image of the suave banker with his JFK good looks. Something had always told her to distrust him.

Mitchell had now put the phone into its holder and stood up. He wore designer duds—a blue gray summer linen suit. He had made a futile attempt at a comb over of his patchy graying hair. He was stocky and his tie hung loosely from his blue oxford cloth shirt collar. He was not much taller than Dita. She looked directly into his opaque eyes—somewhere between brown and gray—encased in steel-rimmed glasses. *He knows something he won't tell me*, Dita thought.

"I'm considering a lawsuit against you and the other board members." Dita had tried to garner the support of her teachers and staff, but they were reluctant to get involved. They were afraid of the powerful men. She didn't tell Shepherd that. "If you have nothing to hide, then why can't we just talk about your decision?"

"The board meets in private sessions. You are not supposed to be privy to our discussions." He started to raise his voice, "Do you know how many hours I donated to your organization. You loved it so much but you couldn't take advice."

"Advice hasn't been forthcoming, seems to me. The board's duty was to listen to the people who run the center. None of you have listened in the past two years."

"I want you to leave, Dita, or I am going to have to call building security. And suing a board of directors

won't be easy—Business Judgment Rule. If you are going to be wrong, do it after careful consideration. Any
lawsuit will be thrown out the minute you file it."

"We'll see about that."

He went over to the telephone again. "I'm calling
building security."

A female lawyer poked her head into his office. She
was plump, clad in a navy business suit and holding a
leather briefcase. "Everything all right, Mitch?"

"I'm trying to convince Ms. Marx to be on her way. I
was going to call building security."

"No need," Dita said. "But this isn't the last time you
will hear from me."

"Don't make idle threats."

Back on Seventh Avenue, Dita waded through
crowds of shoppers, vendors, and garment workers pushing racks of dresses through the streets. She walked to
Forty-Second Street and entered the subway at Times
Square. Arlen had been ignoring her as well and she decided to check out his teaching schedule at Columbia and
confront him there. Maybe Dan and CJ would come with
her. She had come close to feeling a physical threat from
Mitchell Shepherd although he was such an out of shape
slob she could have probably shoved him to the floor if
he had gotten physical.

Several days after Dita's confrontation with Mitchell
Shepherd Dan had gone with Dita and CJ to confront Arlen in the architecture department at Columbia University.

Dita learned that Arlen taught a studio architecture
class Thursday afternoons. Early on in Arlen's association with the center, he had invited Dita and CJ to watch
him teach. Dan went along, too—curious about their new
benefactor. Arlen had struck them as a bit pompous but
he had some good insights, Dan had thought. Arlen read

and admired the works of the Roman architect Vetruvius and discoursed at length to his students on the ancient ideas enduring today. He challenged them to read Vetruvius's ten books on architecture. Then he went on to discuss the project at hand.

The students were designing privately owned public spaces. A new law in New York City required developers to allot a portion of the ground floor area for the public. The examples Arlen cited were the Sony building at Fifth Avenue and Fifty-Seventh Street, The Ford Foundation atrium with its pond and tropical forest, IBM Plaza and 590 Madison. These spaces provided some very nice urban getaways. There was always the problem of finding somewhere to sit in Mid-Manhattan without having to pay for it. After watching Arlen teach CJ and Dita joined him for coffee. He had proposed creating a course in architecture for children from preschool on up. That had been some five years ago but Arlen had never gotten around to formulating it. Dita quickly learned not to count on his participation as a teacher but in the early days he was helpful in connecting them to new sources of funding.

That day of confrontation, Dita had asked CJ and Dan to come along with her. She didn't want to confront Arlen alone like she had Mitchell Shepherd. The center had now been closed for two weeks. The architecture students would be finalizing their projects and Arlen would certainly be on hand. Dita, Dan, and CJ agreed to meet on the steps to Butler library and then make their way back to the school of architecture together. They found Arlen seated at a table in a cafe set up in the lobby of the school. It was practically empty. He was engrossed in a conversation with a tall raven-haired female student. They leaned in close, trying not to let others in on their conversation. She seemed upset and Dita caught the hiss of something about retaliation and grades. *Oh boy*, thought Dita guessing at the scenario. *How like Arlen.* He'd probably tried to get into her pants and she rebuffed him. Dita walked right up to Arlen followed by Dan and CJ. "I remembered where to find you. You've been ignoring our calls so we came over."

Arlen looked flustered. "This is hardly the time and place. I have a studio class to teach."

"We know," Dan said. "This won't take long, but you need to cooperate."

The student rose. "I'll be in the studio," she said to him, gathered her things, and left sullenly.

"Dita, we have nothing to say to each other," Arlen said nervously.

"Look, Van Aiken," Dan said. "You turned the lives of a lot of people inside out. The entire neighborhood is owed a better explanation than you and your board members provided. What were you really doing?"

"Yes," CJ continued. "What were you really doing as a board?"

"Nothing adds up," Dita said, noticing that they were now being watched by a group of students and professors who had come into the cafe on a break for coffee.

"I'm going to ask the three of you to leave. You are trespassing here."

"We're card-carrying alumnae," CJ said, "and we're not going to leave until we at least hear your version."

At this point, the three of them pretty well surrounded Arlen. "I'm going to ask you to let me pass."

A female professor and two of her students came into the fray. "What's going on here, Arlen?"

"Some unfinished business," Dita said. "Sit down and talk first."

Arlen tried to push her out of his way but Dan grabbed his arm.

"Don't get physical here," CJ said, helping to contain Arlen.

"You keep your AIDS hands off me," Arlen hissed.

"I wouldn't go there, Arlen, if you know what's good for you," Dan said.

They had let him pass. The confrontation had come to naught.

 දාල

Once at the precinct, the officers made Dan and Dita wait in separate interview rooms. Dan's clothes were taken away and he was given sweats and a tee shirt several sizes too large. Milton referred to Dan as a "person of interest." He wanted to interview Dita as well about the closing of the center. From interviews Sheila Nadler conducted with the people in the garden, he learned there were a lot of disgruntled people. The closing of the center had had large repercussions in its Harlem neighborhood.

Milton entered Dan's interview room without knocking. He carried a cup of coffee in a Styrofoam-cup and several packets of Cremora. He looked Dan in the eyes as he sat across from him at the small table. He continued to stare as he broke open the creamer packets and dumped them into his brew along with some crumpled packets of Splenda he retrieved from his suit pocket. Dan held his gaze steady. The holstered gun caught in the periphery of his vision. There was really nothing else to look at in this stark little room. No pictures, no windows, no filing cabinet. The interview room was a broom closet without a mop and bucket. There was probably recording equipment but Dan couldn't see that as well. Dan remembered the line in Karate Kid, "The eyes, always look eyes." Milton, he knew, wanted a confession. *How can I convince this detective of my honesty?* Dan thought about what little he knew about body language. He avoided looking down because he thought it would indicate deception. He willed his arms open and leaned toward the Milton, keeping the eye contact.

"Oh, rude of me," Milton said. "Can I get you something to eat or drink?"

"Water would be fine. I've lost my appetite."

The detective went out and returned with a Styrofoam cup filled with water from the water fountain. "No ice in here."

"I don't need ice."

Dan took hesitant sips from the cup. The scent of blood hadn't cleared out of his nostrils and he feared the smell was imprinted in his sense memory. Curse my perfect pitch and sense of smell, he thought. Over his lifetime, others constantly accused him of being oversensitive. But his brain was wired to see different pitches. As a composer he sometimes worked from an image that would take him into music. The key of F major he associated with light grey almost white like icicles. The icicles morphed into organ pipes and he had composed a little fugue and toccata for the instrument. Now he was dealing with the image of Arlen laying there and wondered if given time, he could erase it from his mind.

"Let me ask you this," Milton said. "Your world crashed. You were devastated, according to the gardeners, who love you and your wife, by the way. Did you and Van Aiken argue?"

"Argue with a dead man? I'm not going to say anymore."

"Your inalienable right."

Dan, too, feared, as he remembered the day he, Dita, and CJ confronted Arlen at Columbia. It would probably come out. They had started a scene that almost got violent.

Dan prayed that CJ would arrive soon. Sheila Nadler knocked on the door and entered. She held a folder in her hands. "These just came back from the crime lab."

Milton leafed through the folder. It contained photos of the crime scene, Arlen's body shot from different perspectives. He began to arrange the photos on the table in front of Dan. "Oh, I'm sorry. Does this bother you?"

"It would bother anyone," Dan said.

ℰℐℰℐ

The day after the lock-out in May, Dita had gone in person to tell CJ the center had closed. She was fearful he'd blame her. CJ lived in a deco elevator building on West Thirteenth Street in the Village between Sixth and University Place. The one bedroom apartment, he shared with Neil, his life partner, had a wrap-around terrace crowded with potted fig trees, orange trees, pots of marjoram, oregano, chives and no doubt some cannabis for medicinal purposes. The terrace was littered with droppings from the two Havanese dogs Neil and CJ couldn't be bothered to walk as often as necessary.

Dog shit aside, the apartment had style. The two men were passionate in its creation. "Our projects," CJ called them. Found art in a collection of old parts, the flue from a fireplace, a flattened muffler hanging over the mantle. A giant needlepoint in progress, looking like a blown up Paul Klee miniature hanging on a wall with a basket of Persian yarn under it. Every time Dita visited, a few more squares were filled in. A hooked rug was in progress as well, a giant peachy thing, with barren patches yet to be filled in. A giant poster of Dita and CJ in *Flower Festival*, looking so young and happy, graced the small entryway. CJ had had this made from old ballet school workshop photos. He liked making things larger than the life he clung onto.

Depending on how you looked at luck, CJ had been either very lucky or very unlucky. He had contracted an HIV infection at a time when the disease had become a chronic rather than a fatal one. But the cocktails of meds and the constant vigilance had taken their toll on him.

Sautéed garlic wafted out into the small hallway. CJ had opened the door accompanied by a cacophony of yapping from the terrace. He was barefoot and dressed in boot cut jeans. His purple tee cut out at the neck and shoulder lines to display CJ's gallery of body art begun in the American Ballet School days much to the consternation of his ballet teachers. CJ's dark hair was now threaded with gray. His eyes bordered by thick black lashes were almost violet in color. He still carried himself like a dancer despite his health struggles.

CJ hugged Dita. "We have a surprise, Neil."

Neil, a large black man of Jamaican descent with handsome features, had appeared at the entrance to the galley kitchen wiping his hands on a white chef's apron. "The goddess has ascended into our divine midst." Dita went over and hugged him. Flour from his apron dusted her peasant skirt and tee shirt. Neil wore a citrusy cologne, and Dita caught a whiff.

"The goddess is a bearer of bad news."

"Well maybe we should all have a drink first. Then you can lay it on us," CJ said, steering Dita down the step into the living room. Dita was grateful not to have to blurt it all out. This settling before speaking was a talent CJ had inherited from his oil executive father.

"I'll get the drinks," Neil had said, returning to the kitchen.

"Do you notice anything different?" CJ asked. She heard the whirr of the juicer.

"The rug!" Formerly it had been a patch of threaded parts and bare parts: now a stippled mass of peach and red thread, a pointillism flower enclosed in a border of purple—the calyx—outermost whorl of the flower, the protector of the delicate sepals was now filled in.

"You finished it."

"Yes and now we have to bind it. Neil's job." She knew that that was because the binding needle was difficult to work with, and CJ had to avoid cuts that might develop into infections.

Neil had returned with drinks, a gin and tonic for himself and Dita, and a greenish juice concoction for CJ.

"I hope no dandelion's in it this time," CJ protested.

"They purify you," Neil said, shaking his head in admonishment, as he passed around cocktail napkins and little individual terracotta cazuelas for each of them, filled with shitake mushrooms sautéed in olive oil, garlic, and parsley. He passed around slices of lemon and tiny forks.

Dita began to speak, a mushroom strip dangling from her fork.

"No, no." CJ protested. "Whatever it is, we have to have a toast first."

"Amen," Neil said.

"L'Chayim, to life ever onward. Though, I don't know how." She burst into tears and explained what had happened. "They pulled out the proverbial rug and sent us skidding with nowhere to go."

"There's probably some dirty real estate plot behind this. The center sits on valuable land," Neil had been instantly suspicious.

"We could have run another year at a deficit. Randy can't see the value of anything that doesn't turn a profit— we were a bunch of dreamers in her eyes. I already miss working with the kids. It's so painful."

CJ nodded. He and Dita had been often paired as partners on the stage. What CJ had lacked as a solo dancer, he made up as a solid partner. Dita had implicit trust in CJ. When CJ went and injured his Achilles, she was paired with a younger less experienced male who set her down too hard on her foot. It didn't seem to her that she was injured at the time. But thinking back, she had realized that impact had been the beginning of an injury.

CJ's eyes moistened. The disease and the meds had taken their toll. He had continued to hold his own, but the telltale sunken cheeks and thinning arms shouted HIV.

೪⁄ೱ೪⁄ೱ

CJ arrived at the Twenty-Fifth Precinct in a taxi. The taxi lacked air conditioning and CJ was glad to step out into the August air. He was talking on his cell phone. He'd put calls through to several prominent criminal lawyers. He went through a revolving door and approached the front desk. The desk officer sat high and manned phones with annoyance. He wore a patrol uniform. "What can I do for you?" he finally asked.

CJ figured he probably hated gay men and tried being respectful. "A friend of mine was brought here with his wife a short time ago. Can I see them?"

"What's the name?"

"Di Bello!"

"Nope, you can't see him."

"Where's his wife Dita? I'm worried about her."

"I don't know."

"Who's the detective in charge?"

"That would be The Poet, John Milton."

"Can you tell him I'm a friend, and I want to make sure Dita is okay."

At that moment Milton appeared at the front desk,

and CJ told him that Dita expected him. Milton looked CJ up and down.

"Follow me," CJ said.

# CHAPTER 3

CJ entered the windowless interview room to find Dita white-faced and pacing like a caged animal. "They separated us. They put Dan in a different interview room."

"Gestapo tactics! Did Detective Milton tell you he was detaining Dan?"

"He didn't use those words."

"They call it a person of interest."

Dita sat down at the table and rested her head on her arms as she sobbed. CJ pulled the chair from the other side of the table around to sit next to her. The single fluorescent light in the ceiling began to flicker. If it burned out they would be left in darkness.

"Okay, Dita love, here's how it works, and I'm no lawyer but as you know, Neil has a history, so we've been through the system. They're looking for probable cause. It means a number of elements are in place that make Dan a suspect."

"How are we going to pay a lawyer? When they go over all the evidence, there's got to be something that doesn't add up. I've read enough mystery books to know that they can tell the height of the person wielding the weapon. Whether he is right-handed or left handed. Even spatter of blood tells a story. That's why they didn't read him his rights yet."

"This will get sorted out."

"Not likely. I just seem to have the worst talent for compounding our problems. Oh, I feel the trouble is going to be with us for a very long time. It's going to come out that we confronted Arlen at Columbia. The police are going to think Dan had it in for Arlen. Oh, my God. They could look at you and me as suspects."

"I've got an alibi. I was at the doctor's office all morning."

"I guess I have one, too. I was at Steps, and then Fairway. Getting up town was a nightmare. That leaves poor Dan. Fuck!"

"Dita, you've got to stay calm!"

"Calm? And I didn't tell you yet about another snag in our quickly deteriorating lives: I'm pregnant."

"Well, I'm going to say Mazel Tov, girl. The troubles are temporary, and if you don't have this baby, you never will."

"Something to look forward to after Dan finishes serving a life sentence."

എജ്ഞ

Dita had let herself become pregnant on an impulse. The day after the center was closed down, she'd risen with the sun. For a blessed few waking moments, the reality of their situation had receded. It returned as she stood in front of the bathroom sink, looking into the medicine cabinet mirror—something that couldn't be cleansed out of her mouth, a bilious and acrid taste rising out of her internal organs. She had thought about her flat belly—childless. She'd missed out on that, too. The center had been her child. Over the years, she'd encountered many mothers who had lost children to drugs and violence. *Yes*, she thought, *I too am a victim of violence but my scars are invisible. Something has been violently ripped away from me, severed from me—the toil of many years. I gave my youth to that job.*

She had an impulse to jump back into bed with Dan and fill herself up. A hormonal rush surged throughout her body. She asked herself if women were endowed to handle tragedy and misfortune with a longing for procreation. It wouldn't have surprised her to learn that Eve had bitten the apple because her womb had been empty—and then had proceeded to give birth to two fucked-up kids. Dita was already in her late thirties. Her chances of conceiving couldn't be too great.

As foolhardy as it was, she got back into bed, aroused Dan, and filled herself with him—and filled herself with the idea of creating life with him. She found it sexually arousing in a way she hadn't known. Deeper and deeper, she'd allowed him to penetrate, and she'd climaxed again, and then again. Suddenly, it hadn't been human sex but a karmic connection—her body a temple, she a goddess, and he a part of her. The world in that timeless time could not exist without their connection. When it was over, she had run water in the bathtub and tried to wash it away—the most beautiful lovemaking they had ever known.

CJ's cell phone rang, bringing Dita back to the reality of the drab interview room. "CJ Kroneberg," he answered then listened attentively. "Wonderful!" He covered the receiver. "Martin Duffy!" He made a thumbs-up sign to Dita. "Yes, I'm up here in the Twenty-Fifth Precinct with his wife now. He picked up what was probably the murder weapon before he saw the deceased lying there. There was bad blood between them. Circumstantially it looks like he's in trouble." To Dita, CJ said, "I've got Martin Duffy interested in talking to Dan."

"Who's he?"

"One of the best criminal lawyers around. He's the one who saved Neil's butt."

She had heard the story quite often. Neil had driven some of his friends to an uptown deli, which was in the process of being robbed. When the police arrived, they thought Neil was driving the getaway car.

"We can't afford him."

"An hour of his time could be worth fifty hours of a public defender. You don't want a public defender in a situation like this, and I'm not saying public defenders are bad lawyers. They just lack resources. Arlen could have been involved in some arcane real estate deals. He told us he had a slew of properties—"

She finished his thought for him. "His dealings might shed some light on who else would want him dead."

"Duffy's going to meet us here in an hour," CJ relayed to Dita. "Just try to stay calm. Can I get you anything?"

"No thanks. Do you think they will let us see Dan?"

"I tried."

"They're not going to let him go home, are they?"

CJ put his arms around Dita and she sobbed on his shoulder.

"Why haven't they arrested him already? It's like a game of cat and mouse."

"There's a limit to how long they can detain him without pressing charges but I guess they could hold him here for twenty-four hours without making an arrest."

# CHAPTER 4

Detective Milton braced himself to tell Arlen Van
Aiken's wife, Mindy, that Arlen was dead. He'd
never get used to the routine of notifying the next
of kin. He was glad Sheila was coming with him. In the
case of a family so prominent, access is a many-layered
process. Rich people always made him feel inferior. One
of his officers called the building security to notify them
of his arrival. Milton personally put in a call to Mort
Rothman's office to tell them Van Aiken's family might
need him. Mort Rothman was Arlen's father-in-law and
one of New York City's biggest real estate developers.

Mindy arrived in the lobby with her children moments after Milton and Detective Nadler. Milton introduced himself, and they showed Mindy Van Aiken their
shields.

"Something is terribly wrong, isn't it?" Mindy said.

She was petit with big brown eyes and full cheeks.
Her nose was chiseled—maybe plastic surgery because it
seemed a little narrow on her face. She wore a gray linen
tailored suit and high heeled pumps. A yellow silk scarf
was draped dramatically around her neck and pinned to

her shoulders. Her hand went instinctively to adjust the scarf.

"Yes, can we go upstairs?"

Mindy looked fearful and glanced over at her children who were balancing like acrobats around the rim of the lobby fountain. "Children would you like to stay with Jorge for a few moments while I have an adult discussion?" She indicated the white-gloved doorman who signaled for the elevator. "Is that all right with you, Jorge?"

"Of course, missus. Come on over here, you two, and help me out. You don't wanna fall in there." The kids jumped down and joined Jorge at his desk where he summoned the elevator. The detectives and Mindy rode upward in silence. The elevator opened into the Van Aiken apartment where Flora, a uniformed maid, greeted them.

"I'll be in the den, Flora," Mindy said, as the detectives followed her into a well-appointed room with a sweeping view of Central Park. Fine art was everywhere on the walls and shelves. Milton recognized a Picasso, and his eyes shared it with Sheila Nadler. Mindy closed the door. "Now can you please tell me what this is about?"

They sat beside Mindy on a white sofa and told her Arlen had been murdered. Mindy's reaction was strange to them. No tears, a sort of resignation as if she'd expected that her husband was in trouble. Her face became very pale. "How will I tell the children?" was all she said.

"Is there someone who can be here with you?" asked Sheila.

"I'll call my father."

"We already left word at his office that he should join us here," Milton said. "How did he die?"

"He died from a head wound. Someone hit him over the head with a piece of statuary."

"Where?"

"In the Harlem Arts Center. He was found in the basement," Milton told her.

"He was in over his head. I just know it."

"What do you mean?" Sheila asked.

"Was it the sculptor? He kept calling about his work. Arlen called it tacky."

"The sculptor was in Puerto Rico, and he sent another couple to pick up the work," Milton said.

"You're going to have to make the identification," said Sheila.

"You said his skull was bashed in?"

Milton nodded. "The medical examiner will just show you his face. He was hit from behind."

"And do you know who did this?"

"We thought you might have some ideas. We're going to need access to all of his paper work. Did he maintain a separate office?"

"He worked sometimes with my father. He was trained as an architect but didn't really practice; he taught architecture at Columbia. That was Arlen. He dabbled. Liked things that came easy."

Milton looked directly into her eyes, and she averted his gaze. "What was he dabbling in that could get him killed?"

"He was buying into Harlem real estate for a number of years. He said he paid cash for the properties and was going to renovate them. He really didn't have much experience with construction."

"But he would have had your father's expertise?" asked Sheila.

"My father wouldn't have gone along with Arlen's plans. Arlen was stubborn, said he could manage this on his own. He acquired about thirty buildings. He was involved with several non-profits and that qualified him for HUD loans."

"HUD loans?" Milton asked.

"He said he had dreams of gentrifying the neighborhood. He said regular banks wouldn't lend on the area. He considered Harlem to have some of New York's finest architecture." Mindy hung her head, "I just can't believe this."

"Can I get you something?" asked Sheila.

"No, I'll be all right."

"We will need all the paperwork on those purchases. He was on the board of the center. He was president of the board," Milton said. "We'd like to have the any paper work pertaining to the organization."

"That's just it. There is no paperwork. I went through his things."

"Mrs. Van Aiken," Detective Nadler said. "How would you characterize your marriage to Mr. Van Aiken?"

Mindy hesitated then sighed with resignation. "I didn't trust the lousy bastard. So there, now you have it. He got himself a job teaching architecture at Columbia. Couldn't keep his fly zipped. A student claimed sexual harassment. Arlen claimed she'd led him on. He supposedly had extensive real estate holdings, but there are no documents on any of his properties."

"Where did you spend your afternoon, Mrs. Van Aiken?" Milton asked.

"Don't worry. A thousand charity-minded women can vouch for me."

The maid knocked on the door. Milton opened it.

"Mr. Rothman is here with the children."

"Take the children into the kitchen and feed them supper."

Mindy followed Flora out of the den and returned

with her elderly father. Mort Rothman was short and dumpy—about as tall as his daughter in her high heels. Milton guessed that that put him at about five feet, five inches. His bald head reflected light from the dazzling sky outside of the den window. What remained of his gray hair was scraggly.

Mort Rothman wore a poorly tailored suit and old moth-eaten yellow cashmere sweater vest despite the heat. *Probably once a luxury birthday present*, Milton thought. The man intrigued him. He was a legend. His gruff demeanor softened when he looked at Mindy but returned when he addressed the detectives.

"Mrs. Van Aiken, we'd like to speak with your father alone," Milton said.

She shrugged and looked at her father. "I'll be in the kitchen with the children," she said.

Rothman maintained an air of circumspection when questioned about his relationship with Arlen.

"Mrs. Van Aiken says that her husband worked with you," Milton said.

Rothman snorted. "We were not able to work together, and Arlen went and did his own thing."

"Did he have enemies in your office?" Detective Nadler asked.

"He was a deliberately contentious human being. Always. I think he thought it made him a good teacher. Socratic Method. But I think you can teach better by example," said Rothman, surprising the detectives.

"Do you think being so arrogant got him killed?" Milton asked.

"Was he robbed?" Rothman asked.

"Apparently not," Detective Nadler said. "His wallet was in his jacket pocket, and he was found wearing an expensive watch and pinky ring. So we don't think robbery was the motive."

"Mr. Rothman, can you account for your whereabouts this afternoon?"

Rothman laughed, despite the seriousness of the occasion. "I thought that was coming. Yes, I was in a planning meeting with my team for a building downtown."

❧❧❧

Alone in his interview room, Dan became claustrophobic. The realization that he was in serious trouble sent waves of panic through him. He prayed his heart was strong enough to withstand the ongoing stress of his situation. Why did Milton show him the crime photos? Dan tried to slow his heart rate by breathing in to the count of four, retaining the breath for five counts, and exhaling. Nothing worked. The short panic gulps of air returned as his fear mounted. He tried some stretches Dita had once shown him, but they didn't help him relax.

# CHAPTER 5

The week after the center closed, Dita had become fearful whenever anyone called. She was searching want ads for job listings when the phone began to ring. She was of a mind to ignore it but saw New York Times pop up in the caller ID window. "Ms. Marx, I'm Samantha Elder with the *New York Times*. I'm doing a story on the closing of the Harlem Center for the Arts, and I wondered if you would speak with me."

She'd caught Dita off guard. For the past four days Dita had formulated over and over what she might say to the press. "I was not part of the decision to close us down," she said. "It was done without my knowledge."

"But you must have known the center was in trouble."

"You're talking degrees of trouble. Our tax returns from the year before put us slightly in the red. And that's pretty normal for an organization like us. You know tax returns for non-profits are public record."

"I've seen them. So what so dramatic happened in the past year to make you go so far downhill?"

She had wanted to say, *We acquired another piece of real estate and couldn't make a go of it. And that was the board's decision*. It was too soon to confront the board about it or suggest it publicly.

"I spoke with Arlen Van Aiken," the reporter continued, "and he blames you for gross mismanagement."

"And I blame him and the board and the executive director for not being up to the job of getting us funding. So I guess it's just a pissing contest at this point."

In the infancy years of the center, Harlem was beginning to gentrify. If you looked at it from an aerial view, block by block, a patchwork quilt pattern would emerge constructed from the pattern of squares, some empty rubble-strewn lots, some verdant roof gardens, free standing buildings their old roofs pegged with sculptural cornices, and the myriad makeshift parking lots. The streets were lined with parked cars, ice cream trucks and vendor trucks serving hot dogs, tacos and enchiladas. The two center buildings and the garden were three unusual pieces in the pattern.

Within the blocks themselves buildings ran stoop by stoop, side by side in varying degrees of renovation, from the ungentrified to the posh and polished, but on each and every block stood buildings seemingly abandoned and padlocked, with windows and doors bricked over. These were not ownerless, abandoned properties but rather shells the city under Hizzoner, archenemy of the homeless, had sold to investors replete with all kinds of tax breaks. These owners and corporations promised to renovate them. The renovations never happened. Everyone knew this. Deeds to the properties changed hands as the values went up.

❧❧❧

Dita had been slow to grasp the reality of the closed center. Her last hours with Violet and Marge in the building the day of the lockout had brought a new reality—a silent reality. The center's copiers had been stilled and the pianos locked. Saturday night the center had been alive with the student's annual April recital. It had begun at three p.m., and had lasted until the last student had performed at nearly seven p.m. The audience members shifted in and out of the small recital hall as the performers came on and off stage. There wasn't room in the small recital hall for the entire center family. The students wore their best clothes and had ranged in age from five on up. They beamed proudly at their parents. Albert and Flora danced a pas-de-deux specially choreographed by Dita for their level of accomplishment. Albert was Marge's thirteen-year old grandson and a talented dancer. Dita had been training him at the center from the age of five. Albert's mother was incarcerated and he lived with Marge. Albert and Flora reminded Dita of herself and CJ at the American Ballet School annual workshop. Fresh and not quite adults yet—these two possessed the bones of a good technique. Moreover, she thought, they were gifted musically. The attributes that make a dancer are something of a crapshoot and those two kids had landed all the right ones. Dita swelled with pride. Everyone in attendance claimed her dance a success.

Violet came up behind Dita and gave her a firm hug. It brought Dita back to the closed center and the need to pack up quickly. "Take yourself a souvenir, darling. They'll never notice," Violet had said. "You, too, Marge. Take a dance poster for Albert's room."

"Oh, he'll love that," Marge said.

The center's walls were lined with posters. The performers themselves had donated some of them—a full life poster of Renee Fleming as Elvira. Alessandra Ferri as Juliet—Dita's favorite ballerina with her over the top arches. "I would love to have a poster of you, Violet," Dita said.

"You should have said so years ago."

"Do you think there's any chance in hell that this could get reversed?" asked Marge, thumbing through a stack of posters.

"If you can get an angel with several million dollars."

"And eliminate the job of the executive director," Dita said.

"Fat chance in this day and age. That's how they all think. Never was like that," Violet had said. "Even the money people were part of us. Did I ever tell you how many times Sol Hurok, my manager, went broke? He was a legend. Never afraid to take a chance! That's balls. I'd have never gotten my chance without that man."

"You know, Violet," Dita said. "I feel like I have failed at a career twice. The worst part is that I can't seem to think ahead. I could have been out before it happened. Let someone else with more knowhow try to salvage things. Do you blame me for letting this happen? I feel more awful about your mother's property than everything else.

"Never! Never! Hush honey that's because you're still absorbing. You wouldn't have jumped off this train."

"But I should have gotten wind of what they were doing. Arlen was up to something. I can feel it in my bones."

"This thing is going to be a long hard process for you. Think about it this way, if you were still dancing, what are you approaching forty now? You'd be looking for something else to do. See it as a beginning."

"Is that what you did, Violet?"

"I had to take counsel with myself and listen good to what was coming out of my throat. Vibrato slowed way down. The Carmen days were done. It submerges you, at first, and then you go forward."

"I managed to get fired from a ballet company before I even started." Dita had come to New York City from Poughkeepsie at the age of twelve with a full scholarship to American Ballet School. She'd commuted by train— first with her mother and then alone when she knew the routine from Grand Central Station to Lincoln Center and back to Grand Central well enough. The public school she attended was not supportive and, despite ten hours of physical activity a day, they wouldn't let her drop gym. When she was used in the company ballets, her mother drove round trip. They frequently returned home at two a.m., and attending school became all the more difficult.

By age fourteen, Dita had to live in the school's dormitory, in order to do the demanding program. Her high school education was a correspondence course. Then at the age of sixteen, she had been made an apprentice, and then a corps member of the parent ballet company. Because of the intense exercise, many ballerinas entered puberty late. She hadn't even gotten her period, and she had found herself living in an adult world with little su-pervision and with what had seemed like an enormous salary.

Her former life as a ballerina played out all too quickly in her mind. Everyone had told her how good she was. She was the right size, had good feet. Her technique was clean and dependable. She was pronounced artistic director Percy Fountain's "flavor of the month." Percy trusted her and gave her the opportunity to dance Dew Drop in the *Nutcracker* at the age of sixteen. The music had seemed to come out of the orchestra pit to carry her on its wings. She was vaguely aware of other corps members watching her from behind the piece of scenery where they'd just exited. Her footwork was being com-

pared to the great ballerinas—clean, articulate. She pir-
ouetted center stage, and the light followed her. Dita was
the new phenomena. She had left behind the petty jeal-
ousies in the ballet school but had not been quite compe-
tent to run her own career.

Then at the age of eighteen, when she was too old to
stay in the school's dormitory, she had rented her own
apartment. Then the injuries had begun to happen. A
stress fracture in her right metatarsal, and tendonitis became her constant companion. She was down for so many
weeks at a time that Fountain, finally, called her into his
office and told her they couldn't afford to keep her on
any longer. She had let them all down. It hadn't occurred
to her then that maybe she was pushed too far, way too
soon.

When Dita had migrated uptown into the Columbia
School of General studies, all she had known at that point
in her life was that she had discipline. She had had no
idea where she was headed with it. She managed to com-
plete a bachelor's degree in two and a half years, had
married Dan who played the piano for many of the ballet
classes Dita had taken. For Dan, Dita had always been the
only ballerina in the room. Dita had been well into a master's degree in literature and was considering an arts
management program when she'd opened the center fifteen years ago.

Dita and Dan had finally accepted the stark reality
that Dita would not easily find another job. The *New York
Times* article seemed to favor the board's account of the
closing. Probably a press agent had a hand in the genera-
tion of that article. Dita was frustrated that she no longer
had any resources. The center was cited in the press as a
case of dire mismanagement. Arlen had even given a
quote to the *New York Times* saying that the board was
disappointed in Dita's performance.

# CHAPTER 6

Dita stared at the gray-green wall of the window-less interview room at the Twenty-Fifth Precinct. It had become a screen on which she began to project memories of how the center had changed. Alone in the silent center before the day's activities got under-way, Dita had sipped coffee, planned and read. Incubation time. She'd arrive at six-thirty a.m., just to savor the time. The sound of her day beginning was the music that replayed in her head—Dan's music, music from the ballets she had danced, the childish compositions the center's young students had composed. She often toyed with ideas for a dance, drawing lines on a piece of graph paper and pushing paper clips around to suggest how dancers would fill up the space. Then along would come the cat, barging through her creation in order to lay himself out on her desk and have his stomach tickled. Dita was contented and easy in these hours before the demands could be set upon her, before the copiers had begun to whirr, the coffee had begun to percolate, and the teachers tuned their instruments.

But people had changed, and attitudes had changed. The new board seldom communicated with her, except to tell her that she was overspending, or that they couldn't replace this or that. This was done through Randy Smith-Warren, the board's choice of executive director. The lot of them seemed to be number crunchers, lacking in vision. Why would they want to serve on the board of an organization like the Harlem Center for the Arts? she and Violet often asked themselves. What kind of attraction could it really have held for Arlen and his cronies? Dita continued in her old ways, despite the new frosty climate, thinking about the dances she would make, toying around with scraps of paper, molding them into shapes, thinking about symmetry in body movement, toying with asymmetry. She'd get up from her desk, impelled by visions of the movement and walk through her ideas. Her desk no longer occupied the center of her office. She needed space to move. Dita had loved her work and loved regaling Dan with tales from the day, of her ideas for dances, of kids finally grasping a concept or a movement that felt awkward at first. She and Dan were looking into commissions so that he could compose for her choreography. It was a dream that they seemed close to fulfilling. She felt lucky that she'd found another career to love. Here she was creating something of her own. In her short ballet career, she was a mere puppet and the artistic director pulled her strings. Maybe she was meant to understand this. The center was her calling.

The center was never short on gossip either. Little romances and liaisons had a way of forming. A bassoon teacher fell in love with a flute teacher, and all of the kids picked up on it right away. The starry-eyed couple sneaked kisses whenever they thought the coast was clear. And then it was rumored that Arlen had set his sights on a singing teacher who rebuffed his advances. These thoughts made Dita laugh.

Eventually, Dita had begun to bring home accounts

of stressful situations. She and Dan had thought they only needed to get through a period of adjustment. "The new executive director, Randy, makes me feel like she's infringing on my territory," she'd told Dan.

"How so?"

"She's getting here early, too." She neglected to say that Randy caught her in the act of creating a dance. Dita had had to explain to her what it was she was doing, twisted into an off-balance stance and trying to figure how the movement would end.

Randy just rolled her eyeballs.

"Why should that be a problem?" Dan asked. "Shows she takes the job seriously."

"When she closes her door, I keep wondering what she's doing in there. I don't want to wonder about her. It's my sanctuary time."

"Oh, Dita. Let's not get carried away here."

It would have had to come to a head, and it had. Dita was sure that Randy had lobbied the board to close down the center. The board had thoroughly excluded Dita from their governance processes in the last years of the center's existence. How could it have come to that? She was, after all, the founder, making it all the more painful.

More memories of the day the center closed surfaced in Dita's memory. She had finally found herself alone with Violet and Marge. Rex Turner had left to do Arlen's other bidding, giving them some space, and they worked diligently to pack as much as they could. They had no idea what they ought to be taking out of the building. Dita had heard stories of fired lawyers being escorted out of their firms with one box. Baryshnikitty had mewed in his hastily purchased cat carrier, as if he echoed her thoughts. "I'd better check the skylight," Dita had said out loud. "If this little guy could get out on that roof, then the rain and snow can get in."

"Good idea," Violet had said.

"Well, I'm not abandoning hope yet."

Dita mounted the steps to the fifth story, thinking how two years ago the center had managed to get two million dollars in grant money and had narrowly avoided closure. It had been then that the board had decided to bring an executive director on board. They had picked Randolynn Smith-Warren for her connections to deep corporate pockets—a woman groomed in the corridors of Fortune 500 companies. Randy was attractive, in an equestrian type of way. She was tall with a high forehead and slightly aquiline nose. She had thick but straight brown hair she secured with a tortoise headband and po-nytail clasp. She also had danced at American Ballet School, one of the rich kids that saw *Nutcracker* as a rite of passage. Randy now made the arts her mantra, co-opting and regurgitating Dita's many pleas for funding over the years.

"Give a kid lessons on an instrument, and you have a way into his mind," Dita had said.

A ladder from the fifth story of the brownstone ac-cessed the roof. To Dita's surprise, the skylight egress had been tightly closed, making Dita wonder how the cat had gotten onto the roof. Her thoughts returned to the op-pressive interview room and to her present predicament. *I should have checked the entire building more closely that day. Someone found a way out of there. I know it.*

# CHAPTER 7

Detectives Milton and Nadler returned from the Van Aiken apartment. "What do we know?" he asked her.

"The arts center was closed down by the board after it became financially insolvent."

"We need to follow a paper trail here. Start with Van Aiken's diary." He placed a leather journal on the table in the squad room and grabbed a cup of coffee from an electric coffee maker on a sideboard. Sheila winced. "Do you want me to make a fresh pot, John?"

"You'd make the coffee for me? You're the first female officer to offer."

"I'm in my post-feminist mode, and it's pretty bad when you brew the stuff."

"Even fresh, this stuff stinks."

"Why is it that police precincts can't buy decent coffee like the rest of the world today?"

"Acid gut is part of the job," he said.

She laughed.

"Sheila, follow up on his contacts and put together a team to go through the man's papers. Despite what the wife said, there's got to be something somewhere. See if he had safe deposit boxes—whatever, maybe a self-storage. A guy can't own over fifty properties without leaving a record. He was a busy man, it seems. Always meetings. We need to find out what those meetings were about. We need to talk to all of the center's personnel. Try to get a feel for how things were run on a daily basis. There were parent volunteers, teachers, and staff." They broke off at this point. A desk officer told Milton that Dan Di Bello's lawyer had arrived.

# CHAPTER 8

Dan expected to see a ruddy redheaded Irishman.
Martin Duffy, aka. Duffy, was black. He wore an
expensive summer-blue pinstripe suit and looked
to be in his mid-forties with minor graying that threaded
his short, Afro buzz cut. There was no dancing around.
He grasped Dan's hand firmly. "Let's go over it."

The police had taken away Dan's bloodied clothes
and he was lolling around in sweats and a tee shirt several
sizes too big for him. The police had removed the draw-
string from the pants and there was no way for Dan to
secure them at his waist. When he stood, he had to hold
up his pants with one hand. When he sat, he tucked them
under his butt. Might have been comic in other circumstances but hanging on to the seat of his pants added to
his hopelessness.

Dan recounted how he found the center door open.
Duffy began to write on a yellow legal tablet. "Have you
told all of this to the police?"

"Yes. I felt that I had nothing to hide."

"Less is more when dealing with the police. From
now on, you will not speak with anyone without a lawyer."

"Do you think they're going to arrest me?"

"In their thinking, you had opportunity and motive. Yeah, I think they're going to arrest you. There's going to be pressure on Milton, even if he doesn't believe you could have done it. The circumstantial evidence will be too strong."

Dan then repeated the story of how he found Arlen. "Look, Mr. Duffy."

"Everyone calls me Duffy."

"All right, Duffy. I thought he'd hand me the damned statue at the door. He couldn't have intended for me to take a tour of the wreck he'd made of the place and the fact that a piano worth in excess of a hundred grand was unaccounted for. Dita and I think we are dealing with a real estate scam. We just don't know what. Something went south for Arlen and his buddies. That's for sure. His father-in-law is one of the biggest real estate developers in the city. Maybe he's involved. Dita wondered."

"Mort Rothman has a clean reputation."

"Yeah? Well, maybe he didn't start out that way. How could anyone make that kind of money without bending some rules?"

"Let's talk about the murder weapon. It was missing from the niche on the parlor floor, so you went searching for it as well as for Arlen."

"That's correct."

"A lot of things don't add up here. There's a twenty-minute window of time. If I understand you correctly, the gardener, Tomato Man, saw Arlen arrive and enter the building twenty minutes before you arrived. He saw no one else enter. But could there have been someone else? Could he have been mistaken about the time? You would have seen him or her leaving."

"Maybe Arlen had an appointment with someone earlier and that person came back and was somehow hiding?" Dan said.

"Nothing's totally impossible, but we have to be realistic here."

"I just need to give myself some hope. Could Tomato Man have been mistaken about seeing Arlen earlier? He said he was ignoring him."

"It will be helpful when the medical examiner narrows down the time of death, but don't get your hopes up there either. It will just be a window of time. Before I let you take questions from Milton, I want to speak with your wife."

# CHAPTER 9

Martin Duffy introduced himself to Dita. CJ greeted Duffy but took leave to go and tell Violet and Marge about Dan's predicament. Tough as Violet and Marge were, the shock of Dan's arrest would be too much for them.

"Why do I have to stay in this room?" Dita asked.

"Let's talk first. There's a conundrum." Duffy explained the narrow window of time between Arlen's arrival and Dan's. "That tight time helps implicate Dan. Now one scenario is that it wasn't Arlen entering before Dan's arrival. Tomato Man identified Arlen by the clothes, according to your husband."

Dita sighed. She hated to think of Tomato Man getting grilled, but it would help Dan so immensely if he were wrong. She saw it very clearly. All their friendships and associations were going to be sorely tested by this newest debacle.

"Can you think of anyone else involved in the center who could be mistaken from a distance for Arlen?"

Dita shook her head. "But I'm going to think about it. Only the board members had that designer look about them. And they met elsewhere."

"Is there another means of egress from the basement?"

"Only to the subbasement."

"There's a subbasement?"

"Yeah, it's kind of creepy. The floor was always covered with an inch of water. Violet said that we were over a creek. Sometimes after a big rain or snow melt there'd be more water. Basically, someone would have to be a scuba diver to get out that way. There is a grate. But it's hard to see when the water fills the room. Supposedly, there are all kinds of lakes and streams under Manhattan buildings."

"Could be an interesting tour."

"Do you think there's a possibility a murderer could have gotten out that way?"

"You'd have to find out when and where he could get his head above water. What you're telling me is the stream is always overflowing. But I don't think it is unreasonable to have it checked out. I'll ask The Poet to check out the water level in there today. Hasn't rained in a while. Then I'll have some of my people try to search it."

# CHAPTER 10

Milton scoffed at Duffy's request that he check out the water level in the subbasement, but he complied and verified that there was indeed an inch of water covering the subbasement floor. Milton and Nadler sat at the table opposite Dan and Duffy.

"Okay, pretend I'm blind, and walk me through it all over again," Milton said.

Sheila began to take notes.

"This time, he won't talk freely," Duffy said. "You ask the questions. I decide what he answers. Fair?"

"Okay, how would you characterize your relationship to the deceased, Mr. Di Bello?"

"For the most part it was a second-hand relationship through my wife. I only saw him at fundraisers for the center and, in the last few years, none of the center folks could afford to go to our own fundraisers. They were gala affairs that—"

Duffy stopped Dan. "You don't have to elaborate."

"What was the other 'part'?" Detective Nadler asked.

"I'd like to speak with my client alone," Duffy said.

Milton shrugged but complied. Detective Nadler followed him out the door. When Duffy heard the lock engage, he continued. "What's the other part? I need to know everything."

"A week after the center closed, Dita went alone to visit Mitchell Shepherd, the pro-bono lawyer. She wanted answers. Mitch threatened to call building security. She wanted to get answers from Arlen but was afraid to confront him alone. CJ and I went with her to the architecture department at Columbia. Arlen wouldn't speak with us, and it started to get ugly."

"Are there witnesses?"

"Yes, there are witnesses."

"So it's going to come out?"

"Probably."

"It's my judgment call, but it will look a lot worse if the police snoop and come back for an explanation."

Duffy brought the detectives back into the room, and Dan continued his explanation.

"So, no, I really had met the man on very few occasions. Could probably count them on the fingers of one hand."

"On those occasions were you and he cordial?" Detective Nadler asked.

Dan looked at Duffy before answering. "Before the center closed, we were cordial. We really didn't talk. Van Aiken was aloof. He schmoozed up the rich and famous. I remember one gala for the center when Arlen entered the ballroom, and I thought 'This is unusual. He's making a beeline for me.' So I held out my hand ready to shake. It was the person standing behind me that Arlen was courting. Arlen never noticed me."

"Did you feel slighted?" Milton asked.

"No, that behavior is just the nature of the beast. That's how it works. Everyone involved in supporting the arts needs their crumb of fulfillment. When the day is over, Dita and I laugh at stuff like that. It's an ancient patronage system recycled in modern day America."

"And after the center closed?" Detective Nadler asked.

"My wife wanted answers. The board members and the executive director were ignoring her. She knew that Arlen taught a studio class on Thursdays at Columbia. CJ and I went along in support of Dita. We saw Arlen in the lobby of the architecture school but he refused to meet with us. He was engaged in a heated discussion with a student. All we could glean was that the female student had refused to sleep with him, and her grade suffered as a result. Dita stood directly in front of him, and Arlen grabbed her arm to get away from her. CJ and I restrained him."

"Thank you for being forthcoming," Detective Nadler said. "Would you recognize the student?"

"She was quite striking. So probably, yes."

"How did you feel about the other board members?" Milton asked.

"Can you be more specific?" Duffy interpolated.

"Violet Peters?"

"She might be my wife's closest friend and supporter."

"Did she get along with Van Aiken?"

"To what purpose is this question?" Duffy asked.

"I'm trying to get a feel for the day-to-day relationships between everyone involved," Milton said.

"With all due respect, my client was not involved on a day-to-day basis."

"But he is on intimate terms with his pregnant wife. I take it they shared what was happening in their lives. Seeing her take such a fall must have made you very angry. Your wife had the steady job, I take it, and you don't."

Dan was about to say, *That doesn't mean I don't*

*work, a lot.* But Duffy swiftly interjected, "You don't need to answer that," and, to Milton, he said, "Look, Detective Milton, if you have any other questions, please ask them in a non-suggestive way."

"How well acquainted were you with the layout of the center?"

"I was familiar with several of the classrooms, the parlor floor, concert hall. I knew where the men's room and the copier were located."

"Had you ever had prior occasion to go to the basement?"

"Never."

"The building next door?"

"Not at all. It needed to be renovated."

"And where would the money come from for that renovation?" Milton asked.

"Our understanding was that the work would be financed by the Department of Housing and Urban Development—HUD."

"And what happened to the money designated for that renovation?" Detective Nadler asked, nodding at Milton.

"I guess that's the four hundred and fifty thousand dollar question," replied Dan.

"So the center did obtain loans from HUD?" Milton asked.

"We were told so, yes."

"Did you try to ask Arlen Van Aiken about that?" Detective Nadler said.

"Of course, but he was avoiding us."

"Did anyone else ask Arlen about proceeds from HUD loans?" Milton asked.

"I don't think anybody could get through to Arlen. No one knew what was really going on. None of the board members would talk to Dita and Violet, or answer questions."

"He made an appointment with you for today," Detective Nadler said.

"He didn't have a choice. Arlen had the keys. The Schomburg Center wanted the *Phoenix*. Technically, the sculpture belonged to the sculptor Ricardo Montero," Dan said thinking, *Arguendo!*

"Wouldn't it have been part of the center's assets?" Milton asked.

He was sharp. Dan would give him that. He realized how much he needed this lawyer.

"That's a legal question. My client can't be expected to answer that," Duffy said.

Dan wrote Duffy a note. Duffy nodded his head in the affirmative, and Dan continued, "The sculptor was ready to fight a legal battle to get it out of there. Arlen didn't want to be named in any lawsuits, I'm sure. He was already in the hot seat."

"Okay."

"Why wasn't the sculptor present?" asked Nadler.

"He was visiting family in Puerto Rico when we finally got Arlen to agree to let us take it. Or I guess Ricardo would have been the murder suspect."

# CHAPTER 11

Detectives Milton and Nadler returned to his office and some preliminary findings from the medical examiner. He picked up a marker and began a compilation of what they already knew on a white marker board. "The statue was confirmed as the murder weapon. The position of the wound suggested that a right-handed person had struck the victim. Dan was right-handed. But it would have taken two hands, however, to wield the heavy statue.

Tomato Man is too small to have wielded the *Phoenix*. Arlen was five feet, eleven inches tall, according to the coroner. That rules out the women working in the garden. How tall are Marge and Violet?"

"Those women are in their mid-seventies," Detective Nadler said.

"Still. Di Bello is tall enough to have managed to strike Arlen from behind. The amount of blood and the lack elsewhere in the building confirms that the deadly encounter took place in the basement where the deceased was found. Why was the deceased in the basement? His business was to give Dan Di Bello and his wife the *Phoenix*, and it was on the parlor floor?"

"He went for tools maybe," said Nadler. "He didn't bring any with him."

"Okay, then why bring a heavy object down to the basement?"

"He was followed down there by the murderer when he returned the tools."

"After the statue was removed from the niche? Still doesn't clear Di Bello," Milton said. "You're really not convinced about him are you, Sheila."

"Talk about being caught red-handed. I don't know, John. I just don't know. He could be facing a very long sentence."

"Or he could plea to second degree murder and probably get ten years."

"I don't see that, somehow."

"You're new to homicide. When I started out, I met many a likable murderer. Maybe I'm a cynic now, but, even if Di Bello had closed the door and not reported the body, it would have caught up with him. We'd backtrack through Van Aiken's appointments and we'd have hauled Di Bello in here for questioning."

She snorted. "Then you'd have to investigate the wife, too."

"And we're not?"

# CHAPTER 12

Milton met with the ADA Hugo Torres, and Torres, in turn, met with the head of his unit. There was probable cause to arrest Dan. The public would be alarmed if so strong a potential suspect wasn't taken into custody. "The guy's been dead what, maybe just a few hours? You tell me who else but the guy we've got," Torres said.

Milton read Dan his Miranda rights.

"Can't I have a few minutes with my wife?"

"Dan isn't going anywhere," Duffy said.

"There are too many procedural issues."

"Aw, c'mon. A wife can't testify against her husband. That's elementary."

"I'll give them five minutes, but we will both be present," Milton told Duffy. "Sheila, bring Mrs. Di Bello in here."

Detective Nadler exited the interview room and returned with Dita, who ran to Dan and pulled him tearfully into a tight embrace. When Dan saw her tears, he, too, began to sob inconsolably. What could they say to each other in front of his jailors? They stayed like that for the allowed five minutes and, when Milton approached with handcuffs, Dita said very firmly to Dan. "Someone murdered Arlen, and it wasn't you, Dan. No stone will be left unturned until we find that person."

He felt the cuffs clank closed on his wrists. Keeping his sweat pants up was really a challenge with his hands cuffed behind him. He began to wish Dita would just shut up and let them take him already. He was worn out with worry. He needed to lie down.

"Mrs. Di Bello, maybe you'll find out some things," Milton said. "But I would caution you to let professionals handle this. Arlen Van Aiken appears to have been involved in some unsavory deals. It could be unsafe for you to approach his connections. We don't know what we are dealing with here. You could even make it worse for your husband."

Dita felt her insides turn to mush, but she managed to stand firm. "Why do I get the feeling you don't really think you're arresting the right person, Detective Milton. If you have the right person in Dan, then how could it be unsafe?"

"Dita!" Dan snapped.

"No, let me say it. Having Dan in custody will temporarily take the heat off you. But I'll be on your case should you stop looking for Arlen's killer. And after you have thoroughly dragged us through the mud, caused us to shoulder extraordinary expense, I will still be on your case."

"I'm not going to respond to that," Milton said.

Duffy put his hand on Dita's arm, but she wanted to have the last word. She was desperate. "You need to investigate his board. I think they were in total disarray at the end. One of them knows something. Promise me you'll investigate every last one of them."

Duffy placed his hand on Dan's shoulder and squeezed. Then Dan was led away to a holding cell.

"Those are artist's hands. They are meant to express. Those are not murdering hands," Dita said, watching in horror.

"C'mon," Duffy said, "Let me buy you something to eat. You're going to need strength. Ever been to Amy Ruth's?"

"Of course."

"Smothered short ribs, mashed potatoes, collards?"

"I'll only be thinking of what they are going to serve Dan for supper tonight."

"I know. Well, at least have a bowl of soup. I need to talk with you, out of this environment."

# CHAPTER 13

Outside the precinct, it was already dark. The night was humid and sultry. A tar smell rose up from the street. She had spent hours in that interview room and every muscle in her body had stiffened from the confinement. She needed water. The drinking water at the precinct had seemed somehow tainted. When she requested bottled water they told her that all they had was soda. They'd probably put Dan in one of those cells with a sink on top of the toilet. How could anyone ever put something into his mouth from such an arrangement? She could only imagine what Dan felt right now. Dita's wristwatch read ten p.m. She indeed did need strength from a meal. If she allowed herself to go unnourished, her unborn child wouldn't develop properly. They walked the short distance from the precinct to Amy Ruth's and took a table near the front window. The kitchen would soon be closing. Dita ordered a cup of tea from the waiter and Duffy recommended she order a bowl of the Philadelphia Pepper-Pot Soup.

"I always have that soup before I go into battle," he said. "It has a history. Was served to Washington's troupes when they were cold and starving during the bat-

tle at Valley Forge. You are about to begin a difficult battle. Fortify yourself."

She glugged down water as they waited for their orders to be served. Her bowl of soup arrived and Duffy's
smothered short ribs, mashed potatoes, and a side of
smoky collard greens. He tucked into the dinner while
Dita slowly consumed the soup. Any other time, the tripe
would have been like satiny pillows on her tongue. Despite the soup's rich goodness, it seemed like she was
swallowing pills. Eating because she had to.

"Do you think Dan can make bail?" Dita asked.
That's when her cell phone rang. The call was Violet and
Dita excused herself to take it.

Violet was in tears. CJ had told her what was going
on. "That damned Arlen Van Aiken. As if he didn't already do enough damage."

Violet promised to help with Dan's defense, and Dita
related this to Duffy as she closed her phone.

"You have one thing going for you," Duffy said. "A
tremendous support system."

"What kind of expenses can we anticipate?" Dita
asked. "You know we're kind of flat-out broke."

"We don't know enough yet. This case will, in all
probability, go in front of a grand jury."

"Isn't that just a rubber stamp to bring an indictment?" Dita asked.

"Someone's up on the legalese," Duffy joked.

"I've learned a lot from the people in the center
community. Everyone seems to have a relative incarcerated. I guess we've just joined that club."

Duffy nodded soberly. "That's a big part of why I do
what I do. To answer your question: Rubber stamp? Not
necessarily," he explained. "The grand jury can decide
not to indict. We need an alternative theory to present to
them."

"I'm starting to think the murderer must have been in the building when Dan stumbled on Arlen," Dita said. "Dan's never been violent, ever. You have to believe me on this."

"I do believe you. But it's only a theory right now that someone else could have been in there. But one worth holding onto," Duffy said.

"Will we be allowed into the building?"

"When the police have finished with it."

"I don't trust them."

"I'd like to begin by earmarking funds for a private investigator. We need to know more about who was involved with Arlen."

"Who will you be using? Not that I know any private eyes."

"I use Lumen Quirk. He's good. I'll be dipping into the retainer for that expense."

"What do you want for a retainer?" Dita asked.

"My retainer has already been paid."

"CJ?"

Duffy nodded.

"Can I ask how much?"

"No you cannot ask how much. Part of the deal."

Dita began to cry. "God love the man, that CJ."

"I'm going to meet with the prosecutor tomorrow morning at ten before I visit Dan. After I know what the prosecution's theories are, I will be in a much better position to tell you how I see this case."

"Would Dan go before the grand jury?" Dita asked.

"Possibly, but his testimony could be used later at trial if there are discrepancies in his story."

"He'd only tell the truth."

"You have to see it this way, Dita," Duffy said. "There's never one truth. Same facts can mean many dif-

ferent truths. My truth and a prosecutor's truth can be different things."

"Will he get bail? Do they set bail in murder cases?"

"I will request bail at the arraignment but, with a
murder charge, I'm not hopeful."

# CHAPTER 14

Duffy hailed a livery and was putting Dita into it when his cell phone rang. The case was scheduled for review by a grand jury the next day. She returned alone to their empty apartment. At one a.m., she took a long, hot soak in the bathtub then made herself a cup of chamomile tea. The nausea still remained Dita's constant companion. She awakened to it every morning, and it plagued her just before mealtimes. Dita remembered the afternoon she had taken the pregnancy test, and it made her realize how much she loved Dan. Maybe if she had done it earlier, their lives would have taken a different turn, and Dan wouldn't have been at the center today.

She had kept putting the test off and had let three months go by. Three months of nausea and changes in her body that could no longer be ignored. She steeled herself to learn the truth. The afternoon was balmy. A cool breeze mingled with the scent of roses. Gentle summer had come to New York City. She'd decided to make a walk through Riverside Park and buy the kit at a Rite Aid farther downtown.

When she reached the Rite Aid, she'd hesitated and

told herself all over again that she just could not be pregnant. There was a Starbucks next door, and she ordered a chai latte and sat on a stool by the window, sipping. It tasted funky to her, and she immediately regretted the expense. She tossed it into the garbage, exited, and returned to the Rite Aid.

Dita had found the aisle with the pregnancy tests. She was shy about the purchase and felt like a teenager buying contraceptives. She considered which test to buy. Some promised early results but, if Dita were pregnant, she'd be in her fourth month, too late to do anything about it. Had she really wronged Dan by not confiding in him? She couldn't get these thoughts out of her mind. If the results were positive, she would have to share the news with him. Would he be too frightened to entertain thoughts about fatherhood now that they were both practically destitute?

For some reason, she'd bought the most expensive test on the shelf, paid for it, and walked back to their apartment. Dan was composing at the piano. She scooted by him and headed into the bathroom with a paper cup. The tea had activated her bladder, and she had to pee. She peed into the cup, and ripped open the test kit. It said to put the test stick into a cup of urine for twenty seconds and then remove it. If a blue stripe appeared across a little round window, the test was positive. She hesitated to look at the results. She was filled with a sudden cowardice. When she dared look, sure enough, the blue stripe appeared in the plastic gadget's little window. Dita girded herself to share the news with Dan.

"How?" Dan had said, and that was all.

"I don't know how. I think it happened the night after they closed the center."

"I remember that sex."

"You do?"

"We never did it like that, as good as it was."

"I was filling up a big, deep vacuum. Are you going to be angry with me?"

"I can't say it doesn't complicate the situation."

"Maybe we should leave New York. You could teach theory in a college. I could teach, too."

"I don't have a PhD. They'll use me and never give me tenure. Same with you, Dita. We both should have stayed in school longer. Look, I love you, Dita. I never wanted us not to have children. But this, this is overwhelming. And it's probably too late to do anything about it."

"But you would never want me to abort our child?"

"No." He took her in his arms and let her cry on his shoulder.

"I want to make love," she said. "I want tender sex."

He looked wistfully at the manuscript on the piano but let her lead him across the room to their bedroom. That man could not have harmed another human being. She'd heard many stories about husbands of friends who went into paroxysms of anger when confronted with an accidental pregnancy.

These thoughts about Dan's innate goodness helped sooth Dita a little. How could she and Dan have gotten so low? She just wished she could close her eyes and find herself in oblivion. But she couldn't even consider a sleeping pill or a drink right now." She patted her stomach. She had been feeling the first flutters of life within her belly and, as she patted it again, she felt the almost imperceptible twinge. She longed to share it with Dan as the cat hopped up on her lap. She buried her face in his fur and cried. It felt good to cry, better than feeling numb. When she cried, she felt as if she could cope. It was three a.m. before she turned down the covers on their bed. It seemed so large without Dan in it. Dita couldn't remember whether or not she slept at all. She was awake at first light and remained in bed praying for sleep to come again. It didn't. She finally got out of bed and sat on Dan's piano bench with an acrid-tasting cup of coffee before heading into the shower.

୧୬୧

Long and frequent showers had become one of Dita's coping mechanisms after the center closed. It was as if the pulsing water could wash away her fears. Afterward, she would wrap her lissome body in a terry cloth robe and head into the kitchen. One morning, about a month before Dan's arrest, she had lingered in the shower some forty minutes. She had yet to take the pregnancy test and was tied up in knots of disbelief. Her breasts were swollen and her belly rounder than it had ever been.

Afterward, in the kitchen she'd found a carafe of coffee, a pitcher of milk, and a cutting board set out with bagels and cream cheese. Dan was a thoughtful husband. Would he share the joy as well as the burdens of a child? she remembered thinking as she poured herself a mug of coffee and smeared cream cheese on a bagel half. She was on a second half when Dan joined her. Dita had been on the verge of telling Dan about the nausea and then had thought of the better of it. It wasn't right not to discuss her fears with Dan. He had never been against having a child. She had never pushed the issue.

"What if something else happened to us that's worse than what has already happened?"

"Don't get maudlin."

She had let the moment pass. This was not the way to phrase what she wanted to say. No, it wasn't worse, and worse yet, maybe it wasn't true. Still, she regretted the intentional betrayal and wondered if it would come to fester in their relationship at a later date.

Then Dan left to play for ballet classes. Her worries had mounted. They could hardly manage on what he could pull in each week. What price would there be to pay?

She hadn't given a thought to the mortgage and maintenance due on their co-op. Everything was overdue. The mortgage was in arrears. The bank was trying politely to find out where the payment was. As usual, the collectors, at first, called it an oversight on the first pass at collection. Now that they were seriously late, there would be legal action and the co-op board would find out, too. If only they could have managed to live on one of their salaries, they wouldn't be in this kind of trouble. But they had bought into a lifestyle that demanded two incomes.

There had to be some accommodation somewhere. They had discussed the possibility of subletting their co-op but the bylaws only allowed each shareholder a year of sublet time. It seemed doubtful they could turn their lives around in a year. They were squeezed into a corner with too many unpalatable options—choose door A, and it leads to hell. Choose door B, and it leads to more hell. That expression "there's hell to pay" she had now understood.

With Dan incarcerated, it comforted Dita to hear his music in her head. She and Dan had a sort of musical karma together that she was hard-put to describe. The first time Dan seduced Dita, it was with Wagner's Liebestod. It became a joke between them. They could time their lovemaking to Ravel's Bolero. Dita thought about Dan's latest composition. It was a very mature writing. Despite the disruptions in their lives caused by the center's closing, Dan had been very productive in the months following the closing of the center. They'd had a yard sale to help raise a bit of cash, and the apartment was open and empty. "It was actually nice being in our apartment with it so empty," he'd told Dita. "No distractions. I do nothing but compose when I'm here." He'd finished composing the piece he had been working on. He called it a tone poem for the piano. Written originally for orchestra, Dan had despaired of ever getting it played. Now he was glad for this decision to write it for piano. It should be bringing him the break he so well deserved. But Fortuna was spinning downward in a precipitous spiral. Conjuring the piece again brought her momentary comfort. Dita had the capacity to hear music in her head. In fact like Dan, a sound track always played only to be interrupted if she needed to listen to something else. Their child would probably inherit this innate musicality, she mused.

"Can I play the piece for you?" he'd asked her.

She remembered the day fondly. "Yes," she'd said, settling into a chintz love seat that was all that was left of their living room furniture. It had been her grandmothers, and she could never have sold it. Dita and Dan had managed to sell a beaten-up old leather recliner, cat scratches and all. *I'm going to feel like another part of me is missing. So many hours spent curled up in that chair with a book. I have to be tough.* Dita thought of it as the day of the great purge. She wanted to confide in CJ about how far behind they were in mortgage and maintenance payments, but that would have been like asking for money and Dita just couldn't do it.

Dita had closed her eyes as Dan played. The tone poem was lushly atmospheric.

"Probably more difficult than Gaspard," he said, referring to the "Ravel Gaspard de la Nuit," a daunting piece for any pianist. Like the "Ravel" there were references to water. She thought about fluid dance movements—or internal fluids causing motion. Dan's piece led

Dita to conjure images. Dan smiled. He knew where she was headed.

The finished piece of music brought Dan and Dita completeness, and they were glad to allow it to settle over them for a few moments. A ringing cell phone interrupted their reveries. The bank! They both froze.

*ↄↄↄ*

Dita and Dan requested a meeting with some of their co-op's board members to alert them that they might need to sell their apartment and guarantee the board that the maintenance arrears would come out at the closing. They were allowed to present to the board members in private before the board met officially. *Another board in our lives,* Dita thought as they were ushered into the basement board meeting room. Most of the board members appeared sympathetic.

"We were hoping to work something out with you," Dan said. "We understand that you could start legal proceedings against us, and we would like to spare us and the building that expense. We have every intention of putting the apartment on the market and taking the first reasonable offer we get."

"There should be some sort of time limit. The building needs your maintenance money to run things," said a heavy-set women white woman wearing a bandana to tie back unruly hair, scribbling on a tablet.

Dita and Dan thought her name was Hilary.

"Your name is Hilary, right?" Dita asked. The woman nodded and Dita continued. "We'd agree to a time limit as long as this remains secret. We don't want people to think we're desperate, and I admit we are desperate," she said as Dan took her hand.

The board president suggested allowing them ninety days, the average time it took to sell a co-op such as theirs. The meeting had gone well, and Dita and Dan had felt some relief. There would be a little bit of cash left after the bank took its share. They'd have to live with parents until they could get back on their feet. And now with Dan arrested, Dita would have to live with her parents again.

# CHAPTER 15

At two a.m., Dan's hands were again cuffed behind him, and he was transported from the holding cell of the Twenty-Fifth Precinct to another holding cell attached to the criminal division of the Manhattan Supreme Court to wait for possible arraignment. His shoulder's ached and the new plastic cuffs for transport cut into the skin on his wrists. The baggy clothes were taken away, and he was issued an orange jump suit. At least it was better fitting than the sweats he spent the afternoon holding up. He had trouble staying upright in the transport vehicle. When they arrived and he was secured in a cell, breakfast was brought to him by one of the guards—rubbery scrambled eggs, some sort of tofu bacon or maybe it was over processed turkey, he couldn't tell, and white toast. The coffee was the worst Dan had ever tasted.

# CHAPTER 16

Duffy met with ADA Hugo Torres the next day. They met in Torres's office in the Manhattan District Attorney building. Torres sat behind a scuffed, metal desk, partially hidden behind his copious stack of files. The assistant district attorney's face was too young for the baldness that surrounded it. Torres was an obtuse man. When Duffy brought up the idea that someone else could have been lurking in the center at the time Dan found Arlen, he scoffed at the idea. Duffy had skirmished with him before and won, so Hugo's nose was all out of joint. Torres had an unfailing belief that anyone brought before him had to have done something. He offered Dan a plea. Ten years. Charge reduced to second-degree murder. Duffy informed Torres there would be no plea. He had told Dan that there would probably be this kind of offer on the table, and Dan had been adamant that he wanted a trial if it came to that.

"It's in the hands of the grand jury now," Torres told Duffy.

At Dita's insistence that the relationship between the center's board members had fallen apart, Milton tried unsuccessfully to contact the other board members. "Okay," he said. "Probably just a bunch of red herrings.

"Do you want me to try contacting the board members again?" asked Nadler.

"Yes, maybe some persistence will pay off here. This is the strangest goddamned case. A lot of motives, and only Di Bello had opportunity."

# CHAPTER 17

After Duffy saw Dan in the criminal court interview room, Dita met Duffy in his office. She didn't know quite what to expect. The office was comfortably furnished with a black leather sofa. There were stacks of files on Duffy's desk. He offered her coffee but she took out a bottle of water.

"Let's create a list of potential suspects, starting with the board," he told her.

They jotted down the names of every board member.

"Likewise we need a list of everyone associated with the center," he said.

"I've been making a list," Dita said, handing him a spiral notebook.

"We'll go over this in a moment. I got through to the wife of Mitchell Shepherd. She said that her husband was out of the country on business." Duffy scrawled a question mark next to his name. The other names remaining were Ted Callahan, Violet Peters, Rex Turner, Bennett Dawes, and Reverend John Teague. They eliminated Violet and that left Callahan, Turner, Dawes, and the Reverend John Teague.

# CHAPTER 18

Later that afternoon, Duffy went before the grand jury on behalf of Dan. Grand juries met in secret, and Dita was barred from the proceeding. She said she was going to try to visit Dan. Duffy waited patiently while the assistant district attorney strutted cockily before the assemblage. ADA Torres presented his case succinctly, underscoring for the twenty-three stiff, poker-faced grand jurors how tight the time frame of approximately twenty minutes was. In a scoffing manner, he told them, "It's grasping at straws to think someone else could have been on the premises at the same time. The decedent was dead less than an hour when the police arrived on the scene, according to the medical examiner. The defendant handled the murder weapon. Then he made sure the scene was too messy to do proper forensics. But it didn't work in his favor. Only his prints appear on it." Torres had a PowerPoint presentation of the print obtained from Dan's hand, his bloodied clothes, and whatever else had been gathered at the crime scene. It looked very convincing.

When it was his turn, Duffy contradicted Torres. "A lot can happen in twenty minutes. There was opportunity. The ADA cannot rule out the presence of another actor, plus—" And he paused a beat. "—Van Aiken's lack of response when Di Bello called out for him in the dark, dank center could mean Arlen was already dead," he told the grand jury, letting the notion of reasonable doubt linger. Duffy well knew that Oliver Outlaw, aka Tomato Man, only heard Dan call at the front door. Once Dan went for the flashlight and went back into the interior, only the almighty was a witness unless someone was lurking in the building waiting for a chance to escape— Duffy's hope, Dan and Dita's hope!

As was expected, the solemn-faced grand jury voted to indict. Duffy had told Dan that this would probably be the result.

# CHAPTER 19

After Dan's arrest, Dita continued taking her aimless walks. She'd used up her three allowed visits to the Manhattan Detention Center for the week. She was helpless to console or help Dan on those visits. He was brutally pessimistic about his chances to prove his innocence. How could she give him hope? She was on the outside of all that was happening. He lived the reality of the jail.

Dita liked to be near water that flowed onward. The Hudson River had always brought her a sense of possibility. As a young dance student, she'd traveled the train along the Hudson from her parents' home in Poughkeepsie to New York and back six days a week. Today, she walked through Riverside Park alone. The buoyant river beyond the park glinted in the bright afternoon but Dita walked through a veil of tangled shadows, letting dark thoughts control her mind.

She hated to admit to how she would dread the trek out to the prison on Riker's Island should Dan be taken there.

She wondered if she would stop visiting frequently. Unbeknownst to anyone but herself, her loyalty was being tested. She chided herself for anticipating this new situation. It felt all the more disloyal.

As if to mirror her state of mind, the sky began to darken. A fierce flash of light accompanied an odious rumble, and then the crenellated sky shattered. Heavy rain plunged out of bursting clouds onto the green lawns of the park. Shrubbery bowed under the onslaught. The fanfare played for another ten minutes. It was of no use for Dita to seek shelter. She was drenched in an instant. And then it was all over. The sun pierced through the gray sky and, somehow, the world seemed cleansed of a terrible burden. The hydrangeas, someone in the community had planted, picked up their droopy purple heads assured of safety in the atmosphere.

Dita climbed the hill to Riverside Drive slowly, thinking all the while about Dan. The string that seemed to thread through their lives had gotten tangled. It was her job to untangle it. It was a matter of how you thought about something, she told herself.

Her world had always seemed ephemeral and many faceted—one facet didn't always converge with the others. Her mind made lax associations. She knew she needed to find connections.

Why was she so sure Dan hadn't done this deed? How would life pan out if he had truly lost it in a moment of utter frustration at seeing the center ravaged, pianos stolen, and fearful of bringing a child into the world. Would she allow him back into her life if this panned out to be the truth? Could she ever trust him with a child? Then she shoved these thoughts aside as obstacles to be overcome. What Dita and Dan had was too pure. That was how she knew he was an innocent man.

She went on home to change her wet clothes. Dita was determined to get some answers from the center board members as well. She'd begin with Mitchell Shepherd's office. He'd not been in touch with anyone involved in the investigation. Duffy had tried to contact him, and she understood Milton also had tried. The man was hiding from something or someone. She found the address in the Yellow Pages.

# CHAPTER 20

This time, a receptionist the front desk filing her nails. The place reeked of acetone nail polish remover. A jar of sparkly blue nail polish sat on some paper toweling.

"I'm looking for Mitchell Shepherd," Dita said.

"Yeah, you and everyone else. He hasn't been in the office all week."

"Who else came looking for him?"

"For starters, his wife."

"And who else?"

"Clients. He has a closing this afternoon, and no one has heard from him. One of the other lawyers in the firm said she would go to the closing."

"What is her name?"

"Miranda Hochberg."

"Do you think she would see me?"

Miranda Hochberg refused loudly, and the receptionist pulled off her earpiece and put her finger into her ear, realizing that she smudged the wet nail polish in her ear canal. Dita handed her a Kleenex. Something serious was in play.

"Tell her it is very important that I see her ASAP.

Where is her office?" Dita rushed around the reception-ist's desk and headed into the warren of offices.

"Don't' go back there!"

"You can't stop me."

The space was crudely divided. She found a plump and harried Miranda Hochberg on her cell phone at a shared copier. "No, I have no idea where it is. Maybe Mitch has a certified check on him. What the fuck? Who are you?" she said to Dita.

"I need to talk to you about Mitchell Shepherd ASAP."

"What gives you the right to bust in here?"

"My husband was arrested for the murder of Arlen Van Aiken."

"That?"

"Shepherd was on the board. I was the artistic direc-tor."

"I understood he volunteered his time and provided you with legal services."

"He also got us a mortgage we shouldn't have gotten and the money disappeared."

"That's impossible. Look, I have to go to a closing for Mitch in an hour."

"Why do you have to go to a closing for him?"

"Because he hasn't called in, and the client is frantic and, if you must know, there are no funds in Mitchell's escrow account, and I'm going to have to call the authori-ties."

"Holy shit!"

"Yeah, holy shit!"

Dita called Duffy from the outer office. "I'm going to see Ted Callahan." Ted Callahan was the banker Arlen had brought onto the center's board. He didn't respond to phone calls, either.

"Not alone, you don't. I'll meet you there with Quirk. Where is his office?"

"The Hudson River at the boat basin. He uses a yacht as his office, but he works for some bank in Connecticut."

"Again. Don't approach him on your own. We'll be in Quirk's car, and we'll meet you on the southwest corner of Seventy-Ninth Street and Broadway."

It was a bus stop. Dita waited while several busses loaded and unloaded passengers. Busses out of service waited at the West End Avenue corner down the block. The stop was now clear, and Quirk's black SUV pulled up to the curb.

Duffy jumped out and held open the back door for her. "At your service, madam," he quipped. "We're here to keep you out of trouble."

The private detective Lumen Quirk was at the wheel and turned in greeting. He was the lankiest man Dita had ever seen. Between the seat and the ceiling there wasn't enough space, and he had to tilt his head under the visor to drive. He had penetrating green eyes and close-cropped sandy hair. He reached around to shake Dita's hand.

"Nice day for a yacht ride," he said as he made a U turn on Seventy-Ninth Street and headed for the boat basin. He parked the car in the traffic circle at the point where a wall made from cut stone overlooked the docks. Quirk unfolded to his full height and the three of them clambered down the circular stone stairs leading to the boats. In the short time it took him to drive to Seventy-Ninth Street, Quirk had done his homework and he knew where Callahan's yacht moored at the wave wall where there was room for four yachts. Callahan's was not there. Quirk called the dock master who told them that Callahan's yacht had left on August eighth, and had not returned since. August eighth was the day before the murder.

"I tried to find contact numbers for Bennett Dawes," Dita told Duffy and Quirk.

"I had Quirk on that as well."

"I'm not sure Bennett Dawes exists," said Quirk.

"I had met the others briefly at various times but never Dawes. The new board seldom let me address them. I tried making appointments with them individually, but those appointments got cancelled." Dita said. "Violet never met him either. We think he made up the fictional majority that Arlen depended on to do what he wanted with our property."

"That's probably the truth."

"As to Callahan, we need to follow a money trail," Duffy said. "And perhaps it's time to visit the US Attorney."

Not finding Callahan, they headed back to Duffy's office. Dita had begun to research, in order to understand how HUD worked. Duffy explained how easy it was to defraud the behemoth organization. It lacked oversight and was a sitting duck for Arlen and company, if that's indeed what they were doing. She chided herself for not having learned sooner. *Why was I so oblivious to their real estate machinations?* she'd asked herself. The answer was very simple. She learned that individuals could only get financing on only one property, but not-for-profit organizations could acquire many properties. Had Arlen been somehow using not-for-profits to acquire property? The HUD mortgage gave the buyer half of the money for a down payment on the purchase. The other half should have gone into an escrow account that could be drawn down upon as construction proceeded. But if he was taking the cash out and stashing it away somehow, could this be plausible? she asked herself.

Violet, Marge, and Dita made a trip together to the hall of records to search for property records in the name of board members and they were coming up with dead ends. Arlen was not mentioned, but more not-for-profits kept popping up, and the lender was always the same—the La Grange Trust Company. "Someone knew something," Dita said. "The thing that scares me most is that no one will look into it because Dan got caught with fucker Arlen's blood on his hands."

# CHAPTER 21

The *New York Times* reporter Samantha Elder had gotten wind of a scandal about to break, and it had come to murder. Dita hadn't spoken to her since the contentious telephone encounter in May. When news reached Samantha about Dan Di Bello's arrest, she had been working on an article focusing on individuals who had tried to buy Harlem property. *So You Want To Own A brownstone*, it was provisionally titled. The purchasers had relied on their lawyers and title companies to assure them of clear title.

Her impression was that the purchasers were a greedy bunch, in denial about the truth of what they sought. She was having trouble being their advocate in a news article. Her editor had suggested that it was almost a human-interest story, and it could help to plug a gentrifying neighborhood. To Samantha, it was a story of the gullibility of home-buyers. When she learned one of the properties in question was now owned by the defunct arts center, it made Samantha very curious. A quiver of excitement coursed like electricity through her veins about a possible huge story, and she called Dita.

"Why should I talk with you?" Dita demanded.

"Because I can possibly help you."

"I don't want to be quoted in any article you are writing about the center. It could harm Dan."

"Dita, hear me out. I'm learning things. It can only help if I share what I learn with you. I know you didn't run the organization into the ground. I know I was lied to by Arlen Van Aiken."

"Yes," Dita said. "Arlen was involved in an enterprise of some sort to defraud HUD. It's come to light since the murder. But I should only talk to you through Dan's lawyer at this point. But oh, shit! Please find out anything you can." She paused for a breath. "Well, let me start by telling you what I know and what I don't know."

"Fair enough."

Dita told her about her visit to Mitchell Shepherd's office and that Callahan had gone fugitive.

"That's news worthy," Sam said. "I learned he has other offices in Darien, Connecticut. I actually went all the way there. He wasn't there, either. Something is going on."

Samantha didn't know about the yacht. A huge exhale was Samantha's response. Dita could almost feel the wind through the receiver.

"So they both might be fugitives?" Sam said. "Furthermore, there is another board member named Bennett Dawes"

"I don't think Bennett Dawes is a real person," Dita told her. "He's the vote who gets the board the majority." She imagined the conspirators laughing when they came up with the name. Could it symbolize something? She'd play around with it.

"I couldn't find him, either."

"There's a couple I met who tried to buy the building next door," Dita told her.

"The Carsons?"

"Yes, how did you know?"

"I interviewed them for an article on Harlem real estate. They seem to have moved on. Are you in touch with them?"

"I met up with them at Fairway. I had seen them come and go from my office window last year with their architect and engineers. I was hoping they'd be able to purchase the property." Dita prefaced what she said by explaining to Samantha what it was like for her after the center closed. "I had never been introduced to them. They didn't know I existed until I ran into them at Fairway."

"At Fairway Market?"

"Yes, at the fish counter."

"And you introduced yourself and got into a discussion with them?"

"Sort of like that. At first I wasn't sure they were the same people. And I was so out of sorts by then. After the center closed I became a jobless shopper to fill my time. Don't laugh! Before the closing I scarcely had time. But since, shopping groceries for dinner was looming pretty large in my daily agenda although we were broke. Even with Dan in jail I wander through places. You know that ballet La Sonambula?"

"Sure! And I like the opera."

"Well that's what I've become, a sleep walker. It all started early on. What else could I do? I'd lost the strong sense of direction that had always driven me. I had managed to combine the shopping with long pointless walks. That's how I spent my days until Dan's arrest. There were no job leads to follow and let's face it. I'm tainted. He might never get out of prison. I might never get a job again. So I Just wander around the city like a bag lady. Oh, why am I telling you all this?" She needed to unburden herself even though part of her knew that the reporter could misconstrue everything she said.

"No, continue," I want to understand what you went through. It puts a human face on it all. I can't imagine losing my job. I've always taken the pursuit of a story for granted. Something I love."

"Thank you." Dita felt herself melting inside and warming toward this woman who began their acquaintance as her detractor. So she talked on. Dita explained how sometimes she'd pay a penny at the door and wander through the Metropolitan Museum. "You can pay what you can afford there and as an artist I have no compunction about entering for a penny. Besides I didn't have enough cash to wander through the Guggenheim or the Modern."

Samantha laughed.

Dita threw caution to the wind and continued to pour out her soul. It just felt good to tell someone how she felt. "I hardly see the art anymore. It seems such a sad irony that Dan's incarceration is what throws me back into action. So about a month after the center closed," Dita explained to Samantha, "I finished with the day's wanderings and was contemplating the trout on the seafood counter at the Fairway Market. Big moment in my day! I thought it would be a nice and inexpensive treat for Dan. Poached, skinned and slathered with melted sweet butter. Comfort food! At least to me anything with butter on it is comforting."

"You make that sound so yummy. Do you like to cook?"

"It is simple and yummy and I do love to cook. Dan once did some accompanying in Aspen, the summer music festival, and there was this place you had to reach by ski lift, and all they served back then was trout prepared that way. Place is probably out of sight pricewise today. I doubt we'll ever get back there. But at least I have a talent for knocking off recipes."

Samantha laughed and Dita continued to tell her how she met up with Marla and Brett. Samantha could imagine the scene. Dita was beginning to fascinate her with her food wanderings as a coping mechanism. *Moreover, she's a dancer who cooks, eats, and stays skinny*, Samantha thought.

Dita reconstructed the scene at the Fairway market vividly. Samantha, who also had a love of detail, let her ramble. The lady was writing an article and not realizing it. If the center hadn't closed she would have made a great profile piece.

"When I don't want to confront something I think about food a bit too deeply. The trout sat behind a glass partition, on a bed of shaved ice, garnished here and there with curly kale leaves. It reminded me of a skating rink the way the fish was set out. Fillets seemed to curl and dance around the whole fish. Could have been a painting of turn of the century New York. Whoever does the displays has a sense of humor. I really appreciate that."

"So did you buy?"

"I was not won over by the clarity of the fishes' eyes," she said. "Fish eyes become more opaque with each passing hour out of the water I've been taught. That's how you decided if a whole fish was fresh. With fillets—it's another matter. I was checking out the piles of fluke, flounder, English fillet of sole when I became aware of a tall man standing beside me. I noticed the length of his legs and trim butt in khaki slacks—the kind of legs that go on forever."

"That would be Brett?"

"Gorgeous man! He was wearing a plaid button-down short-sleeved shirt. His coffee colored face and almond green eyes stirred my memory, and then he was joined by a petit strawberry-blond with a down-under accent. His shopping cart was laden with grocery items.

'You see anything you want, love?' he asked. 'Not sure,' she said. Those same voices drifted through my office window a little over a year ago. They couldn't have seen me, but I felt an intimacy with this couple that I can't explain. I said to them, 'You were looking at a building in Harlem a year ago.' They looked at me, shocked. He said cautiously, 'Yes, how did you know about that?'

"'I worked in the center next door,' I told him. 'I was the artistic director. My board closed the center. That is, after we purchased the building you were looking at. It destroyed us. I knew it would end badly. What happened with you?'

"'What didn't happen?' the woman said. 'It was a very bitter experience.'

"Brett asked me, 'How were you able to buy the building? There were some very unclear things in its prior ownership. We finally gave up after wasting thousands of dollars on architects and engineers. Then we had trouble getting back our down payment.'

"'Did you buy anywhere?' I asked them.

"'Yes, a co-op apartment. It was a much simpler closing. I'm Brett Carson and this is my wife Marla.'

"'Dita Marx.' I didn't say that I already knew their names from overhearing them spoken by the people they had consulted. How much more eavesdropping could I confess to without sounding like a total creep?

"'Do you own somewhere?' Brett asked me.

"'Yes, a co-op in Morningside Heights but we need to sell it. When the center closed my job ended.'

"'Ouch,' Marla said. 'I'd actually like to hear about how the center acquired the property.'

"'Do you want to exchange phone numbers?' I asked.

"'Good idea,' Marla said.

"'Same here. Let's meet for coffee,' Brett said. 'Our place.'

"It was one of the last times Dan and I socialized with anyone," Dita told Samantha. "Let me explain…"

eↄeↄ

The Carsons lived on West End Avenue and Ninety-Seventh Street. Marla had opened the door of their two-bedroom apartment to Dita and Dan.

The center hall was painted white on white with a hint of yellow. It had a long cheerful hallway. A new oriental runner covered the length of wood floor freshly scraped.

"Well, we would still be wearing hard hats if we had gotten the brownstone," she had said with a crusty irony. They all laughed. Brett appeared in a navy blue denim chef's apron from the kitchen at the end of the hall. Cooking scents redolent of cinnamon filled the air.

"I made us some muffins to have along with our brew." He ushered them into the kitchen. It ran the width of the apartment and extended into a cozy sitting area with a breakfast table. Someone had taken out the maid's bedroom to create an eat-in kitchen.

"Looks like you did well," Dan said.

"We would have liked to have had the rental you get with a brownstone. But that business got too difficult."

Marla went about setting out stoneware mugs and filling a matching creamer. "We like real cream."

"So do we," Dita said. "Have to have the real thing in my coffee."

Brett proffered the muffins. Everyone stirred cream into the coffee. The muffins were densely rich with whole grains and not overly sweet.

"These are terrific," Dan said, alternating bites of

muffin with sips of his coffee. "And the coffee is the best."

"So tell me what the center was about?" asked Brett.

"It was Dita's baby," Dan said.

Dita explained her first career as a dancer and how Violet, CJ, and she'd conceived an arts school with the real estate donation of Violet's mother's house, empty corner lot and start-up money from CJ's parents. "Violet's mother was Ella Peters."

"The jazz pianist?" Brett asked.

"Yes," Dita said, surprised.

"My dad was a fan."

"She ran a way-station for jazz performers passing through New York. Some pretty famous artists couldn't book the hotels because of the color of their skin. Violet grew up with the best of the old time jazz players, and then she discovered the opera."

"So the center building is a piece of history? What a shame. I had no idea there was other interest in our place. We bid and had gotten our bid accepted, and then all the hanky-panky started."

Dita sighed. "It never occurred to me that my board would want to acquire another piece of real estate. We were always struggling as it was. We were supposed to bring in this incredible rental income that would float the center. There was supposedly money to make the repairs. I must have had my head in the sand, but there was nothing I could do. My concern was running the program."

"It's very impressive that you were able to start something like that at such a young age," Marla had said, "and you kept it going for quite a long time. We would have been volunteers for you. I always wanted to be in the kind of urban environment where people pitch in and share."

Dita had laughed. "I actually fantasized the same

thing when I would hear you coming and going with your engineers. I was praying that after you moved in, all those other shells would get bought up by people who wanted to live on our street."

"So what happened when you tried to close? Did you actually sign a contract?" Dan asked.

"We did indeed," Brett said, "and it came back with a disclaimer that if any industrial pesticides were found on the property that the seller had no responsibility for its removal. And that if we didn't close in thirty days, we would lose our deposit."

"Pretty onerous!" Dan said.

"I thought, by that point, they were trying to renege, had something else going. We should have walked, then and there. But we signed and then the seller sat on our check until I went over and screamed at his lawyer to cash it already."

"What were you going to pay for the building? If you don't mind my asking," Dan asked.

"No, we don't mind," Marla said. "With a HUD mortgage you can only get up to four-hundred-and fifty thousand dollars. So we made a bid of one-hundred-and-ninety thousand that was accepted, and that left the rest to do the renovations. The place wasn't really habitable. We had to have architects plans to be accepted for the mortgage and that was fifteen thousand dollars that came right out of our pockets."

Dita's face had become very pensive. "The center paid well over three hundred thousand dollars, and I was told we qualified for HUD because we were a non-profit. Something just doesn't add up. I think we should have a lawyer go over the real estate deal, Dan."

"Wow. I can see why," Brett said.

"It stinks. It seemed to me, back then, to be a matter of a seller getting a better offer after he accepted a bid,"

Marla said. "I mean that's what we thought at the time. There are people walking around with plenty of cash, too."

☙❧❧

"So you see," Dita told Samantha. "We became friends, the Carsons and Dan and I. It helped me shed some of the blame I put on myself. I realized that none of the center's woes were really my fault. We were defrauded. I hope it can help free Dan."

"I can't imagine putting up engineering fees for something so tenuous. But I'm hearing the story over and over again," Samantha said. "People want to live in those houses. It's New York City's last frontier."

"If something seems acceptable, then people do it, Samantha. How could anyone know Arlen and company were going to clean out the center and sit on it just like they sit on all the other properties all over Harlem. The value would spiral. But something happened, and Arlen ended up dead. I tried to fathom what the personal connection to Arlen and, maybe, Randy was."

"Who is Randy?"

"She was the executive director."

"That's Randolynn Smith Warren. I just didn't think of her as Randy."

"It was difficult for me to think of her that way, too," and Dita proceeded to explain Randy to Samantha. "She was so hard-nosed. But Randy sometimes had seemed at odds with the board. Her presentation of the purchase had somehow lacked enthusiasm. I felt."

"Do you think Randy was in on whatever went down?" asked Samantha.

"I just don't know. I remembered thinking the relationships were very confusing—toward me, mostly adversarial. And there was a program to run. I wanted to rely on someone like Randy. But she didn't seem to have a clue as to what we were about.

"Several months into her tenure as executive director Randy had presented to me the idea of acquiring the adjacent property. 'The center will not only get more space for its operations, the rental values alone will help float it.'

"'Well, I don't know anything about real estate,' I had protested.

"I assumed the young couple I now knew as Marla and Brett had closed on the building. I didn't mention them to Randy. Randy's announcement surprised me, but I let it pass, remembering how the wind carried the musical cadence of his voice upward into my office. I had found it soothing as Randy made me more and more nervous.

"Randy had paced the floor before each and every speech to board members and potential supporters, adjusting her scarves and glossing her lips. The board had complained that I was never persuasive enough. And Randy took over this aspect of my job.

"I had to admit that I have never been fully at ease with the donors. I understood that they, too, needed to find their crumb of fulfillment by being involved. I had seen donors turn fickle when they suddenly understood that the center was not about celebrity as many bigger arts organizations were. Only Violet, CJ, and Dan shared the small pleasures of seeing the place turn on its own axis.

"Once she had established her persona, Randy had gotten down to the business of going over the everyday details of the center's operation. Not hesitant to walk in on a private lesson to survey a piece of equipment, she had made copious lists, annotated by questions. Ballet slippers, music stands, sinks, toilets, the center's fifteen pianos, an umbrella stand, copiers, coffee makers—even things like an ancient microwave that had been brought in by my assistant Marge didn't escape Randy's listing. And then because there was no intercom, Randy had taken to calling the personnel on their personal cell phones.

"I had been enrolling a perspective student the first time Randy had called my cell. "'Dita, I need to see you ASAP.'

"'I'm with a parent.'

"'Let them wait.'

"'Absolutely not. I'll see you in ten minutes.'

"Ten minutes later, ensconced in a walnut Victorian parlor chair with a jacquard seat and back cushion, I faced Randy, who had been arranging a new glass bauble into the curio cabinet—a paperweight filled with glass rose petals.

"'What's on your mind, Randy?'

"'I think we're having some problems here.'

"'You know I'm always busy with students and parents in the after school hours. The timing wasn't good.'

"'I called you to ask you if you knew how many pianos the center owns.'

"I hesitated. 'I don't know.' I counted on my fingers. 'There are three baby grand pianos in the main teaching studios then ten studio uprights in the practice rooms and the concert grand in the recital hall. So that makes what, fourteen.'

"'I counted fifteen,' Randy said. 'There's a Mason Hamlin baby grand on the third floor.'

"'It's not usable,' I said. 'Someone donated it just to get rid of it.'

"'And who paid to haul it in here.'

"'It was a mistake made by me early on.'

"'So, what I want to know,' Randy had pressed on,

'is how often do you tune all of these pianos?'

"'Quarterly, except for the concert grand in the recital hall which we tune before important concerts.'

"'And keyboards don't have to be tuned?' she asked.

"'We only have one keyboard that we travel to schools with. Where are you going with this, Randy?'

"'I figure fifteen hours of tuning every three months, repairs, et cetera. If we could get keyboards donated, we could save thousands of dollars a year on piano maintenance.'

"'Most of these kids don't have pianos in their homes,' I said. 'Michael, our piano tuner, was a student here. He went to Steinway after high school and learned to tune. He is also a song writer.'

"'You don't need a piano for most of the instrumental lessons.'

"'Those kids play in their own ensembles,' I said. 'They need a place to practice.'

"Randy threw some paper onto her desk in front of me. 'Here is a bill I am most reluctant to pay. Fifteen hundred dollars for the registration of the concert grand.'

"'That piano belonged to Violet's mother Ella Peters. She was a jazz legend. Her history is in this building. How could we not maintain her piano?'

"'All I'm saying is that, by tightening the reigns on our piano expenses, we could save the center thirty thousand dollars a year,' she told me. One fifth of Randy's salary! Can you imagine that, Samantha?"

"It's pretty shocking, the gap between the salary of the executive director and the artistic staff," said Samantha. "A lot of grassroots not-for-profits have hired executive directors these days."

"Well, it sure didn't pay off in our case."

"I searched property records and came up with a string of corporations," Samantha continued. "Fly-by-night names. To pin a conflict of interest on any board member would take more than a search of public records. The layers of ownership are nowhere transparent."

"They were forced to let the garden stay open," Dita said, "and I had determined that I would spend time helping in the garden. I'd enjoy it anyway, and I could keep a wary eye on the center real estate. I knew that could have some advantages. I tried to watch their comings and goings. But mainly Rex Turner, the handy man came and went and, when he finished desecrating the center as per Arlen's instructions, he didn't return. The center sat there vacant until Dan and I made an appointment to get the *Phoenix.* How can we possibly prove there was hanky-panky?"

"Did you try to search the title?"

"I had a lawyer friend order a title search on the center and the property next door. The title on the center property was straightforward. Violet's mother had purchased the property in 1935. Subsequently, she lived and worked in the building until she died in 1980. She had acquired the empty lot in the 1960s after a fire destroyed the building next door. Violet inherited the property from her mother, and that transfer of ownership was clearly represented in the chain of title, and the new deed was registered. Then Violet deeded both properties to the Harlem Center for the Arts, as the center was legally known. But you are so right. The title chain for the adjacent property acquired by the center under Arlen and, maybe Randy's, guidance was not so straightforward. I know something about that because of Violet Peters. A Forrest Watkins had acquired the building in 1945. Forrest Watkins was a jazz trombonist and friend of Ella Peters. They had spent a lot of time in each other's company, according to Violet. But Ella had wanted to remain independent.

Violet had always suspected that Forrest was her father. But her mother never would say."

"That stuff makes for a good story," said Samantha. "I think I remember that Forrest died way before Ella Peters."

"Forrest died in 1950. In his will, he'd left the property to Mae Johnson, his common law wife. Mae Johnson moved south and sold the property to Gloria Brown who turned the property into a boarding house and lived in the property until her death in 2000. The property was left in such a state of disrepair that it was closed up by her heirs, who didn't have the funds to renovate it. That was the glaring gap in the chain of title," Dita said. "Nothing was registered until the center bought the building from the St. James Church Corporation. The title showed a lien on the property for four hundred and fifty thousand dollars from a HUD insured mortgagor The La Grange Trust Company. The mortgagee, The Harlem Center for the Arts. Likewise, the center was responsible for a mortgage on the property next door."

"So, tell me. Where was the money?" Samantha asked. "A search for properties owned by the St. James Bank Corp came up empty except for the church building on One-Thirty-Fifth."

"I knew it was famous for its basketball program. My assistant Marge Bliss has her grandson Albert enrolled in it. He would have spent the summer at the center if we were still open. He has a great love of dance. I had met the director Reverend John Teague in community organizing meetings. Then Arlen brought him onto our board."

"It was apparent to you," said Samantha, "that the center had been allowed to acquire a building without a clear title. Yet the bank approved them for a mortgage.

Has to be someone on the take at the title company. This thing has many tentacles out there."

"For sure! Something wasn't right. But what could I have done? I put a call through to Arlen that went unanswered. I tried to put a call through to Randy. It, too, went unanswered. I was determined at this point to get some answers. CJ said that we needed to report our findings to someone. Maybe we should have taken our questions to the U. S. Attorney. But then Arlen was killed and you know where I am in this now."

"You should have called me."

"But the murder happened. And, to be quite honest, I wasn't exactly happy when you quoted Arlen in that first article, saying that I mismanaged the center. I didn't want to bring more blame down on my head. The real issue is that all of these things went on under my nose, and I would end up looking like some naïve and hopeless dreamer."

"It was too early to have reported the closing any other way, and I have to remain objective. I don't apologize but, in light of what we now know, I think I can help you find out some things."

"Okay, I'm in agreement there." When she hung up the phone, Dita remembered that she wanted to play around with the name Bennett A. Dawes. She began by writing the corresponding number for each letter in the name. She came up with 2514145202014123519. She stared at what she had written. Could it be some sort of bank account with routing numbers? With so much money missing, it very well could be. Maybe there was a way to trace the missing money? Like make a deposit into the account.

# CHAPTER 22

Dita was excited and thought she'd pay a visit to The La Grange Trust Corporation. See if any of the numbers in their deposit slips corresponded to Bennett A. Dawes. It couldn't hurt. She might have stumbled on something important, she reasoned. It couldn't be dangerous to visit the offices of a bank. Their stated address was an office in a garment center building on West Twenty-Ninth Street. She rode a rickety elevator to the nineteenth floor and had found the bank's office at the end of a dirty grey hallway. The occupants of other spaces were video artists and a recording company. Some enterprising person was renting out rehearsal space by the hour and a cacophony of show tunes, Shakespearean speeches, tango music, and copious vocalizing issued out into the hallway. She too, sought 1901. "There's no one here," Dita told her.

The door for 1901 had no nameplate, and when she knocked, no one answered. The elevator arrived again at the nineteenth floor and a woman stepped out. "I didn't expect to find anyone here."

"Oh, my, you're Samantha Elder in person. I recognize your voice." This was not the person she imagined over the phone. She didn't put forth a tough exterior. She was petit with flowing dirty blonde hair and a heavy canvass bag with pockets was slung over her shoulder.

"So we had the same idea. You should have said something," said Samantha.

"I tend to do things without telling anyone. If I say something to Dan's lawyer, he insists that I don't go alone."

"Well, he might be right about that."

"I replaced the letters in Bennett Dawes name, and it looks like some sort of bank routing number."

"Well, that's very interesting."

"So, I thought maybe I'd get a hold of some of their deposit slips or whatever. Then maybe even make a deposit into the account to find out who cashes my check and find out whom it belongs to."

"You're amazing, Dita. But I hate to tell you, it might be committing fraud, and you'd be dealing with a federal offense."

Dita shrugged. "Well, let's just see what's here."

They went to open the door. It was locked but loosely.

"There's not much locking this door," Dita said.

"And I just got a whiff of something pungent."

"Smells like the dead rats in the subway."

"We're nineteen floors above the nearest subway. But something smells very dead."

"I think we should call someone," Samantha said.

"Something is really wrong," Dita said. She gave the door a shove. Only the bottom lock was engaged, and it didn't line up properly so that the door flew open. The smell became stronger, but there was no one there. "Hello!" they both called out. The interior consisted of a reception area from which flowed a long room containing unoccupied cubicles. It was barely wide enough to call it a room—a hallway divided up. There was little furniture and what there was generic and scuffed. Not very banker like.

Then they both saw it at once—a form beyond a desk—presumably a man, sprawled across the floor. Dressed in what might have been well tailored clothing had the body not been so bloated. There was a designer jacket slung over the chair. Two empty Dewars bottles stood on the desk along with a plastic glass with the scotch drying up in side. The victim had probably been drinking heavily. Blood and fluid stained the cheap gray indoor, outdoor industrial issue carpet. The cause of death was not immediately apparent.

"It doesn't look like he was shot," Dita said.

"The fluids are leaking because he is decomposing." Samantha covered her mouth.

"People drink themselves to death," Dita said, remembering a ballet student who almost succumbed to alcohol poisoning in the ballet school dorm after a night of heavy imbibing.

The smell became overwhelming. They exited back to the hallway, and Samantha called 9-1-1, then her newspaper. *So much for deposit slips*. Dita thought she would gag and put a call through to the Duffy who told her to stay put but out of the way of the crime scene. "And don't you touch anything."

In a flurry, the police converged on the offices. Dita and Samantha explained that this might have something to do with the murder in the Harlem arts center. The responding officer called Milton.

දිරිස්

Milton snorted with disdain when he saw Dita there with the police. She explained that she and Samantha had wanted to visit the La Grange Trust Company.

"Since when do you go about helping the press?"

"In this instance, the press has been very helpful to me," Dita retorted.

"Why wasn't I informed?" Milton asked. "If you have information, I need to know."

"Well, with all due respect, Detective Milton," Samantha asked. "Would you have checked it out right away?"

"Considering you already have someone in custody," Dita said. "Listen, the real estate is at the heart of the matter. More than the real estate stinks. Surely you won't try to pin this one on my husband."

"We don't know how long this latest victim has been here." Milton gave Dita a frozen stare and went back inside to the scene of the murder. He was eager to hear what the medical examiner had to say.

Duffy arrived with Lumen Quirk.

"I seem to be becoming a magnet for maggots," Dita said by way of greeting Duffy and Quirk. "This is the tawdry La Grange Trust company. And this is Miss Samantha Elder from the *New York Times,* who might be able to shed some light on some real estate deals gone awry."

Duffy and Quirk shook hands with Samantha. A chilly look passed between Duffy and Samantha that made Dita think they had some history together. She'd find out about this as well but Milton heard Duffy arrive and came back out into the corridor, interrupting her thoughts. "You should tell them about the bank routing number," Samantha told Dita. "They can probably check it out."

"Check what out?" Duffy said.

"Dita made another discovery. Tell him," said Samantha and Dita explained how the name Bennett A. Dawes seemed to translate into a bank account routing number. Duffy whistled. Samantha nodded. "She was thinking to make a deposit, but I told her that might be fraud."

"And a federal one at that."

But then Milton came out into the hallway. "Does the paper know about this, Ms. Elder?"

"I called my editor."

"Please don't post anything until we can identify the victim." And then he turned coldly to Duffy. "Tell your client's wife to stop snooping," Milton said. "It could get her killed."

Duffy looked sternly at Dita. "I just came from a visit with Dan. He's terribly worried about you." To Milton, he said, "My client's wife happened on to something you might want to check out."

From her handbag, Dita pulled out the piece of notebook paper on which she had written the name Bennett A. Dawes and the corresponding numbers. "What if this is the account Callahan used to launder money from the HUD loans? And Bennett A. Dawes is the name they created out of the bank numbers? Hell, Bennett A. Dawes is the fictitious board member. Maybe the name is the password."

Milton looked at Nadler then said to Dita, "Can I take that?" He was somewhat chastised but wasn't letting Dita know that.

Dita looked at Duffy, who said, "He has more resources to look into something like this."

Dita handed him the paper.

Then Duffy said, "Can you take a statement from them? The wife of my client needs to go home and put her feet up. Right, Dita."

"Sheila!" Milton said.

Nadler dutifully wrote the account provided by Dita

and Samantha. Samantha went back to her paper to pre-
pare a story.

# CHAPTER 23

Duffy tried to halt Dan's arraignment pending more information about the latest murder. Judge Jerome Horner felt the link between the two murders was tenuous at best. He reasoned even if it were there, it wouldn't matter. Dan was arraigned at midnight.

Dita, CJ, and Violet sat in the row behind the counsel tables when Dan was brought in. Samantha took a seat several rows back complying with a glare, indicating she should stay away, from Duffy. For the arraignment, Dan was wearing a navy blue suit Duffy had picked out for him, instead of the neon orange prison garb. The suit looked so good on Dan that Dita thought maybe Duffy brought his own tailor into the prison as part of his legal services.

A stone-faced clerk spoke in a loud monotone, "The People versus Daniel Di Bello, on for arraignment. Counsel, please state your names for the record."

ADA Torres stood, gloating, "Good Evening, your honor."

The judge consulted his watch wearily. "Morning." Torres flinched and emitted an awkward laugh.

Laughter. A collective weariness pervaded the assemblage witnessing the proceedings. The judge, with a sarcastic comment, underscored the weary mundanity of a courtroom so clogged that prisoners were processed around the clock—his luck to get the midnight shift.

The ADA continued. "Hernan Torres for the people of The State of New York."

Duffy stood. "Martin Duffy for Daniel Di Bello who is present."

The judge continued, "I am informed that an indictment has been returned in this matter. If you and Mr. Di Bello will stand please for arraignment on the indictment."

"Do you waive a reading of the full indictment, Mr. Duffy?" the clerk asked.

Duffy had explained to Dan that it was considered poor courtroom etiquette to insist on a reading of the full indictment.

"We do," Duffy responded.

After the arraignment, Dan was cuffed once more and led out by the guards. He had completed one more step in the removal of his tethers to his own world. What he shared with Dita, he now thought of in the past tense. He gazed straight ahead and refused to make eye contact with anyone. He was shutting down, and part of him knew that that would worry Dita. He needed to muster enough self-centeredness to cope. The few times he had played concerti with orchestras, he had needed to cut himself off from those he loved and knew, then and there, that a concert pianist's life was not for him. He preferred a more introspective world of music. He would now be taken to Riker's Island to await trial. God only knew what could happen to a man accused of murder in that place.

# CHAPTER 24

S heila Nadler brought the *New York Times* and put the article in front of Milton. He pulled a pair of reading glasses out of his breast pocket and squinted closely. Samantha hadn't written the article. He figured that because Samantha had found the body at the La Grange Trust, her editor wanted another reporter to write about it.

*The New York Times' Samantha Elder along with Dita Marx, the former director of the Harlem Center for the Arts, and wife of Dan Di Bello the composer accused of the murder of Arlen Van Aiken, found another possible murder victim at the offices of the La Grange Trust Company. The deceased has not been identified. Elder found out about irregularities at the trust company researching an article about disappointed Harlem Real Estate buyers. Marx and Elder had teamed together to find out how a property lacking clear title could be acquired with HUD funding by the center. The La Grange Trust appears to be a front for an enterprise to defraud HUD. Miss Elder and Ms. Marx found links to funding for other properties that are only shells. The shells were never renovated but the funds for those renovations have disappeared. The police*

*are treating both murders separately despite an attempt*
*by Di Bello's lawyer to stay his arraignment.*

Milton laid the paper on his desk with a twinge of
annoyance. "And our Mrs. Di Bello is now credited along
with Samantha Elder as the lead investigators. I hate this
case."

Nadler shrugged and laughed sardonically. "Credit
where credit is due. They did manage to find another
body and who knows what kind of story the Bennett A.
Dawes idea might tell?"

# CHAPTER 25

D ita waited hours in the cold sterile visitor waiting area of Riker's Island for a visitation with Dan. She was allowed the usual three visitations per week. This was her first visit to the prison. This was where Dan would stay to await trial. The waiting area hummed with babies crying, people shouting over one another, the nervous activity generated by sheer frustration. Whenever someone's name was called a momentary hush descended, and the din returned as the party followed a guard behind a locked door. Mothers with toddlers, diaper bags, strollers shared their stories with one another. She heard the word plea over and over again. Most took what they could get she supposed. Then there were the parents of adolescents looking bewildered—mostly poor people.

In the center community, practically everyone had a loved one incarcerated including Marge. Dita wondered how many times Marge had waited with Albert in a similar area so that he could know his mother. What did she say to Albert? Her crime was taping nickel bags on the tires of parked cars so that the drug dealer clients could pick up their drugs, allowing the dealer to remain anony-

mous. It was her first offense. Albert's mother was an out
of work single mother. Under the onerous Rockefeller
Drug laws, the judge had no discretion and handed down
the maximum sentence. Marge loved Albert but she was
spending her retirement years and retirement income as a
second time around parent.

Would Dita someday wait with other mothers with
the baby she and Dan created just to let him see his baby?
she wondered.

When she finally heard the name Di Bello called
over the din, she steeled herself to face the fact of Dan's
incarceration. Up until now everything had taken on a
surreal and absurd aura. It had been less than a week
since his arrest and her old life seemed so far behind her.
She walked through the motions of living—not tasting
her food, not sleeping but not staying awake, beyond
worry, pacing and thinking, and pacing some more. The
guard led her into a small viewing room with a glass partition. There was a heavy black phone receiver. More
time passed before Dan was led in once again wearing an
orange jump suit, his hands cuffed behind his back. The
guard removed the cuffs and then removed himself off to
the side to somewhere beyond the entry door catapulting
Dita and Dan into a zone of profound aloneness. They
picked up their respective phones. "So near yet so far,"
was all Dita could say. "I feel a chill."

"And I can't hold you and make you warm."

"Tell me what has been going on."

"A lot of hours passing slowly in a cell surrounded
by the most abject of humanity. And I'm now one of
them."

"No, you're not."

"Oh, but I am. I don't get any kind of special treat-
ment in here for being white and educated. I'm a murderer to them. Maybe I should just enjoy it and say boo. To

the guy who mugged a grandmother I'm a scary dude. Up for murder."

"We have support, Dan," she said. "CJ, Violet, Duffy. Samantha Elder is in our corner."

"Duffy doesn't trust her."

"Did he tell you why?"

"He's pretty close-mouthed on the subject of Ms. Elder."

"She knows a lot about the real estate. She was writing an article on Harlem homebuyers before the murder. It confirms what we've been thinking about Arlen and a real estate scam."

"Not that it'll do me any good."

She told him about Bennett A. Dawes being code for a possible bank routing number and Dan whistled.

"We're going to find out who did this," Dita said, adamant.

"Who is we?"

"I'm not going to just trust those cops. I know how to get information. People are going to say things to me. People will know things they don't know they know. It's all in their subconscious waiting to be triggered. The way the murder happened will become apparent to us. I feel it in my bones. There's a missing piece."

Dan sighed. "That's totally naïve, Dita. Your flaw is that you take too much on. Duffy tells me he's never had a client with a wife like you. It's okay to play plumber with a clogged toilet. But the center doesn't exist anymore, and it somehow provoked a murder. We don't really know what was at stake."

Dita smarted from Dan's criticism. "I'm so frightened you'll be convicted by a jury on circumstantial evidence. This has got to get solved before it can go to a trial. That Detective Milton is a milquetoast."

"Just don't do anything stupid. I'm not the murderer, and someone out there sure as hell is. Duffy worries you're too involved. Please stay out of this." His voice shook with emotion and she reacted.

"How can I not be involved? People have always talked to me. It's one of the gifts I discovered after I stopped dancing."

His eyes were wild with helpless fear. "Don't confront anyone and don't push anyone's buttons by knowing too much. Dita, you are carrying our child."

"I promise not to do anything stupid. Is there anything I can get sent in here for you?"

"Can you ask someone about some staff paper and some pencils? I've got to make something of all this wasted time. I want to see if I can hear music, despite everything. I've got to tap all of my resources to get through this."

# CHAPTER 26

Mindy Rothman Van Aiken and her father watched the morning news in his office.

"Bail was denied today in the murder of socialite Arlen Van Aiken. Rumors are circulating that Van Aiken was involved in more than a charitable enterprise. The US Attorney has begun an investigation of allegations that have come to light in the murder of Van Aiken."

"So," Rothman said and got up and snapped off the television. Mindy loved the simple comfort offered by her father. How had she gone so wrong in the choice of a husband? Her marriage hadn't lasted much beyond the honeymoon. Arlen was twenty years her senior, seductively handsome when he was still in his forties, with a Harvard architecture pedigree. At twenty-five, her mother recently deceased from breast cancer, Mindy was swept off her feet—she missed her mother more than ever now.

The children should have brought them together, but their births caused the wedge to open further. In therapy, she learned that Arlen was the classical narcissist and jealous of her as well. Sometimes, he would refer to her as his "little peasant," implying that money couldn't buy class. He made her feel ugly—a form of abuse and control.

She had become increasingly involved in charitable work. There was something in her that needed filling. Now she wished she could grieve, but all she could think of was damage control. Mort Rothman was never one to criticize his only daughter. He wasn't one to say, "I told you so," even to an employee.

Security in her father's office was tight. There was a bulletproof window with a view to an outer lobby, and any visitor had to pass through several other security stations. But Rothman's office hadn't changed in the fifty years he occupied it. No sign of modernity. No computer but filing cabinets, a desk, an old sofa. The television was so old that it didn't use a remote. The one concession to modernity was a Time Warner cable-box for reception. Rothman presided over his extensive real estate empire from this simple room. There were other's working for him who designed buildings on computers, kept extensive records of tenants, both commercial and residential, plus a battery of in-house legal advice.

Rothman knew construction—big and small. He had a mind for the minutest detail, coupled with infinite patience. His powers of concentration were legendary and allowed him to focus on whatever task was at hand. They had been discussing how much the children—Julie age eleven and Josh, age nine—should be told and how much they would probably hear from others.

Both investigators from the US Attorney's office and the NYPD had spent the week at her house removing files from Arlen's den. As Mindy had told Detectives Milton and Nadler she couldn't find deeds, loan documents, or paperwork connecting Arlen to the ownership of more than fifty properties. They swarmed over Arlen's office at Rothman Real Estate as well. Eighteen million dollars was presumed to be missing. The total borrowed by the enterprise from HUD. The estimate was based on Arlen having told Mindy that his real estate holdings were probably valued at that amount. Arlen's account was depleted. It appeared that someone had made transfers out over a long period of time. Had Arlen laundered money himself? There was no sign that he had overseas accounts.

Dan Di Bello's lawyer had made an informal request to interview Mindy. He would make more formal requests if she denied this one. Her father arranged for her to be accompanied by both himself and his personal lawyer.

# CHAPTER 27

Duffy called to tell Dita that the body she and Samantha found had not yet been identified. He reiterated that Dita needed to stay home and away from this investigation. "Keep your feet from swelling up as well," he told her.

"My feet aren't swelling up but your head is."

"You can insult me. Just stay home."

"What are you doing about the Bennett A. Dawes thing?"

"We agreed to let Milton track that. I'll keep on him, but the process of money laundering goes through a lot of steps. The idea is to get the money to cross many borders to make it undetectable, and if Bennett A. Dawes was the first step, then chances are the money is long gone. Callahan might have gone to Hong Kong and purchased a shit load of casino chips that he will gamble with some and then convert the rest into currency. It's the stuff of international thrillers. We need to focus on a defense for Dan."

"So you are sure Callahan left before the murder? What if he positioned the yacht somewhere else and flew back to murder Arlen?"

"I think he already had what he wanted. Dita, keep to your armchair. That's the only kind of detective work you should do."

# CHAPTER 28

Dita did not stay home with her feet up. Without telling Duffy, she went to the St. James Church to speak with another center board member, the Reverend Teague.

She wasn't totally reckless. She checked to see that the boys were assembled on the basketball court. *Safety in numbers*, she thought. *And Teague had more to gain with Arlen alive. But so did Rex*, she reasoned.

She knew, through Duffy, that these boys were the reverend's alibi.

Teague greeted her with a wary cordiality and invited her into his parish office. It overlooked the new basketball court. "Arlen did that for my boys," he said, indicating the court. "So sad that he passed."

"It's a beautiful court, Reverend John," Dita said.

"Arlen's done a lot for my guys. I was so sorry the center couldn't stay afloat."

"Times, they do change. I want to ask you about other real estate St. James church owns."

"This is it," Teague stated simply and Dita plunged on.

"Look, Reverend John, there's a deed on record

showing St. James sold the building next door to the center. Who did you buy it from?"

"Ah, we participated in the sale sort of as an agent for you through the HUD process."

"What? I never knew anything about it."

"It was an opportunity for us to put eleven thousand dollars into our coffers."

"That might not have been legal, you know."

"No, it's common practice. We issued a letter of authority to the board."

"It's called being a straw man, Reverend John. Did you do that on any other occasions?"

"We did. It was for the boys."

"Can you make me a list of the other properties?"

"I don't know if I'd be able to."

"I surely won't be able to ask Arlen. Two buildings owned by the center are mortgaged for close to a million dollars. The money was never used for us."

Reverend John looked incredulous. "How could that be? Arlen had the boys at heart. I'm sure of it."

"He wanted you to think that he was doing it out of love. Just think what the basketball program could have done with two million dollars. He was probably buying other properties with the money from those mortgages. I think they call it flipping. No one knows where the money is. Reverend John, you were his straw man. It's difficult to believe you didn't know you were doing something illegal."

He stood abruptly and Dita flinched. She needed to leave. He was a very tall man. But then one of the boys entered the office with a bloody knee.

"I'll go now," Dita said and made her exit.

# CHAPTER 29

On the walk home, Dita called Samantha and told her about Reverend John.

"Wow! That colors things very differently," said Sam.

"Apparently, we were right. Arlen was involved in an enterprise of some sort."

Sam snorted. "Bastard! And Reverend John?"

"Man of God?" Dita asked. "Doing it for the boys."

"There are probably other straw persons as well," said Samantha

"I thought about Rex. He was Arlen's handy man. He stripped the properties of anything of value and probably took a cut. And whatever groups or persons were needy enough to get involved with Arlen. He promises a tidbit in exchange for what amounts to a major windfall for the enterprise."

"I want to talk to Reverend John and Rex," Samantha said. "This is why property is so difficult to acquire. HUD is a nightmare and the mayor's policies contributed to the fraud."

Samantha broke the story the next day, mentioning Reverend John's basketball program—raising questions about a possible enterprise to defraud HUD. It made the front page of the *New York Times*. An irascible press officer from the mayor's office called Samantha. "You're alluding to links that the mayor has with an illegal enterprise. It simply isn't true."

"It raises a lot of questions. Why does your office allow these properties to be flipped without making repairs?"

"We neither allow or disallow."

"Oh, c'mon. Spare us both."

# CHAPTER 30

Dita and CJ sat in front of Duffy's desk. She told him about her visit with Reverend John, and he was livid that she had gone to see the man. "As her friend, can't you get the woman under control?"

"He's right," CJ said to Dita. "You can't just run with an idea because it seems right at the time. You've gotta weigh in everything, girl."

"Amen," Duffy said. "How am I going to impress upon you that you are taking a risk—short of locking you up, too?"

"The second body would never have been found if Samantha and I hadn't gone to the La Grange Trust offices. The murderer didn't wait around for the body to rot. I can assure you there was no danger in going there, except that was the worst thing I ever smelled."

"Yuck!" CJ said.

"He'd been decomposing for days," Duffy said. "I'm hoping that the medical examiner will be able to tell us when he died."

"Hopefully, after they arrested Dan."

"Yes. They are still treating both as separate cases."

"But you know in your heart of hearts that they are connected."

Duffy nodded.

"Does anyone know about the money that was in Mitchell Shepherd's escrow account?" CJ asked.

"The theory is that he was about to flee and laundered it through the Cayman Islands or someplace like it. The police found a one-way ticket to the British Virgin Islands on his computer—first step on the way to being a fugitive. But Shepherd never got to the airport."

"But Arlen's money is missing, too. Was he planning to flee, too?"

"Somehow, I think Arlen was duped by the other two, and then Callahan duped Shepherd," Duffy said. "Like I told you before, following laundered money is not easy. In this day and age, a billion dollars can be sent a world away at the click of a mouse."

"Do you think the second body will turn out to be Mitchell Shepherd?" Dita asked.

Both Duffy and CJ turned to her.

"Now what would make you say that?" Duffy asked.

"If he didn't flee, then he must be dead."

"I was hoping they'd find him, and we'd get some answers. I'm assuming Arlen trusted him. A crooked lawyer was crucial to what they were up to."

"Arlen was pretty arrogant. Probably thought his co-horts worshiped him," CJ said.

"There's that. He brought them on board initially," Duffy said.

"But he needed them to falsify documents and help conceal other illegal activities," Dita said.

"Probably."

"Do you think we will ever know for sure?" CJ asked.

Duffy laughed. "You both are too much. By the way,

are there any physical plans for the properties?" he asked. "It would help us to understand the layout."

"Marla and Brett Carson," Dita said out loud. She explained who the couple was.

"And I put all the papers from the center into storage," CJ said. "There were some very old blueprints in a cardboard tube from Violet's mother's time. I was afraid to handle them. Didn't want them to disintegrate."

"Aren't plans registered?" Dita asked.

Duffy shook his head. "Not necessarily, but as to the Carsons, they or their architect should still have the plans. We are going to need access to the center and the building next door to see what's possible. How could that person leave a property that was swarming with police three minutes after Dan called nine-one-one? I want my private investigator to go over the building as soon as I get the word from Detective Milton. We need to learn more about the physical layout of the center's property. In short, we need to find someone else with motive and opportunity. We need the results of the police physical examination of the property. We need to demand all of their evidence and start telling our own story with it."

❧❧❧

Marla and Brett had heard about Dan's arrest and subsequent arraignment on the evening news. They'd called Dita the night of Dan's arrest, both of them in tears. "We want to help in any way we can," said Brett. Marla was on the extension and added, "You are our new friends and we know our instincts are right about Dan. He couldn't have murdered that crook. I would have murdered him if I had known who he was."

Now Duffy dialed the number and put them on the speakerphone.

Brett answered on the first ring. Marla picked up the extension. "There is something you could do." Dita told them.

"Ask," said Brett and Marla in unison.

"Do you still have the plans your architect drew up for the other building?"

"As a matter of fact," said Brett. "For some reason, we were reluctant to part with them after paying so much money. You are welcome to them. It would be some irony if they could be of use. Where do I send them?"

"I think to Dan's lawyer's office."

Duffy confirmed with a nod.

"I'll bring them to him first thing tomorrow," said Brett. "I understand them very well if you need help reading them."

Dita gave Duffy a "thumbs up" sign as he closed out the call. CJ would bring the center blueprints. Being armed with drawings of both buildings could potentially put them ahead of the police.

"Can CJ and I go with you? We'll be able to tell if something looks out of place," Dita asked Duffy.

"That would be all right, so long as you both understand who's in charge."

"You're the man," CJ said.

"He gets it," Duffy said to Dita.

"You have to trust me, Duffy. I know everyone in the neighborhood. It's very difficult for me to wonder what is being uncovered and what is getting ignored," Dita said.

"You know, Dita," Duffy said. "There's something called a fresh perspective. Don't knock it."

"I'm not knocking it."

"You are when you constantly take these risks."

# CHAPTER 31

Brett delivered the blueprints to Duffy's office on the dot of eight a.m. He pulled a set of keys out of his pocket. "I never returned them," he said and wished Duffy luck as he left for work.

Dita arrived soon afterward, as did CJ with blueprints, and Lumen Quirk.

"We should have access to both properties," Quirk told Duffy and Duffy dangled the set of keys. He had obtained permission from Milton to go through the center but made no mention of his plans to go through the building next door.

"That sure as hell makes things a lot easier. Have the police gone over the other building yet?" Dita asked.

"I don't know the answer to that. Milton made no mention of it. But we will have an advantage if we can get there first," Duffy said.

"Well, let's go," Quirk said.

They all crowded into Quirk's SUV and headed uptown, catching the green light on Sixth Avenue, then following the roads through Central Park until they reached 110th Street where Quirk segued over to Adam Clayton Powel and onto the center's block where, as luck would have it, someone vacated a parking space. Private eyes got parking tickets galore in New York City. Only the press, police, and medical doctors had privileges—oh, and clergy. Dita remembered seeing a "pastor on call" sign on a vehicle parked by the fire hydrant near the center one day. It turned out that it was the van Reverend Teague used for his basketball team. He'd had business with Arlen when he first joined the board.

"Let's look at Brett's building first," Duffy said.

Quirk provided four hard hats. The paved front yard led to a ground floor door under the stoop. The door was badly in need of repair and was covered by a metal security gate that was unlocked, and swinging on a single hinge. Quirk swung it open and inserted the key into the rusty lock of the wooden door. At first it didn't budge but with enough nudging and prodding he was able to get the lock to turn. "Didn't think I could ever see the inside of this," Dita said. The electricity was turned off and the windows boarded-up as were the center windows. They heard a scurrying as they entered the little alcove.

Quirk had provided each of them with flashlights. He shined his upward to where a jagged gap in the ceiling let them see through into the parlor above. "The ground floors of these buildings are usually rentals," he said.

"What a nice lifestyle to occupy the other three floors," Dita said. "I can see why someone would take the risk."

"Can we get a light on those plans?" Duffy asked. There was really nowhere to unfurl them. Quirk held them against a wall, and CJ held down the bottom while Duffy and Dita shined their flashlights on them.

Dita noticed that Brett's drawing showed approximately an extra nine square feet of space in a corner of the kitchen. She went over to the space. "It's a dumb-waiter."

"Be careful!" said Quirk and Duffy in unison, and she stepped back.

"Allow me," said Quirk, relinquishing the plans to CJ. He went over to the dumbwaiter. There was no floor. He could shine the light into the basement. "Could take a nasty fall in there."

"Is it safe to peek inside of it?" Dita asked. "I'll hold on."

"I'll hold onto you."

"Yes, I'd like to see the inside of it," Duffy said.

"Better yet, let's go to the basement," said Quirk.

The basement had an old-fashioned laundry—an agitator washing machine with a ringer on top and a mangler stood in the center next to a large metal table. "Maybe a business taking in laundry," CJ said. "The dumbwaiter shaft must have been extended to the basement. I don't remember the one in the center going that far down." Quirk shined his light upward into the space and the others bent around the wall to look up. The light traveled three stories upward to a ceiling laced with cobwebs. The iron rails for the mechanism were still attached to the walls. But the dumbwaiter had been removed.

"There's another door on the parlor floor," said Quirk.

"So the dumbwaiter traveled from the basement up to the parlor floor," Duffy said.

Dita put her hand over her mouth. "The dumbwaiter! Someone could have hidden in it."

"We kept bookshelves in front of the dumbwaiter doors. We were afraid of a kid falling in there," CJ said.

"But a strong adult could push the shelves and then what?" asked Quirk.

"It's possible. But it sure as hell could help us develop an alternative theory. If we could just place someone in the vicinity and figure out how that person left the building unseen," Duffy said.

They finished the tour of five decrepit floors. Every room furnished with a sink. Old stained toilets and other debris accumulated in the center of every room. They checked out the basement and subbasement thinking there might be some sort of passageway between the two buildings. There wasn't. Both subbasements were wet. Both homes were built over the stream.

"We should check out the yard," said Quirk.

A windowless metal door led to the yard. They were able to open it. The yard was crammed full of debris and was enclosed by cyclone fence at the south end, topped by rolls of barbed wire, and it shared walls with the properties on either side. The yard contained chunks of cement, rock, old brick, and more old sinks and toilets. Dita sighed. "This building is a metaphor for wrecked lives."

"It's surreal," CJ said.

"I've seen enough here," Duffy said, also dismayed. "Let's visit next door."

They entered the center. Dita felt a chill crawl down her spine—that old avoidance mechanism.

"Let's begin in the basement," Duffy said. "I want to get a feel for the crime scene. What do you think, Quirk?"

"Good idea to work our way up. We need to check out every square inch of this place including the roof."

Relics of the crime scene investigation remained— Brown stains on the gray cement indicated where Arlen had fallen. Tools had been removed from the workbench probably to test for fingerprints. Dita expected a chalk outline of Arlen's body but Quirk laughed." That happens in mystery books. The crime scene was photographed from every angle. Technology gets better all the time. Sometimes the detectives will leave an outline for photojournalists after they finish with the scene. Outline of the body is less gory. Using chalk at the scene initially could mess up crucial evidence."

Arlen's prints had been found on a wrench and a Philips screwdriver as were Rex Turner's. Milton had taken prints of everyone who might have had access to the basement. The theory was that Arlen had borrowed the tools to remove the statue from the niche. He was probably returning them when he was struck from behind.

"The workbench was set up by the parent we lost in the World Trade Center. He kept everything in repair. A volunteer much missed," Dita explained.

On the garden level they easily located the dumbwaiter. The bookshelves had been removed. Bookshelves were also removed on the parlor level above. In the center, the dumb waiter did not descend to the basement. The dumbwaiter mechanism had been removed at the center, and what remained was a two story empty shaft.

Quirk checked to see if anyone had shimmied the walls to get onto the parlor floor. "Nothing's disturbed on the walls. I think he just waited until Dan was in the basement. I'm going to take photographs of the floor. There's a mélange of footprints," Quirk said, arming himself with a digital camera. "But I'm not hopeful for anything."

"Next question is how does he get out with the windows boarded up, if he couldn't or didn't want to walk out the front door?" Duffy asked.

"Why wouldn't he just walk out of the front door at that point? I'm missing something," CJ said.

"He feared being recognized by the gardeners," said Quirk.

"But how about when Dan went to the car for the flashlight?" Dita asked.

"Yes," Duffy said, "that's also a window of time, albeit a very brief one."

"So it has to be someone we all know rather well," CJ said.

"People know each other up here," Dita said. "The bodega owner knows all the kids and their parents. Someone saw something and didn't know it."

"I think I agree with you, Dita," Duffy said.

"I'll start canvassing the stores on the avenues. We'll find that someone who saw something," said Quirk.

"Can CJ and I go with you?" Dita asked. "We know all the store owners well."

"But you let Quirk do the asking, agreed?" Duffy said.

"You guys can be my sounding board," said Quirk to Dita and CJ.

"When we found out that we were locked out, our cat was locked in, and he kept going on the roof," Dita remembered. "I thought the skylight had been left open, but I found it closed up tight. So the cat must have gone out some way and back in. Do you think that has something to do with this?"

"Possibly," Duffy said.

"They were actively stripping the center of anything of value," Dita said. "Dan had focused on the missing pianos and stained glass windows. How right Ricardo was to want his sculpture returned to him."

"What would be the value of the center's pianos?" Quirk asked.

"A lot of money. Maybe upward of two hundred thousand in all," Dita said. "They were good instruments, and Violet's mother's Steinway concert grand carried the distinction of celebrity with it. That adds to the value. Her piano was the one in the parlor that Dan loves so much."

"And there is no record of how the center's property was disposed of," Duffy said. "It bears investigation. Quirk I want you to do all you can to track the center's property."

"Yes, siree."

"You can track piano ownership by the serial numbers," Dita said.

"I think I have those numbers written down somewhere," CJ said.

"Randy might have them as well. She made a big deal about our piano expenses," Dita said.

"I'll call around to piano showrooms," Quirk said.

"What if they were sold privately?" Dita asked. "For quick cash. Someone savvy would put an ad in the *Juilliard Journal*. But any potential buyer would want the serial number. Then there are piano tuners who refurbish and sell pianos."

"Well, I guess I'm getting an education," Quirk said.

"I will say something to Milton about that as well," Duffy said. "Let's focus here right now."

"Dan said he went upstairs first to look for Arlen," Dita said. "The murderer could have gone to the ground level and entered the dumbwaiter when he knew Dan was on the higher floors."

"And escaped when Dan was in the basement?" asked Quirk. "Let's check out both floors."

"I'd like to see the garden as well," Duffy said.

"The garden is walled in and there's no egress," Dita said, "It was a lovely and very meditative spot."

"At the parlor level the fire escape would let one climb to the roof?" Duffy asked.

"The person would have had to go up. The fire escape has a fold out ladder that descends to the garden but it was so rusted that is was impossible to release it. We were even failing in our safety measures at that point," Dita said.

"How do we get to this meditative backyard?" Quirk asked.

"There's a back door at the garden level," Dita said, "But I'm sure it was boarded up as well."

They descended the stairs. To the rear of the garden floor they located a wide doorway. It was boarded up like the windows. "What were they thinking when they boarded up a door as well?" CJ asked.

"They're glass sliding doors and pretty new," Dita said. "I guess they attempted to sell them also."

Duffy just stood there, shaking his head. Today he was dressed in jeans and a tee shirt. Dita had never seen him out of a suit. His back was very straight. She imagined him strutting before a jury.

"What do you think we ought to do?" Duffy asked.

Quirk brushed blond hair off of his forehead and pulled at the plywood panels. His eyes got a green intensity when faced with a problem to solve. "I have tools in my car," he said and exited quickly. He returned with a tool kit and began to assess how he was going to remove the heavy plywood. He brought out a screwdriver, crowbar, and hammer. The plywood was secured to the doorframe by a sort of brace with long screws. It took Quirk almost a half hour and intense effort to pull off the boards.

When the backyard finally came into view, Duffy said, "It's not like someone could have lifted a board and sauntered out." They entered the yard. It was paved with red brick in a herringbone pattern. There were benches, planters and a sand box and a picnic table. Whatever had grown in the planters was now dead and dried. "Such a shame," Dita said. As she had told them, the garden was completely walled in. "Violet's mother had had that wall built. The building on the garden lot had the reputation as a house of ill repute. She had wanted to be distanced from it. One night, it caught fire. After the fire, when she acquired the empty lot, she had windows made in the side of the brownstone that overlooked the garden." Today, they could hear the lively chatter from the community garden, but it was blocked from view by the twelve-foot high brick wall.

"Looks like the only way out is up," Duffy said.

Dita observed the back wall of the building. "I kept a ladder against the back wall but it seems to have disappeared."

"So someone could have scaled the wall into the yard next door," Duffy said.

"But it's a long drop without a ladder on the other side," Dita said. "And you saw the debris. Landing on it could injure someone seriously. And again, there's no egress with all that rusty barbed wire. Tetanus heaven."

"For sure," Duffy said. "Even somebody desperate wouldn't want to get skewered on that."

"So let's assume for the moment he went up," Quirk said, observing the back wall. He used his long hands as a visor and squinted upward. The others did likewise. The back wall of the building glowed warmly in the sun's path as it ascended. When it began its western descent, the garden would be shady.

"Could he have gone onto the roof and escaped down the fire escape of another building?" CJ asked.

"The problem is how did he leave?" Quirk said. "Let's walk the entire place again. We're missing something."

"Wouldn't someone from the garden have noticed a person on the fire escape?" Duffy asked.

"Not if they were looking down gardening," Dita said. "We used to climb out the window and sit on the fire escape when there were no children around. We were pretty well hidden from view."

"Couldn't set any bad examples," Duffy said. They all laughed.

"You'd have to try hard to get the gardeners' attention," Dita said. "Their noses were pretty much aimed at the ground."

"And there's that shed thing next to the wall," said Quirk, referring to a piece of makeshift red and white plastic awning installed to give the gardeners relief from the sun when they took breaks. "It would prevent them from seeing someone on the fire escape as well."

They trudged back inside their eyes adjusting once again to the lack of light.

"That must have been some nice garden," Duffy said.

"We used it for receptions. We had some wonderful parties with goodies from the garden and potluck from some of the best cooks ever. I wanted to build a deck but got out voted by the new board," Dita said. "All the good just came to a halt and everything became about money. You can't see it, but the building has such a nice flow. The kids loved running up and down the staircases." She could hear their patter. It felt ghostly.

They climbed to the parlor level once again. Something nagged at Dita. She couldn't retrieve it from her subconscious, but she knew that she knew something and said so. "I keep thinking I am missing something."

"Do you want to walk through again?" Duffy asked.

"Yes," Dita and Quirk said together. This time, Dita found the ladder leaning by the entrance to the parlor.

"If he used the ladder, there is no sign that he could easily have used it to leave." They went around and tested all of the plywood panels to see if any were loose but all the panels were unyielding.

Dita cast a last glance around the parlor. What was she seeing that she couldn't see?

When they were once again on the sidewalk, Dita remembered something else. "The day that Dan was arrested, there was someone on a roof down the block. A shadowy figure, he or she disappeared quickly. Maybe he lived there and was just observing the excitement. Can we walk by?"

"Absolutely," said Quirk. "Do you know which building?"

"About four doors down."

They walked down the block. The forth building was a shell. "I guess I'm not sure," Dita said.

"No roof," Quirk said.

"Could someone walk on the cornices?" Dita asked.

"Sometimes they lay scaffolding when they start to renovate these shells," said Quirk. "That could provide a platform for someone to walk on."

Duffy turned to Quirk. "We need to find out who owns the property. When we get back to my office, we will start going over our lists of people who hung around here.

"We didn't exactly find the alternate theory, did we?" Dita said.

Duffy huffed. "I sure as hell am going to try to plant one. I'm getting more and more convinced that someone was in there when Dan found the body. But he'd have to be some sort of Houdini not to be noticed by anyone. And if he walked out over a roofless shell, then he's a high-wire artist as well."

Quirk replaced the boards on the garden level doorway and they returned to Duffy's office and a spread of sandwiches, salads, fruits, and beverages on a sideboard in the conference room. There was a message from Detective Milton. Dita had been right about Bennett A.

Dawes being a bank account in which the enterprise deposited the proceeds from the HUD loans but, as expected, the money got forwarded on. Callahan had changed the password for the account so that Arlen and Shepherd couldn't access the cash.

"That was good guessing," Quirk told Dita.

"Well, I see how hard this is," she said. "Disappointments right and left."

Violet joined them at Duffy's office as well. Violet had had her hair cropped close to her skull and wore hoop gold earrings. The short haircut brought out her huge brown eyes. Violet was well into her seventies with hardly a wrinkle on her face. Just smile lines crinkled her eyes and mouth. When Dita admired the new do, Violet said, "I always wore a wig in the opera. When I quit singing, I felt I had to grow my own wig. But my mother always told me my head was perfectly shaped. So I thought I'd try this again."

"You look beautiful," Duffy said.

Quirk and CJ concurred.

They all filled their plates and took them over to the massive conference table. Quirk used Duffy's lawyer search engines to track the title to the shell four doors down. "The owner is listed as a not-for-profit called Carecorp," he reported. "There is a mortgage on that property as well from the Lagrange Trust. Oh, my! Carecorp has offices on DeKalb Avenue in Brooklyn. I'll check it out."

"Probably another shell. Arlen had tentacles all over," Duffy said as he began to write on a huge white board at the front of the conference room. It had a trough filled with magic markers and erasers. Duffy took a black marker and wrote: *Witnesses. They come in three flavors—friendly, hostile, and neutral.*

"What are neutral witnesses?" Dita asked.

"Hopefully, witnesses with no relationship to either party. Neutral witnesses could be a clerk in a public office or a hospital admin. A neutral witness would have information about only one facet of an investigation, in all probability."

Dita frowned. "And if a person was an unwitting witness to an event an offender wanted to conceal, he'd be in danger, would he not?"

"Yes, he would be a threat to the perpetrator," Duffy said, holding her eyes with his dark brown ones.

"So by solving this we could be saving another life?" Dita said.

"I like the way you think, Dita. Good lines of thought," Duffy said, continuing. "If only we could control your impulsiveness."

Then Dita's cell phone rang. She saw the name Samantha Elder on the screen. "I think I should take this."

Duffy nodded.

"Samantha?" Dita asked. She listened for a moment. "Mitchell Shepherd? I'm here in Martin Duffy's office. Let me tell him." She turned to Duffy. "The body at La-Grange Trust was Mitchell Shepherd. Two million dollars is missing from his client escrow account."

Violet's hands flew to her heart.

"Well, you don't say?" Duffy said. "Two people involved in the enterprise are dead."

"Mitchell Shepherd, I was told, donated his legal fees," Dita said.

"Figures," Duffy said.

"Shepherd?" CJ said.

"That's the scumbag that represented the sale of the next door building as far as we can tell," Quirk said.

"The one Samantha Elder and I found in the offices of the La Grange trust company. He was—how should I put it delicately, more than dead."

Duffy whistled but then he told Dita to end the conversation.

"Thanks, Samantha," she said.

Duffy looked at her seriously. "Samantha is not your ally."

"Methinks this is personal."

"It is. All you need to do is remember she's a reporter first and foremost. She's throwing some bones your way." He neglected to tell her about the high-profile case he lost because of Samantha Elder. They'd been seeing each other but never openly. They were in love with each other, but neither could sacrifice a career. He was defending a rabbi accused of murdering his wife and was close to getting the guy off. When Samantha covered the trial, a woman came forward and said she had been the rabbi's lover. The direction of the trial changed at once. Duffy knew he was being irrational. Samantha was just doing her job, and his guy didn't deserve to get off. The rabbi subsequently admitted hiring goons to kill his wife and was now serving a life sentence.

"Let's not get ahead of ourselves," he said, wincing from his memories. His stubborn pride also made him fight for his clients. "You had seven board members prior to Nine/Eleven. What were their names?"

CJ sat up. "We had Arlen, Ferdie Forbush, Josh Grogan, Violet, Jesus Avila, Pastor Don Brownlee from the Baptist Church, and Dr. Grimm, a local pediatrician. Ferdie, Josh, and Jesus died in the World Trade Center. Pastor Brownlee has since passed on."

"So to reiterate, initially you had a supportive board and those in support of the center were in the majority."

"That's right," Dita said. "They were one-hundred percent behind us. Even skanky Arlen appeared to be a staunch backer. Dr. Grimm took us to task with her questions, but that was her way."

"So then after Nine/Eleven the board reconfigured?"

"Arlen brought in Theodore Callahan, Bennett Dawes, and Mitchell Shepherd,"

Violet said. "They began to hold the board meetings on Callahan's yacht. I get seasick. That's how they took to meeting among themselves. Would come to the meetings with decisions already made. We'd have been outvoted anyway. The first I got wind of it was in 2002, when they brought that Randy Smith-Warren and introduced her as their choice of executive director. Now I know why I never set eyes on Bennett Dawes." She removed the top slice of bread off of an egg salad sandwich and chewed thoughtfully.

Dita snorted. "Funny that. His vote sure counted—what blatant behavior!"

"We should ask Randy about Dawes see if we can catch her off guard," Duffy said, making a note. "The executive director reported to the board but the board would have voted in a private session. Randy was not on the board and has that going for her."

Duffy wrote the names on the board as the discussion continued.

"And Dr. Grimm remained on the board?"

"Yes, but she was getting very elderly. Kept missing meetings. All sorts of ailments," said Violet.

"And was there no board member from the neighborhood to replace Jesus Avilla?" Duffy asked.

"Yes, Rex Turner, but he'd go along with anything they wanted. He was a paid board member, if you know what I mean, as was the good reverend," said Violet. "I do hope my mother isn't turning in her grave over this."

"Okay, so Turner knew the layout of the center pretty well and probably had access to the tools," Duffy said. "He took his wife to her physical therapist. They had a one-fifty appointment. It checks out. He was on time."

"Could he have stopped at the center on the way?" CJ asked.

Dita could see he was starting to look tired. He'd spent a long day with them.

"We've got to ask ourselves what he would gain by killing Arlen. He was a pal of Arlen's. Arlen kept Rex in work," Dita said. "He was a difficult man to read. I always felt that part of his work was to eavesdrop and report back to Arlen. But he seemed to be conflicted. I'd get glimmers of friendliness, and then he'd be all business—Arlen's."

"Quirky, go talk to the Turners while you're at it," Duffy said. "And get me some background on them."

"Yesiree."

"So to summarize," Duffy said. "We are still lacking motive and we're still lacking opportunity for everyone but Dan."

"Should we be looking at the Rothmans?" Dita asked. "Arlen was a philanderer."

"Mrs. Van Aiken has an alibi for the time of the murder. She was running a charity luncheon at Lincoln Center that hosted almost a thousand women. She was at all times in front of the assembly," Quirk said. "I nosed around pretty good there. Gossip was forthcoming, and I learned a few tidbits." He related what he knew. "When Mindy married Arlen, Mort Rothman had tried to involve him in the business. Mort wanted to gradually increase his responsibilities. Arlen's career had been mostly academic. Arlen was too old to be treated like a young associate. He was basically promoted upstairs and out of the way. Mindy confirmed this. According to Mort Rothman, he'd told Arlen about a small building in the West Village very near the highway that they owned in partnership with a group. 'They need an architect for the project.

It's a rehab. You should go talk to them and put your best foot forward. It won't be my decision.'

"'I'm reworking my CV to represent more of my architecture and less of my academic credentials.'

"'Good for you. Let me know how it goes,' Mort said.

"Mindy told me that, later in the week, Arlen had confided to her, 'Your father is playing a game with me to get out of recommending me outright. I didn't get hired.'

"Mort had called Arlen into his office and spoke in a blunt manner, saying that the group was dismayed that Arlen put projects on his CV that were never actualized—including an imaginary building at Hollywood and Vine in Los Angeles.

"Arlen sat in front of Mort and argued that his plans were construction ready—worked out in detail. 'The Harry Paulsen house got built.'

"'The rock singer?' Mort asked.

"'Yes, it's some of my best work.'

"'Then I suggest you get a reference for that.'

"I contacted Harry Paulsen," Quirk said. "There had been problems between Arlen and the contractor on the house. The contractor had told Harry Paulsen that he needed builder's plans with more specifics. Arlen had argued that the contractor didn't know what he was doing. The contractor had said that if he built according to Arlen's blueprints, the structure would not pass inspection. Harry Paulsen believed his contractor."

# CHAPTER 32

Duffy received a discovery packet from the district attorney's office and asked Dita to go over it with him. Among the many documents culled by the different investigative agencies, they found Arlen's curriculum vitae.

"Would it be okay for me to call some of Arlen's former clients?" Dita asked.

"Dita, here we go again. It could be a motive for murder," Duffy said, exasperated.

"Here's one from fifteen years ago. He calls it the Sackler house. It's in Putnam County. I want to get a feel for his work."

"No, Dita! I want you to meet with Quirk this afternoon. He has a way of getting people to remember things."

"What, he's going to hypnotize me?"

"Well, not exactly."

"He does have something of the Svengali about him."

"He's a man of many talents."

# CHAPTER 33

Quirk bought Dita coffee in a Pain Quotidien near Duffy's office. She sat across from him over a rough timber table stirring raw sugar into her brew and watching people pass on the crowded sidewalk outside of the window. He held a notebook at the ready and stared at her with his green eyes. "Dita, I want you to remember each and every event leading up to and after the lock out."

His questions unleashed a flood of memories. He was a very fine investigator, she told herself and began to explain. "We were in a state of shock. I can't help feeling that I saw things I can't remember. I think adrenalin wiped out my memory banks. Rex Turner returned with the key to padlock the building. I suppose Arlen was afraid to show his face again. Turner stood there watching us. He was measuring the windows, I guess, in order to get materials to board them up. Not once did he bother to help Violet, Marge, me, and Violet's driver to cart stuff to Violet's car and to a livery station wagon we were forced to hire as well. It didn't occur to me that day to check on the entire building. Maybe I would have seen something that could have allowed the murderer to get out of there. An opening somewhere.

"We watched Turner close the padlock and walk away with the key before we drove off. He apologized for the way things were in a kind of gruff way. Said to me, 'You're young, you'll get back on your feet.' It was as if his life offered no choices anymore and it was his way of asking for some sort of absolution from me as if, in my pain, I could give it to him. In the back seat of the car, Violet had taken me into her arms. Both of us were stunned."

Quirk led Dita from the day of the closing to its aftermath in her life. A waiter refilled their coffee cups.

*ଔଔଔ*

She remembered coming home that fateful day. The building porter had helped to unload the boxes from the livery and stood there in her living room until she remembered to give him a tip—a ten-dollar bill. She had nothing smaller. Left alone in the quiet of her living room crammed with boxes of treasures from the center, Dita had finally cried. She cried for the many books and papers she and Violet were unable to pack up; for the dances she would be unable to make; cried for the indifference she had endured for more than five years from her supposed supporters; cried for the relief that accompanied the shock; cried for CJ, who battled for life with cocktails of medications; cried for Dan, who self-published his compositions, many of them dedicated to Dita; cried for his hours away from composing to play dance classes; cried for the artists friends and their shared humanity; cried that she could no longer imagine herself with them in this world of her own choosing.

The evening after the closing, a rapid succession of

SOS knocks had announced Dan without a key. Dita opened the door and buried her face in his shoulder. "Whoa!" He set down his shoulder-stooping, leather brief case, bought at some fundraising rummage sale for the center, and held Dita. Then he had taken in their shared living room with his dark, widely set eyes, his hair sparkled with gray, sweat circles on his armpits from hours at the piano. "What is this? We're moving?" he had asked, surveying the mass of hastily packed boxes covering the Pottery Barn Sisal rug.

"We might actually have to."

"You've been crying. What's going on, Dita?" Dan stood five feet, eight inches. On her toes, Dita equaled him in height.

"Arlen and the board closed the center, Dan. They did it behind my back. I didn't even suspect that this was the way it was going to be. We were locked out." She told him everything.

"Oh, man. That's not fair play. Bastards!" He crouched and rummaged through a box. "I would have loved to have seen those kids drench Arlen. That's really funny, you know."

"This constant crisis of money never seemed real until today. Why did I think we would have been rescued again?"

"Because you deserved to. People depended on you. Business people have no business minding our business," Dan had said, his anger rising.

ഛഇഛ

"Dan was really fuming about it," Dita said.

"And Dan confronted Arlen with you," Quirk said.

It chilled Dita to think about the confrontation and how it further implicated Dan. Pain Quotidien was filling up with more customers, and now they had to talk over a rising din.

"Arlen was infuriatingly indifferent! I was so frustrated. I felt I had a responsibility to try to help the kids replace what was lost so I kept calling around to other programs. It was too late for most things."

"Sad and mean thing to do to kids who are so vulnerable," Quirk said. "It stinks. Let's go sit on a bench in Bryant Park. This place is getting too noisy."

He paid the tab. They walked three blocks east and found a spot that wasn't too crowded near the edge of the park overlooking Forty-Second Street.

# CHAPTER 34

Quirk led her through more of her recent history. He instructed Dita not to edit but to let it all come out. She had been fearful of reliving the trauma but if it would help Dan, then she would face it. In the weeks following the center's closing, Marge had checked in with Dita on a daily basis. The bond with Marge was a permanent one like the bond with Violet. It had survived the trauma. "I don't know what I'm going to do to keep Albert in motion now there's no dance classes," Marge had said. "I put him into that basketball program. But he says it's only okay. He wants there to be music. But Reverend John thinks he's good at it and wants him to stick it out. Probably good at it from all the dancing."

Dita laughed, imagining Albert pirouetting on the basketball court. She'd have to tell Dan about this. Maybe he would include Albert in a game of hoops. "I'll find somewhere to give him a class."

❧❧❧

It was now five o'clock and the sun was heading west and glared in their faces. Dita and Quirk needed to change positions. They sat on the steps of the Forty-Second Street Library. The sun was behind the building. When they were comfortable again, Dita continued. "Several months after the center closed but before Dan's incarceration, I had arranged for some of my promising dance students to continue with classes," Dita told Quirk. She hadn't spoken to or been in contact with Margo, the director of the ballet school, in many years. She'd see her former company colleagues in the public classes at Steps and Broadway Dance. There was a cycle to the ballet life. It showed in a ritual physiognomy; from the fresh, young, hopeful faces, hair pushed back into tightly coiled buns; to the cropping of hair and slovenly warm up outfits of the older professionals, many of whom looked as if they were ready to move on with their lives—their bodies no longer finely tuned and cooperating with the rigors of the profession.

Dita shrugged. "I took a different route and ended up at the same point on the dancer life map. If I had the money to take class again, it would feel good to be in that world again." She explained to Quirk how she wanted to watch the wealthy devotees who took class every day just to watch the ballet stars and maybe live vicariously. By night the same devotees frequented the orchestra seats of whatever company was in season. Dita laughed thinking about the public classes like Steps on Broadway. In addition to the students, professionals, and stars were the eighty-year-old women who refused to give up their point shoes.

Margot Duprez, the director of American Ballet School, had been in her office and had picked up the phone herself when Dita called. It had been late afternoon and most of the students were still in classes. Her office looked out over Lincoln Center Plaza—the terrazzo pavement gleaming in the sunlight. Dita could imagine

Margot behind her desk—ageless, the posture impeccable her hair was almost fully gray when Dita was still a student. Margot must be in her seventies now, Dita thought.

"Dita Marx, I do think of you. To what do I owe the honor of this call?"

Because Dita had not kept in contact, she was surprised to be so warmly greeted. "I explained the closing of the center to Margot and the need to find a place for some of the very talented students. Margot was willing to look at them and suggested that I bring them on the second Wednesday in June right after the yearly workshop was finished."

Dita had then called CJ to tell him that their former school would look at their kids. "I'm coming along," he'd said. Then Dita had spent the afternoon trying to contact the parents of the kids. That was always frustrating, since some families were without phones. Her main contact with them had always been at the center.

Dan had been critical of Dita's plan to take the center dancers to American Ballet School. "The center kids are going to have a difficult time in that environment. Can you just see it with all those private school kids and their social X-ray moms?

"Inverse snob! They respect talent."

"Especially talent with money."

"Money drives its wedge further. Cut it out, Dan. Margot will look, and we will see."

"That's when I started to suspect that I was pregnant," she told Quirk. "Do you have kids?"

"Not even a wife or a girlfriend right now," Quirk said.

Dita remembered how, the night before the appointment for the center kids to take class at American Ballet School, she had dreamt she was floating on a rubber raft at sea. The waves tossed the raft as she clung on desperately, trying to stay afloat. She thought the dream had made her seasick. She spared Quirk the details. The water was a murky cistern—endlessly deep like a tarn. She had awakened to waves of nausea. Waves wafted over her as she lifted her head from the pillow. Oh no, I must be sick, she thought and had run to the bathroom in time to fling her head over the toilet bowl. There'd been little in her stomach and what spewed from her mouth was a bilious liquid. After a shower she'd felt remarkably better and thankful it wasn't the twenty-four hour bug. This was the fullest day she'd scheduled since the closure of the center.

Dita had forgotten that Sally Wilcox, a sales associate specializing in co-op marketing, would be at their apartment at eight-thirty sharp to advise them and probably pressure them into giving her a listing. Dita had made the appointment the month before. With her appointment book now practically empty, Dita would forget to look at it. She surveyed the apartment. They needed to move their clutter. She and Dan hurriedly found spaces under the bed and stacked boxes of stuff into already tightly packed closets. It pleased them to create a vista to the door and the windows. The airiness was why they fell in love with their apartment in the first place. They hoped something would come along to reverse their fortunes before they were forced to sell. The schedule was tight because Dita had the eleven a.m. rendezvous at American Ballet School.

She showered and shaved her legs. Dan has always said that when Dita was shaving her legs, he knew she was up to something. Dita toweled off and wrapped another towel around her head. The bed was unmade and Dan was in the kitchen. She could smell the coffee brewing. She'd stepped into a peasant skirt and tee shirt, draped a leather strap belt with silver baubles around her hips below the waist. Tossed the bed together as best as she could without removing the blankets and sheets. She threw pillows at the bulges under the duvet. The cat was curled up on Dan's pillow again. CJ had said to get a water gun and spray him when he went where he wasn't wanted but they didn't have the heart. He was so cute, all curled up like a ball.

Dita and CJ had planned to meet in the fifth floor lobby at American Ballet School by the marble receptionist desk. Dita's visceral response to seeing the bank of marble was to check her bun as she patted her head she realized that her hair was loose. Loose hair was never allowed in the dance classes. There were so many strictures—almost military concern with hair and dance attire. Very few children could commit to a program of ABS intensity. Dita had picked out seven children whom she thought had the body type and gift of dance. A parent, Bernadette Colon, chaperoned her own daughters Tash and Rosie, and three other girls from the center—Flora, a little blond girl with green eyes whose family recently had immigrated from Brazil, La Toya, already a star according to her name, a lanky thirteen year old who seemed to grow taller as one watched, Cam, a tomboyish blond with freckles across her nose and kinky hair from her afro American father. Albert was the only boy, and he could hardly contain his excitement. Dita stared wistfully at Albert remembering when Marge had first brought Albert to the center. He was a scrawny five-year-old whirling dervish.

"Nothing can keep this kid still," his Grandma Marge had said. "Maybe you've got a class that can keep him in motion long enough to wear him out?"

Albert became one of the two boys in the pre ballet class at the center. He possessed an uncanny gift for the language of dance. He was quick to pick up steps and quick to create his own. He was now almost thirteen years old and growing lanky and long. He had turn out, beautiful feet and was always sad when class was over. American Ballet School could give him enough classes to develop him into a dancer.

Albert ran from the outer lobby to the open doorway of a studio. It was a partnering class with upper class men and women.

CJ grabbed Albert and brought him back to the group. "We need you to go into the dressing rooms and change into your tights."

"I got mine," said Albert unbuttoning and pulling off his baggy jeans.

"Okay man, you go stay in the doorway and watch and don't wander around. That room is where you are going when the class is finished." Albert began to bolt again. "Don't leave your jeans there in a heap."

Albert picked up his jeans and put them into his back pack,

"Where are your ballet shoes, Albert?"

Albert had looked a bit sheepish. He'd forgotten them. The girls followed Dita and Bernadette to the women's locker room.

"This is an audition for real, man. You know Dita and I used to go here. Remember when we took you guys to the Nutcracker?"

"Do you think they'll put us in it, too?"

"Gotta work hard."

"That's not work," Albert had said, "That's fun."

"Oh, it's work!"

Albert had begun to twirl around. Some boys from the inner Lobby stared at him obviously impressed.

"Would I be the only black kid?" he'd asked CJ.

"Now why would you say a thing like that?"

"These kids are all pink."

"These kids all want to dance. That's what this is all about, not what color your complexion is. You got that, Albert?"

Albert had twirled off in acknowledgment.

The dressing room lockers looked more worn than Dita remembered them. In Dita's student days, the locker room was the scene of many pranks—some malicious and some just fun. She had been friendly with a little girl named Christine who was also involved in gymnastics. An only child, she attended the best private school and was expected to succeed academically as well. Christine confided in Dita that she was afraid of gymnastics and only wanted to do ballet. On a play date at Christine's apartment the mother overheard the girls talking. She called Dita's mother and accused Dita of putting ideas of fear into Christine's head. "Please tell your daughter not to discuss gymnastics with Christine."

To which Dita's mother retorted, "I certainly will do nothing of the kind."

"Mrs. Marx, you have feet of clay."

After that Christine was instructed to have nothing to do with Dita. The little girls became enemies. Once Christine lost an expensive pocket book. She accused Dita of stealing it. The mother marched into the administration offices to try to have Dita removed from the ballet program. But by this time, Dita was recognized as the more-talented dancer. Christine disappeared from the program. There were rumors she suffered from anorexia and had to be hospitalized. Dita often wondered what had become of Christine.

Bernadette and Dita emerged from the dressing room with the girls now dressed in black leotards and pink tights, hair tight in buns. Bernadette's girls wore cornrows.

The audition was a class given by Margot. From time

to time other teachers poked their heads into the room. Flora placed herself at the bar behind the other girls. Dita and CJ knew what would happen, she would go into her own world, barely listening but somehow executing each and every combination at the bar.

At first, Margot barely looked, and then she raised her eyebrows.

Dita's eyes moistened. "But then what about Albert?" Dita had asked. His grandma Marge hadn't wanted to come with them today. Dita had pleaded but Marge remained adamant. "He needs to do this on his own, you understand, I can't go along. You've told me so much about this Russified world. I don't want to register disappointment if they don't like him."

"But if they take him, he's going to need your support."

"He'll have that and more."

"Oh, but Marge, he is so talented. I've never said it to you. Now his window of time is beginning."

"You really think my grandson can be a ballet dancer?"

"I do. He has the love."

"I always hoped you'd start a company, Dita, and he'd be your star."

"So did I, but that just didn't happen. You know that saying about all your eggs in one basket?" she'd laughed.

Marge had started out as a volunteer, a position she'd created for herself. She'd bring Albert after school for his lessons and peruse ladies magazines while she waited. One day she wandered into Dita's office and asked if there was anything she could help with. They were sending out a mailing and needed to seal and stamp envelopes. Marge took a pile out to the waiting area and in less time than it would take to drink a cup of coffee, she had the stack finished. "Mail I'm good with. Worked for the post office more than thirty years. What else have you got?"

Knowing she'd ask for something else, Dita pulled out boxes of music donated to the center but that had been sitting in boxes for so many years no one knew what was in them. Marge had them alphabetized and filed by the time Albert emerged from his ballet class, hungry and thirsty. An advanced piano student had been so delighted to get a volume of Beethoven's early sonatas. Marge had balked when Dita first suggested that they could pay her something, but Dita had told her to put it away for Albert's future and so Marge had become Dita's assistant.

Albert needed to learn to work inside himself, Dita had thought as she watched him cross the floor with his uncanny sense of space. His movements were almost feline—a leopard maybe? Would the pomp and seductiveness of the big arts center make these kids lose their special focus? Who would pay for the pointe shoes?

Dita always remembered how her own mother had paid for the Freeds of London pointe shoes and didn't leave enough in the bank account to pay the utility bill. The check bounced. Her father was furious at her mother. *Our Con Ed bill is overdue*, she thought as the audition class was winding toward the end with pas de chat. Next would come the reverence, the traditional ending of the ballet class in which the teacher thanks the students and the students thank the teacher. Flora's port-de-bras breathed elegance. Albert finished in first position with a manly stance. The other children did well, too but were not on the same level.

*Sometimes you can't teach a student how to work*, Dita thought. Albert and Flora had an innate understanding of the process. Margot told Dita and CJ to join her in the office. "You've done very well by your students," she said to Dita.

"That's a great compliment for me. I'm choreographing now, Margot."

"We should certainly consider having you choreograph for the choreography workshop."

"I would love that," Dita said. Percy Fountain was still the artistic director of the parent company, and he watched the workshop closely. Dita felt a tingle of the old excitement that had been deadened after the center closed.

"As to who we can accommodate in the school," Margot said, "The boy Albert and the girl Flora can attend. They will need scholarships, I imagine."

"They will," CJ said, "And I will make a donation to the fund."

"Very nice of you, CJ."

"It would be my pleasure."

Margot continued, "I will send them official letters. I don't want to disappoint the other children, so just keep this to yourselves for now."

"Certainly we will," CJ said, grabbing Dita's hand.

# CHAPTER 35

When she'd returned from the American Ballet School audition, the lights were still on, she told Quirk. The apartment was serene. Dan was reading want ads at the kitchen counter. He had made a salad and an omelet and had waited for her.

"'I'm going over to the gym to shoot hoops,' Dan told me when we finished supper. Do you play, Quirk?"

"The only thing right about me and basketball is my height."

"Dan said his feet dragged on the court—the combination of too much food and too much on his mind. He managed to hit the rim of the basket to the disgust of the other player. Dan was too distracted so he left and went to the West End for a beer. I joined him. Seated in the old West End Bar, now an upscale eatery, Dan pondered our next step and doodled on score paper. We'd reached a real impasse. The shock of the center's closing became a banal nothingness settling in between us. We said little."

"Had enough for the afternoon?" asked Quirk.

"I'm hungry and tired," Dita said. "Talking about all this is so emotionally painful for me."

"We will continue another day," Quirk said, and they shook hands.

Dita headed uptown on foot to her apartment. It had been an intense day, and she didn't want to ride public transportation in rush hour. She continued up Sixth Avenue from Bryant Park and entered Central Park at Fifty-Ninth Street. The playgrounds were thronged with children and their parents, many adults still in work clothes. She wondered about the strange day with Quirk. Her mind replayed some of the things she had told him. She'd opened up to someone she barely knew.

# CHAPTER 36

As Duffy worked to construct a plausible defense for Dan, questions about Randy kept cropping up. Dita tried to sort out Randy's relationship to Arlen. Could she have been part of an illegal enterprise? Randy represented many things that Dita found distasteful. She was a bottom liner and anything that wasn't producing money had no value for her.

At first, Dita had welcomed the idea of an executive director for the center Dita explained to Duffy. It was late afternoon in his office and sunlight was dwindling. He flicked a remote and electric light illuminated the space. A close shave with closure and last minute rescue the year before had chastened Dita. Having Randolynn Smith-Warren aboard, she hoped would clarify her own role. Since CJ's departure, Dita had taken on more functions than she could have reasonably juggled. Scheduling had never been her strong point, and she had hoped someone would check the teaching schedule to prevent the double booking of rooms that frequently had gotten the ire of her staff. In addition, the center had lacked a regular maintenance schedule after the death of Jesus Avilla. Arlen had brought in Rex Turner. Jesus, and Dita had a really close working relationship. Turner was Arlen's man and, if she made a request, he'd tell her it had to go by Arlen. She was losing control over the center. Sometimes Dita felt Rex lingered by her open door too long when she took phone calls but maybe she was imagining this. She wanted to close her office door, but her policy had always been open door so the students wouldn't be afraid to seek her out.

Not so, Randy! Randy had chosen two rooms situated in the back of the second floor, removed from the hubbub of the center whereas Dita had a tiny room behind the front office that opened to the main hall of the ground floor. Because the kids and faculty always had access to her, sometimes she found herself settling squabbles between children or between staff members. She enjoyed this role also and had wondered if she was headed on a collision course with Randy.

Randy's office overlooked the community garden— She even supplied rose bushes in the space just under her windows—as if she disdained the idea of being winked at by a towering sunflower or morning glory on its vine. Randy spent the first week decorating her office. She rummaged the center walls for the best posters. She personalized her office with a collection of glass curios she kept locked away in a mirror backed and glass fronted cabinet as if she was afraid some of the center clientele might steal them.

"To my annoyance," Dita said to Duffy, "Randy's perfume of choice was tea roses. You can't imagine how much I hate that scent and, when Randy wasn't there, the scent still wafted through all of the corridors to me a malodorous passing spirit."

Duffy laughed at the idea of a rose-scented ghost inhabiting the center.

# CHAPTER 37

How do you buy property in Harlem?" Dita asked Duffy on another one of her visits to his office. "I'm trying to understand exactly what Arlen was doing."

"You can go through real estate brokers like everywhere else. Or you can make secret deals with secret connections."

"How do the brokers get in on the game?"

"Real estate in Harlem is making Miss Ruggles and some of her colleagues piles of money," Duffy said. "But sometimes the listings slip through. A guy like Arlen comes along and offers the owner cash. I assume that's what he was doing. Or that's how he got into the game."

"And then he was leveraging them out and keeping the cash."

"Seems like that's the way it happened."

❧❧❧

Dita paid a visit to Miss Ruggles in her storefront real estate office and asked pointblank if she knew Arlen. Unabashed, Ruggles related her dealings with Arlen to

Dita. "I'm not surprised he got himself murdered. Skanky guy. A train wreck waiting to happen. I tried to protect some of my elderly sellers from him, but he offered cash, and I never got the listings. I sure hope they can prove your husband didn't do it." Miss Ruggles seemed happy to talk about it. Arlen had slighted her.

Two years before he became involved in the center, a "for sale" sign on a five-story Harlem brownstone had led Arlen Van Aiken into the office of Ruggles Realty. "You could see," she said, "He was feeling like his entrance had caused an event of sorts." Arlen had asked about the listing. 'Now, that's going to take some work,' I told him. 'Are you looking at it as an investment, Mr...'

"'Van Aiken. Possibly.'

"'Well, here's the situation. The daughter recently came to me for some advice. She wants her mother to move south to be with her. She's ninety-three years old and living alone in a five-story brownstone—five stories of steps. Ella Mae Archer, that's the mother, lives on the parlor floor. Her son has an accounting office on the second floor. What they did is fix the parlor floor so she could have everything she needed at that level. So her son added on a bathroom, and a kitchen."

"'Is it legal?' he asked me.

"I met his eyes. 'You'd probably have to take it down.'

"'Could you take me through it?'

"'I've got instructions,' I told him. 'Don't show on canasta days. That's Monday, Wednesday, and Fridays.' The canasta players—Ella Mae Archer, Shirley Simmons, and Patrice Brown—have outlived a child each. The three, now in their mid-nineties, meet rain or shine, snow, or ice to play canasta. The fourth member Lou Ann passed on earlier in the year, in her ninety-eighth year, forcing the others to modify the rules of the game—a game best played by four. I know the ladies from my church."

Dita thought the real estate business kept Ruggles going to church.

"Those women are the rocks of stability up here. I paid my respects when Lou Ann died. The other three were shook up by it. Talked more about selling. They talked about how Lou Ann never did get back home. These are my people," Ruggles went on. "Tight friendships we enjoy—the loss of the friend was still raw in our collective memory. We share our Southern roots. These ladies are home-owners, rocks of stability in Harlem. We get one incompetent self-interested leader after another. Paving the way for an Arlen Van Aiken, is what they do. Those ladies were the weary and tolerant spectators to every incarnation of salvation government around here could devise. And you know who I'm talking about."

Dita nodded wearily, making Ruggles laugh. "You're going to regret getting me started—the futility of it all. Take a look at the every mounting rubble. The ever-changing owners keep confining it by new installations of cyclone fencing. No one's fixing up anything."

"Very discouraging," Dita said. "So what happened? You showed him the property?"

"I took him through on a Thursday. He stayed quite a while. Trying to charm the old lady when he was really twitching his nose. Cooking smells lingered in the curtains and the paneling that covered the addition. Place needed a thorough going over. The addition looked like it could have been knocked down with a broom. Someone with the money could do something with it. Made me cry, thinking about it.

"In the front parlor a beautiful bay window over-looked the street—no trees. We had a tree program a while back that provided saplings but no one had followed up with care. The saplings died with their support wires still stuck in the dusty ground. That was the view from Ella May's parlor."

Dita imagined Arlen in Ella May's parlor. She'd seen many properties like it with the bones of a wonderful residence.

"I told her she could get upward of ninety-eight thousand for her brownstone. Ella May sold to Arlen for seventy-five thousand cash. He bought the brownstones of her friends for cash as well."

Ruggles pulled some fliers out of her desk drawer and handed them to Dita. They contained a promise of cash for properties. "These were circulated by Arlen," Ruggles told Dita. "I'd pull them down whenever I'd see one."

Dita laughed.

"No laughing matter to me. He'd ruin my business. All those shells got tied up by Arlen and people like him. I'm a family real estate broker. I like to help good families move in up here. And yes, I've done well. But I've done it by playing an honest game," Ruggles said.

*ⱸↄⱸↄ*

Detectives Milton and Nadler struggled to fill in the blanks. They continued to ask serious questions of Van Aiken's family. They learned that Arlen had spoken to his father-in-law Mort Rothman about acquiring some other properties and shared this knowledge with Duffy.

"Too many unknowns." Mort Rothman had told him. "Why should I play there? Did you count the number of sinks? That tells you if it's been a boarding house. I can't back you in this, but I can't tell you what to do with your own money."

"So Arlen Van Aiken had discovered that he had a nose for distressed properties," Milton said. "In addition to circulating the flyer offering cash, quick closing terms, he encouraged Mitchell Shepherd and Ted Callahan to form an investment group with him. Arlen met Ted Callahan at one of Mindy's charitable events. He'd been the underwriter. Arlen would meet up with him at the Harvard Club to play squash, followed by drinks and dinner, according to Mindy. Callahan was astonished when Arlen told him what he paid for his buildings and what they were worth not renovated six months later. 'You could get loans on the properties and buy more,' Callahan suggested. 'But you can't get the banks to loan up in Harlem,' Arlen said. This much Mindy had overheard," he said.

"That's when they decided to form a non-profit and create their own bank. They needed a lawyer to do the documentation. According to the bank Callahan worked for, Callahan had used Mitchell Shepherd on some low-level foreclosure deals. Maybe Arlen hadn't intended to do anything illegal but, with Callahan as the catalyst, it just happened. Callahan created the La Grange Trust Company and a slew of non-profits, and Mitchell Shepherd provided false documentation on the loan applications. The enterprise was vertical—everything under one roof. It seemed too simple. The Department of Housing and Urban Development (HUD) was not equipped to oversee its loans.

"The conspirators soon discovered lots of Ella Maes out there and from 2002 to 2005 they had acquired more than fifty properties and sought financing. They also discovered the world of not-for-profits, and that the mayor's office wouldn't deal with individuals who sought to rehabilitate a property as a primary home. If the city owned them, they were sold off in bulk to developers with the requirement that the properties be rehabilitated. With no oversight and real estate prices spiraling, the shells got traded like commercial paper and Harlem suffered the rat-infested shells on each and every block."

☙❧☙

Mindy had known very little about Arlen's secret life—his enterprise as it was to become known. Milton shared some of his investigative findings with Duffy, who relayed them to Dita: The police investigation put Arlen and Mitchell Shepherd at the Oyster Bar in Grand Central Station the day before Arlen's murder. A waiter described their impatience as Arlen and his cohort had waited for a third party. The gray-haired dude he said slapped down a credit card down on the check and stood while the waiter went to put it through. Arlen left a not so generous tip, and the men rushed out of there. Arlen's steps were traced to a taxi because he used a credit card for the ride. Mitchell Shepherd was still with him according to the driver's description. The cab took them to the boat basin.

"They must have discovered that Callahan's yacht was missing," Dita said.

"Seems like it," Duffy said, leaning back in his desk chair. "The picture so far looks like this: Arlen had brought the other men onto the center's board of directors. Callahan chartered a bank, in order to avail themselves of loans through the department of Housing and Urban Development, and Shepherd, a lawyer had helped submit false documentation, in order to obtain the financing. He also created fictitious non-profit organizations to receive the loans. Their scheme had depended on the spiraling property values in the Harlem neighborhood of upper Manhattan. They could take the cash from the loans because they would flip the properties for far more than they paid for them."

"And nothing was in their own names?" Dita said.

"That's correct, so they had to trust one another. Arlen had trusted Callahan to earmark funds into a separate account for himself. When he went to access it, he found the password had been changed. It was no longer Bennett A. Dawes. I can assure you of that. Mindy heard him screaming on the phone about a password. Not just the arts center, all the other properties would be in default if they continued to be unable to access the cash fund. Their property-flipping scheme was imploding. They had to know for a certainty that Callahan had betrayed them all."

"Oh, my," was Dita's only response. "But how can this help Dan."

"The old conundrum!"

# CHAPTER 38

With Dita's help, Duffy tried to sort out the relationships of the other board members to each other. From Reverend John, he had learned that, shortly before the closing of the center, Rex Turner had approached him after the Sunday morning service. He pushed his wife Becky in her wheelchair. She had wanted to attend the coffee fellowship after the service. There was no elevator so they had needed to unlock another exit and push her through the basement door into the community room.

Becky had always been a robust woman—large boned and blonde. She was nurse at Harlem Hospital. Rex had had a used car business. He'd buy vehicles at police auctions, fix them up, and sell them. He had found a van for Reverend John's basketball team and John had been grateful for this.

When Becky's condition had begun to deteriorate, Rex had found it impossible to provide for her on his salary alone. She was suffering from a rare neurodegenerative disease—MSA or Multiple System Atrophy. In its early stages MSA could be difficult to distinguish from Parkinson's. But MSA progresses more rapidly. Becky had now needed a full time attendant. Rex needed to make money. John had introduced him to Arlen, and Rex had become the caretaker for the properties Arlen and his cohorts now owned. "Caretaker" meant stripping the properties of anything that had value, selling it off for cash, and bricking up the shells. Rex had done other favors for Arlen that had put even more cash into his pockets. Rex had been able to move Becky into a ground floor apartment. Rex told himself that there was no one to look out for him and Becky but himself. He had pushed aside any ethical inclinations he might have had. Arlen had paid cash according to Rex.

Rex had hated seeing Becky helpless he told Milton. "Becky, I have a surprise for you," Rex had told her. She had tried to repeat the word "surprise." An idea would take hold but she couldn't get it out of her mouth anymore. Her speech had begun to deteriorate. Rex had picked her up and carried her down two flights to their building lobby. As her muscles had atrophied she had become lighter, almost weightless. The door to a ground floor apartment was open and he carried her inside and put her on a sofa.

"We're moving in here so you can get out more."

Tears had come to Becky's eyes.

# CHAPTER 39

The medical examiner put the time of Mitchell Shepherd's death as on or about the same day of Arlen's murder. The toxicology reports hadn't come back. The body was so decomposed it was difficult to ascertain if Shepherd had been wounded. They were tentatively calling it a murder. Was someone on a spree, Milton asked himself. He said to Nadler, "Can we place Di Bello in both places?"

"Aren't we jumping the gun here?" Nadler said.

# CHAPTER 40

Dita met with Quirk once again, this time in an Italian restaurant on Columbus Avenue. It was two p.m., and the lunch hour was just about over. Several patrons lingered over espressos. Quirk and Dita sat at a table by the window and watched the place empty out. After a table was vacated, a waiter swooped down and changed the butcher paper covering red table clothes. Dita would have liked to order the lobster ravioli but the restaurant had sold out. She ordered a linguine and clam sauce instead. Quirk ordered the same, and they continued the memory game.

She sighed. "It was like maggots feasting on garbage. In the weeks following the center's closing the bill collectors began to feed on us. Early on Dan and I were helpless to make even small payments. We had begun to measure our days by when bills were due, and how long they had gone unpaid. There was no cushion. Stacks of statements began to accumulate on the dining room table. Reminder notices covered the stacks of collection notices. Eight-hundred and eight-eight-eight numbers were now the predominant caller identification numbers that popped up on the phone window. There was a pattern to the collection efforts: At first an automated voice message suggested that an oversight had occurred. Then the serious and intimidating collection efforts commenced, with a human being on the other end of the line. I tumbled into a vortex of numb fear. I didn't want to burden Dan with more anxiety."

"It's very frightening to be out of work. Most people don't have any cushion at all," he said.

"Knowing I had taken the chance of getting pregnant made me all the more anxious to find a job." She'd gone to the district school office in the basement of a public school. The center had now been closed for several weeks, and she had no leads on a new job. It was seven-thirty a.m. She'd brought her Columbia University diploma, and an unofficial transcript. She'd have to make a trip to the registrar's office if they required a sealed transcript. She had hastily mocked up a one page resume neglecting to state that the activities and work she had listed was all done at the center at the one job, beside the ballet, that she had ever known.

She'd passed children in the hallway that she had known from the center. They'd recognized her too. "Hi, Miss Dita," Miranda an eight-year-old girl with pretty feet and a natural turnout had said. "When do we get ballet lessons again?"

"Since the center closed, the summer dance program had to be canceled as well," Dita told Quirk. "Working parents depended on it. It provided three classes and activities each weekday for seventy-five children." She remembered saying to the little girl, "I'm going to be calling your mother sometime soon. We'll see if we can't get you into some other school. Maybe even American Ballet School. Those kids dance in the Nutcracker." She'd been immediately sorry she'd said this to the child. The ballet school could take very few children.

After talking with Miranda, Dita saw the head of the district. Mrs. Lowe, a light-skinned black woman, had been dressed immaculately in a navy skirt suit with white lapels and spectator pumps to match. She knew Dita and beckoned her into her office. "Just wanted to say we all are going to miss you and we wish you the best."

It had been difficult for Dita to accept these condolences. "Well! Actually, I came by because I was hoping to get onto the sub list. I need to find work."

"I can imagine. You were left high and dry. Well, our kids would be lucky to have you for a day."

"Thanks, Mrs. Lowe. I don't have any education credits, but please think of me if something opens up that's right for me. I feel worse for the kids. I'm going to try to find the places for lessons."

People waiting for Mrs. Lowe had begun lining up outside of the open office door.

"I know you will. Let me take you over to Cynthia Moore, she's the one that keeps the sub list."

Cynthia Moore had greasy scraggly blonde hair and an overworked air for so early in the morning. She'd beckoned Dita to a chair and had taken her name and phone number. Dita had become a file to her. She would become a new file to many people throughout the day, and the weeks that followed.

❧❧❧

"There were no responses to my job queries," Dita told Quirk. "The school district never called to give me substitute teaching. No one called, except bill collectors. The bills lay in stacks on the dining room table. Poverty is an oppression of paper one is helpless to confront." There was nowhere to eat except for the tiny kitchen—a galley with an under the counter niche for two stools—or the bedroom in front of the TV on which there was nothing she desired to watch.

"Even after Dan's incarceration, I spent my days cooking. Working with my hands is soothing, restorative. I liked the idea of the completeness of a meal when everything else was fragmenting. Food anchors me," she said winding the linguine around her fork against a soupspoon. She cooked everything from scratch rather than stand on line and part with their now scarce dollars. She had found a cellophane bag of tree ears in the rear of a cabinet that must have been bought for a stir-fry dinner several years ago. To the eye and nose they were perfect and she'd decided to add them to the filling consisting of greens and ricotta.

Dita smiled at Quirk. "Dan's incarceration certainly didn't deter the bill collectors. They continued to heckle me day in and day out. I was again making ravioli again even though I knew I would be eating it alone. Greens and ricotta filling is my favorite. I dried the wooden board and put three cups of Italian flour onto it making a well in the center in preparation for the pasta."

"I'm amazed at how you can eat and still ramble on about food."

"I guess I'm just a foodie."

Because Quirk was encouraging Dita to use sense memory, in the hope she could remember something helpful, she described to Quirk how she had cooked up a bunch of endives and mustard greens from which she squeezed the liquid out of with her hands. She would save it to bathe the ravioli in their final cooking.

She'd chopped the ball of greens and squeezed it more. Against what she now considered to be her better judgment she had bought Parmesian Reggiano and a creamy handmade ricotta from Zabars. She should have bought the Poly-O brand the supermarket offered half price. She mixed the chopped greens into the ricotta and grated the Parmesan into the mixture with several eggs. "Making the ravioli made me think about the stories my mother-in-law had heard from her mother who had grown up poor on the rocky coast of Liguria. Dan and I have always wanted to go there to the cave hotels carved out of mountains dipping into the sea. We want to savor the Ligurian cuisine we've heard so much about. Grandma's favorite dish was fava bean puree, greens, and a crusty piece of bread. My ravioli is a legacy from Dan's grandmother. One, two, three eggs, I broke into the well, and as I began to stir the phone rang. The call was from Citibank MasterCard. A Mr. Frost, darkening his voice to sound ominous, asked for me by my first name.

"'This is Dita.' The card said Edita. He wanted to make sure he had the right person. 'Oh you have me, all right.'

"'Do you know that your payment is now ninety days overdue?' It was now more than four months since the center had closed," she told Quirk. "I bristled and decided to negotiate. 'Sure I do, but the way you guys add fees and charges, there's no way I can pay.' We had accumulated late fees, overdraft penalties, and what had been two thousand dollars was now closer to thirty-five hundred dollars.

"'So what you're saying is you're not responsible,' the jerk tells me.

"He'd tried to intimidate me with a patriarchal tone." She tried to conjure up a face to go along with it. "I sensed he was young. 'What are you twenty-two years old?' I asked.

"'That doesn't matter. I'm calling about your debt.'

"'Well I'm asking you to cut me some slack. The add-ons are reprehensible. I'm responsible but I've just lost my job.'

"'You and everyone else,' the man said.

"I neglected to say that my husband was also incarcerated. He would probably figure me for a crook as well as a bad debtor. The egg had begun to clot at the edges of the flour and I stirred it furiously with the fork bringing more and more egg into the flour."

Quirk laughed at this.

"'I don't know about everyone else,' I said.

"'So then maybe I can expect a payment in good faith?'

"I stirred even more vigorously. The dough had formed a soft ball, and I needed both of my hands to work it. Finally, in exasperation I said, 'I can't even give you a payment with another card. Don't you get it? No cash.'

"'You're not saying the thirty-five hundred wasn't spent by you?'

"'No, it was spent by your company with all their add-ons and fees. It's usurious. You know what?' I asked. 'You're lucky you have a job right now. I bet you even get benefits.'

"'Look here, I have a degree in finance.'

"'So why are you into this harassment crap? I'm trying to make ravioli here. It's the cheapest dinner I can think of, and you're making me dry out my dough.'

"'Four years of college and then some.'

"'So you can harass people? You should be qualified for something better than that. But maybe you need outlets for your sadism.'

"'Four years of college so people like you can take a fucking ride.'

"'Watch how you talk to me,' I said. I was getting flour all over the receiver, the floor, and the counter. The dough was drying onto my hands.

"'I'm talking a free ride,' he said.

"'Speaking of rides, I bet you drive something fancy and you're stuck with that.'

"'I drive a piece of shit because people like you take free rides.'

"'Who put that idea into your turgid little brain?'

"'I told you because I'm not a freeloader.'

"'You're calling me one? I've been working since I was sixteen years old, and I'm approaching forty. I lost my job of many years, and you dare to call me a free-loader? You know what, buster? You get to work your way up the corporate ladder.'

"'No, there are too many rungs missing. No one can climb any more,' he said. 'Gotta fucking eat!'

"'You're going to get fired for talking this way.'

"'That's when I eat my gun.'

"'Listen!' But he was gone. I punched buttons on the phone to retrieve the number. But the caller was lost in telephone cyberspace." Dita sighed. "The animals knew something was amiss in the world. The Pomeranian next door began to yap mercilessly. Baryshnikitty arched his back, mewed, and dove under my seat."

"Debt collectors are a sick bunch," Quirk said.

"Do you think knowing we were in this kind of trouble makes Dan look guiltier?"

"There is this tendency to blame the victims. The nineteenth-century Brits sent debtors to prison."

# CHAPTER 41

Shortly after the American Ballet School audition in June, Albert had begun to ask Marge for little freedoms. She was standing at the kitchen sink, washing their lunch dishes. Albert was excited that American Ballet School had accepted both him and Flora. There were preparations to be made. He would be on his own sometimes. They needed to find a school program to accommodate his twelve-thirty men's class. He would need to walk by himself from school in time to take the class and return at two o'clock for the last academic class of the day.

There was La Guardia High School, an arts high school a block away from his dance school, but since the school had its own dance program. It wouldn't accommodate Albert and Flora. Professional Children's School was expensive and geared toward kids making fortunes acting in commercials. Marge decided to home school Albert. Dita helped Marge set up some tough parameters. Albert promised to do two hours of schoolwork before he left the house and two hours in the evening. He was so excited, he would promise anything, but Dita told Marge he'd get more done with less pressure.

"Grandma, can I go over to the bodega and get a fruit pop?" Albert now had a little bit of fuzz over his lip. He was a full-blown adolescent.

"I'm still cleaning, Albert," Marge had said, "maybe in about an hour."

"I can go myself?"

It was always difficult for Marge to let Albert go out on the street by himself, her daughter, his mother, had been so vulnerable. But Marge also knew that he needed to.

"Well, I guess you can. Take your cell phone with you, just in case." *The cell phone is such a blessing,* she thought, pulling a small wad of bills out of her apron pocket. She handed a five-dollar bill to Albert. "We can use some dish soap, too."

"Okay, Grandma!" Albert had literally danced out of the front door. He needed to pass the center to get to the Bodega and found its door open. A pickup truck loaded with plywood had been backed up onto the sidewalk. Albert wandered inside. Boards had been placed over all the windows on the garden level. He heard hammering on the parlor floor and climbed the stairs. In the concert hall he found Rex Turner who had startled and jumped nervously.

"I don't like people sneaking up on me," Turner screamed at Albert. "You're not supposed to be in here."

"I'm sorry, Mr. Turner," Albert said.

The wall air conditioner had been removed from its sleeve and stood on the parlor floor. It dripped forming a small puddle of water. "I'll tell you what," said Turner. "You can help me carry this to the truck. It has to get fixed."

Albert trudged down the parlor stairs backward, holding onto the heavy machine while Turner guided from above. When the machine was secured in the back of the pick-up truck, Rex Turner had handed Albert a five-dollar bill. Twice in an hour Albert had gotten a fiver. He was delighted and thanked Rex. Rex told Albert that, if he was around over the summer, he might have more work for him to do. That pleased Albert. He wondered if he should tell his grandma, but she was so negative about everyone involved in closing the center.

June passed into July. As the summer wore on, Marge had been hard put to keep Albert in activities. More and more he needed to have his freedom. Unbeknownst to Marge, Albert's helping Rex had become a regular job by late June.

"You wanna do some work for me?" Turner had asked.

Albert had a broad smile on his face.

"You have some time right now?"

"Yessir!"

"But this stays between us, buddy. I can't offer every kid in the hood a job."

"Mum's my word." Albert followed Rex into the center.

"We need to remove some stained glass windows. The one's that run floor to ceiling in the center parlor. They're very heavy mind you." Albert steadied the ladder while Rex unhinged them. Then they wrapped them in mover's blankets and loaded them onto the truck. Rex gave Albert another five-dollar bill. He bought candy at the bodega and thought he needed to hide it from his grandma. She would wonder where he got the money for it. Albert decided it would be best not to tell Marge that he was working for Rex.

# CHAPTER 42

Baryshnikitty sensed Dan's continued absence with an increased cat neuroticism. He wouldn't let Dita out of his sight. The way he followed Dita around the apartment reminded Dita of a faithful little dog. He'd bat her with his paws when he wanted her to guess what he wanted. He'd jump to the kitchen counter and lunge for her when he wanted to be fed. Dita, Dan, and Baryshnikitty had only begun their tenuous life together when Dan was arrested. For the cat, the loss of freedom near his foraging grounds had brought the new comforts of a home. It had taken him all of three minutes to discover the queen-sized bed and take over Dan's pillow. No more nights locked up in an empty institution without human contact.

Dan had tried to move him off to a space between them onto the quilted coverlet. The cat mewed with indignation. His mewing had become the dominant voice of the household. The litter box had taken over space under the bathroom sink. The cat scratched the leather recliner until it revealed a faux backing. It was already old, and even if it wasn't real leather, it was comfortable. He manicured his claws on the hooked rug CJ made for their wedding present. And so a silly black alley cat with white tuxedo markings and three white paws made Dita and Dan a family, at least provisionally, because it had become clear to them that the apartment needed to be sold. Now, no Dan's head competed for space on the pillow.

# CHAPTER 43

Dan was now incarcerated almost a month. Duffy was becoming increasingly frustrated that they hadn't been able to place anyone else in the center with Dan the day of Arlen's murder. Dita sat in chair in front of his desk. He contemplated her folding his long fingers into a steeple.

"I don't mean to offend you, but I'm really trying to understand how Arlen got control of everything."

"I don't understand it myself. It was the structure of the arts. I let the possibility of the money tantalize me. That's my history. No money but lots of connections to people with money. It's difficult not to become some kind of whore. When I was in the company, I was very young. The dancers were expected to socialize with the donors. Taboos found in regular society were broken in the ballet world. We got the message that we were expected to keep the rich donors tantalized. Many dancers are so young they don't know how to watch out and not cross certain lines with the people who keep them in work. When we'd go on tour, I'd sometimes get on the bus taking the company to the airport not knowing what city we were going to. We were totally taken care of. I fell into that role again when I reconnected with Arlen. He had history with us. I rue the day that brought him back into my life."

She explained to Duffy how a few years after opening the center and maybe a year before the collapse of the World Trade Center in 2001, she and CJ had been invited to a seminar on the revitalization of upper Manhattan. The guest speaker was the mayor's current Commissioner on Homelessness Tommy Thompson. It had been held in a seminar room at the Columbia Presbyterian Medical School—a mixture of academics and neighborhood forces like Dita and CJ. They had sipped Perrier water and had eaten carrot sticks, doughy canapés and cut up fruit, stabbing squares of precut cheese with toothpicks. Mr. Thompson, flanked by his two assistants, clearly had come there to stem the notion that the mayor was inhumanely forcing the homeless out of Grand Central and Bryant Park to the delight of suburban commuters but at the expense of Harlem and Washington Heights. It was clear to Dita that from time to time some of the center's kids and their families had gone homeless and she had been there to learn as much as she could about the system.

Dita had asked a pointed question. "Mr. Commissioner, what about the properties the city has sold to individuals with the understanding, the properties will be improved. Every block up here has several and it seems the turnover in ownership is rapacious. We all know these shells are rising in value yet no one is making the required improvements. How can this be allowed?" Someone kicked her leg under the table.

Across the table she saw a gray-haired, well-coifed man. He cleared his throat and pointed to his nametag—Arlen Van Aiken. She realized she knew him.

"Ah, now I know who you are. Blast from the past!"

she had said to him. It had been seventeen years since she last saw him.

"It was through Hy Rosen," he had said.

Her utter naïveté had come back in waves of warm shame. Dita, eighteen, ensconced in her first apartment .The crazy roommate Leslie—then an International Affairs student at Columbia. There had been two other roommates as well. These had been the pre Dan days as Dita called them, the only other guy Dita ever dated— Bruce, a med student. His father Hy, a ballet supporter, had followed the dancers, had taken them for dinners, had bought them tickets, and had lavished them with gifts. Hy had been a voyeur. Dita had remembered him as warm, funny with an edge of brutality that his friends had seemed to enjoy. He had been their ringleader. He had called them boring, and they had opened their wallets for the ballet company. They had taken it with good humor. Arlen had been one of the donors. "You know the name Van Aiken," Hy had said in jest. "It's a big deal. Might even be some Jewish blood."

Hy's wife Ellen had seemed to share his interest in the ballet world—she had served on boards, had raised money tirelessly. They both had been Dita's friends and they had encouraged her to become involved with their son Bruce. The week Bruce had taken his boards, Hy had invited Dita, Marla, Maddy, and Ghisla to the ballet—the other company—the one Dita was so sure hers was superior to. Hy had brought along a friend for each of them. Arlen, Jules, and Mike. Rich guys, their wives away in the Hamptons including Ellen, Hy's wife. Arlen must have been in his early forties then; that would make him about fifty-seven, Dita had thought.

"You stopped dancing, didn't you?" Arlen asked.

"Injured too many times."

"It's a tough life, kiddo. Wouldn't let my kids do it.

Hy, he was a sucker for the ballet. Did you know he passed away?"

"No, I didn't."

"He was diabetic. Needed heart surgery but they couldn't because of the diabetes."

"That's too bad. And Ellen?"

"Don't see much of her. Heard she has a significant other in her life now. Ask me about their boy Bruce."

"Okay." The last time she had been out with Hy and Ellen's son Bruce, she sprained an ankle in the Village. Bruce helped her into a taxi because he had to study for an exam. The injury kept her out of action for six weeks, she recalled ruefully. Bruce called three weeks later. Dita was already involved with Dan.

"What about him?" she said but his eyes admonished her to let it wait.

Their encounter had been interrupting the flow of the seminar. Arlen returned to the packet in front of him and Dita did likewise. He slipped her a note: *I'd like to catch up. Can you join me for coffee?*

She nodded in the affirmative and showed the note to CJ who had raised his hand. The moderator Dr. Hanley had given CJ the go ahead to speak, and he'd spoken directly to the commissioner pursuing the thread Dita had begun. "Dita is right. The vacant shells in these blocks are rat infested and the rest of us suffer. Shouldn't the city step in and warn the owners to get their acts together and clean up. Better yet develop these properties."

Arlen, a serious fa away look on his face, had added, "Part of the problem is the permitting process. I speak from experience. I'm involved in some housing on One-Hundred Thirty-Eight.

CJ had continued to prod. "It is well known that there is retribution by the mayor for anyone who disagrees. Commissioners and aides turn over almost as quickly as upper Manhattan real estate. Can you address this, Mr. Commissioner?"

"You know not everyone can be made happy."

"Something like you can please most of the people some of the time and some of the people all of the time?"

"Yeah, something like that. We are faced with very complex variables."

*Love that word, variables*, Dita had thought. It had been the biggest excuse word she could think of. This was too blatant just to let it go. CJ pressed on, making the other seminar attendees very uncomfortable. Dita watched as all eyes settled on CJ—almost a suspenseful waiting game. "But no one is saying why these shells get traded like commercial paper. Am I mistaken? You are unwilling to answer my question?" CJ was unwilling to let it drop.

The moderator, a medical school dean, finally intervened. "Let's move on, shall we? We are invited across the street to the armory to watch an outtake exam of an HIV homeless man," he said, looking at his Movado wristwatch. Movado supported the ballet company. Dita had once appeared in a Movado ad printed in the company program. She had gotten to wear one for the shoot. She was so young she thought that they would probably give her a watch afterward. She was not paid to model for the ad. It was just another thing the company expected of its dancers.

More memories had flooded Dita's mind. While Bruce studied for his exams and Ellen played on Long Island, Hy had played host at a dinner party for Arlen, and his friends Jules Greenblatt and Sydney Crumb. Dita, her roommates, and close friend Annie were considered their dates. Sydney had owned a jet airplane and had insisted that they all have lunch in Martha's Vineyard before returning for steaks on Jules's East Sixty-Second

Street terrace. Dita had had a performance the next day and had returned home alone without her friends that night. But she had been wasted from the afternoon of imbibing.

The men, her father's age, had foisted drinks on the young women. She had remembered the flight through the corridors of clouds, the landing at the small airport with a waiting limousine. Drinks and more drinks, Steamers out on the dock, boats floating by. They had been back in the airplane by late afternoon. The plane's bathroom had been well stocked with toiletries, condoms, hairspray, and moisturizing cream. Coffee, more drinks. She had realized that she had procured her girlfriends for Hy and Arlen, and their good buddies.

Dita remembered her last conversation with Bruce.

"Bruce, would you care if your dad had an affair?" Dita had asked.

"It wouldn't surprise me. My mother doesn't believe in sex."

"How do you know?"

"I know she drives him from the bed."

"You know this because she tells you this?"

"Not in so many words."

"Why do you always block off when it comes to discussing women? Maybe he drives her from the bed?"

"Oh, my little Dita, maybe you will be one of the lucky ones. He's worked like a dog all his life, and she drives him from bed."

"She doesn't work?"

"She raises money."

"Isn't that work? People like her keep me dancing."

"It's her hobby. She can do it because my father worked like a dog, and now he's finally doing his dream."

"What else could she do? I don't think you see your mother in a fair light. I mean what else could she really do?"

"Be a better wife. Be a better mother. Given what she's given."

"You mean just when somebody wants to give it; powerless to get it. I think you are being very selfish, Bruce. Just think about her. How was she not a good mother?"

Dita had thought about her own mother and her solidly middle class background. Her mother had had a freedom Ellen had lost to the need to be bound by fashion, the right schools, replete with an entire list Dita could have cited from her skirmishes with the moneyed people. Her relationship to them had been as a kind of steward—to think of things they couldn't conjure up for themselves. As long as you kept the Hys, Ellens, and Arlens of the world in a state of titillation they remained in your palms. They loved the youth and beauty of the dancers. But, for Dita, it was like holding onto something diaphanous—this thing of their creation. Bruce, she could have never married.

"You cannot even begin to imagine. You come from a very middle, middle class background. You romanticize wealth. But it's not what you think. You are naïve in a good sense, Dita. You have been spared the extreme neuroticism." She thought of CJ.

එඑඑ

Over coffee with Arlen directly after the homeless seminar, CJ and Dita were, at first, serious. They had been across the street to the armory that housed homeless men where they watched a physician do an outtake exam of a homeless HIV man whose disease, they were told, had progressed to encephalopathy of AIDS. He had been given a bus ticket to return to his mother in South Carolina and twenty dollars. He couldn't answer the simplest questions about who he was, or where he was. Dita still wondered if he even got to the Port Authority. *How could that have been?* she thought in chilly retrospect. *There were more questions I should have asked at that seminar.*

They seated themselves in a booth in a Dominican restaurant. A Formica table divided CJ and Dita from Arlen. "Heavy!" Arlen sighed. "You get the luck of the draw. Well, what'll it be?"

Dita ordered a caffé con leche. Arlen and CJ ordered coffee.

"You know, CJ, that was a bit irreverent," Arlen said. "The man is a commissioner. They get points on you for that kind of uppity."

"Uppity is a term with other connotations," CJ said.

"Well, you know what I mean. You're a bright boy."

"No, I'm not a bright *boy*."

"I'd like to see your arts center," Arlen had said. "Maybe I can help."

Dita and CJ had exchanged glances. Here was an opportunity.

"I have to pass that way to get home." Dita explained to Duffy how they had walked with Arlen to the hospital garage and he drove them to the center in one of his fancy rides—this one a Jaguar convertible—top down. CJ climbed into the small space behind the seat leaving Dita the passenger seat. Arlen stepped hard on the accelerator and had the green light all the way down St. Nicholas Avenue. Dita was glad when the ride was over. Arlen had cut uncomfortably in front of a tour bus. The little sports car would have been mashed in any collision with it.

CJ and Dita had given Arlen a tour of the center. Arlen had written them a check for ten thousand dollars.

Duffy sat back and closed his eyes for a moment then looked at Dita and asked, "Did it seem like a lot of money?"

"No, I knew how far ten thousand dollars could go but he hinted at more. I thought if I could reconnect with his circle as an adult, as the leader of an institution, that I could put up with them. I should have known Arlen was lacking in any kind of moral scruples. It must have galled him that he wasn't as wealthy as his wife and his greed led him to form an enterprise."

"Probably a thrill in it for him. Sociopath."

"You know, Duffy, talking to you and Quirk is like being in therapy."

Duffy laughed. "Except you don't listen very well to your therapists."

"The money made Dan uncomfortable," Dita said. "Always! His failure to play that game held him back as a composer. He'd see lesser composers getting their work played by orchestras."

"Did he have to swallow a lot of resentment?"

"No, he guided our lifestyle in a very frugal mode and still we got into trouble."

"I remember a different, less expensive New York City," Duffy said. "I'm glad I got to enjoy that."

Dita smiled. "For example, the day after the center closed, I went to the village to tell CJ and Neil. When I came home, I found Dan, seated at the dining room table, with our latest bills sorted out in front of him. I looked at him miserably and started to cry. 'We're going to have to decide what gets paid here,' he'd said and threw up his hands. His voice gets a scalpel edge whenever money's the subject. He can't discuss money in a loving manner. But, Duffy, that's as violent as I've ever seen Dan. So I want you to know this. This, to me, was the most disturbing aspect of our marriage—my fear of angering him about money. His insecurities run deep, yet when I saw an opportunity, Dan seldom opposed it. His parents had advised us not to invest in New York real estate but to buy a modest house in Bloomfield, New Jersey. In fact, they had offered us very affordable terms on their own house, the one Dan had grown up in. His parents, at that point, were ready for a condo and retirement winters in Florida. But Dan and I both wanted to be near where we worked and also, with New York real estate snowballing in value, we believed the hype and thought it would bring us the great fortune, our jobs would never provide. So we bought our New York City co-op. And we're about to lose it."

"You are not alone with that."

"The down payment and lender fees wiped out most of our savings," Dita continued, trying to explain herself. "There'd been no paycheck in my bank account that week the center closed, the unemployment hadn't started and is too small to carry our obligations. It's about to end soon. We weren't able to pay the mortgage and maintenance. It was shocking. The world just kept closing in. Dan paid the electric bill and that left nothing to pay our charge cards. We kept going on those until we maxed them out. Our credit is a mess. 'We have to prioritize,' I told Dan.

"'How? There's nothing to prioritize with,' he told me coldly. I was desperate to find a solution, was grasping at straws. I signed up for to do substitute teaching and temp work, anything. Now I'm the notorious wife of a murderer.

"'Not going to happen overnight. We're fucked,' Dan had said to me.

"'I supposed I am totally to blame,' I remember saying.

"'I never said that," he told me, and I thought our

marriage was on a collision course and would end over this. And I said, 'Oh, Dan, we can't let this wreck us. That would be the final price to pay. We can work this out, but we have to do it together.'"

"So, Dan had his back pushed up against a wall?" Duffy said. "He seems like a well-grounded guy, despite what's going on."

"Oh, he is. That's why I married him. He offered to take on another job. I felt so guilty about that. I wanted him to finish his symphony. He was really down on himself. 'It's not going to get performed anyway. I don't know why I started it in the first place. I sent it out to a bunch of orchestras, and I haven't even gotten a rejection letter. I should know better and stick with smaller things.'

"'You need sometimes to work big and see where it can go,' I told him. He'd shrugged and showed me his list. One side the pros, the other the cons. Get rid of the landline and just use cell phones. Well, what about the Internet subscription, and sports channels? No magazine renewal. That's a must. We don't read them anyway. We subscribed to *Music Educator*, but the center should have been picking up that anyway. Fuck them. No vacation. He had accompanied at a ballet festival on a lake each summer—where I sometimes had taught beginning class to the small children. We've never taken a real vacation. No eating out. We preferred our own cooking. We're going to cut into what we don't do anyway, I thought. How did we get so close to the edge?"

*The edge*, she repeated in her mind. She remembered this moment of realization well. It had become part of a cycle of sangfroid memories to which she steeled herself. The dining room had seemed to close in on Dita and Dan as the sun faded over the horizon and night descended. The room's lighting was never adequate, and had made Dita squint. In the distant sky, the moon had been full and opaque, a blind eye with curdled river running through its core. An inky haze had drifted past it blending into the deep night.

The moon had reminded Dita of pearls, the coldest, yet the most common of jewelry, a string of pearls—obligatory in a woman's wardrobe. She'd modeled clusters of them for the company jewelry ads. They made her shiver. She remembered being dressed in an expensive necklace for a shoot. Dita, in everyday life, wore the dime store variety. They had accompanied another couple to an auction upstate at the Stair gallery the month before. The husband had wanted to buy his wife a pearl necklace. The couple frequented auctions. He studied the offerings ahead of time—beyond the auctioneering blurbs. Up for auction had been the pearls of the Countess of Muhlenberg, the pearls had adorned the collar of a gown, and were subsequently made into a necklace for her granddaughter Theresa, the most recent owner the estate of the Hand family—but this set of pearls had graced the neck of Helen Hayes. Everything the couple owned they had considered an investment. Someone would no doubt auction off the center's assets to people like them who could acquire things in the course of a Sunday's entertainment. Why was she thinking like this? It wasn't their friend's fault that she and Dan were momentarily down on their luck. They always had been supportive of the center financially, but it had made Dita queasy to think that a bottle of wine bought at auction could easily have provided weekly lessons to ten children.

"When this is over," she said to Duffy, "I'll make us a meal. I comfort myself imagining that there will be something to celebrate."

"I'll hold you to that," Duffy said. "Let me get back to work on Dan's defense. It helps to understand who you both are."

Dita wanted to ask Duffy about his relationship with Samantha Elder, but she also wanted to keep Duffy in his present, less irascible mood.

෯෯

It was now early July. Violet, Marge, and CJ had come over to Dita and Dan's apartment on a Sunday to help sort out documents pertaining to the center. Albert had received his acceptance packet to American Ballet School and was thrilled. Today Albert helped to lift the boxes of center documents and stuff. He had agreed to do the basketball program over the summer as long as he could take a ballet class somewhere. Dita found a boy's class in a private studio that met twice a week but then found out there were openings for boys in a summer dance program at Ballet Hispanico. Albert ended up attending both the basketball program and the dance program, and Marge thought she could stop worrying about him. A brief perusal of the papers in front of them raised questions in all of their minds. There were mostly bills, demands for payroll taxes from the State of New York, and attendance records of the center students.

"Whatever Arlen and Randy were working on they must have kept," Dita said. "They must have cleaned out their offices way before they closed the center. Randy had lists of possible donors and all kinds of notes on how to cut spending." She had begun to cry.

"Where's all this going?" CJ asked.

"Part of me wants just to toss it all," Dita had admitted out loud, eyes bleary. "Who are we kidding? Maybe this is just best forgotten, buried."

"You want to have a record. Like you said, the records are incomplete," Violet said, and CJ and Marge nodded.

"Looky here, fifteen years of my appointment books," Dita said. "Right now, I don't even need an appointment book. Should I toss?"

"That's who came, who went, who you talked to," CJ told her.

"Do you have yours?"

"Yes. And we should go through both of our records and make lists of everyone who was ever associated with the center."

"A dumpster was outside the last time I walked by. I did it the other day. I don't know why I went there. Rex Turner had just boarded up all the windows. He was carrying tools out of the place and lumber. Sullen as ever."

Albert gave Dita a funny look. He didn't know why she called Rex sullen.

"It was a day hard to forget," Dita said. "With temperatures climbing to record highs—felt like one hundred degrees in the shade." Walking up Columbus Avenue that day, she had passed restaurant after restaurant. The sidewalk café tables had been all set with butcher paper cloths over linen ones, wine goblets, and slim bottles of extra virgin olive oil glinting green in the intense sun. Probably ruined by the high temperatures. The air was stagnant in the harsh sunlight. Even the awnings couldn't provide shade in this heat.

No one sought to sit outside. The few customers who had ventured outside their homes in this heat clustered in the dark interiors around the bars and sipped tropical drinks.

She had continued uptown in the heat, stopping to sip water from a bottle. On a whim she'd headed over to Central Park West and hopped a bus. The center's community garden bustled with people under makeshift shade makers. Sheets, towels, old rugs strung across on clothesline tented the tiny garden beds. Children splashed in the fire hydrant. They recognized Dita and ran towards her. How she loved them.

"Everybody miss you," said Tomato Man. "Gotta see what we grown."

She was about to enter the garden when she caught sight of Albert licking a fruit pop and clutching a brown bag in his hand. His pockets were filled with candy. He joined Dita.

"Where are you coming from?" she asked. "Looks like you struck it rich. I'll come say hello to your grand-ma Marge after I see the garden."

The garden was truly verdant: Squash and cucumbers weighted splitting vines; Tomatoes, firm and fleshy rip-ened by the hour; flowers—sunflowers, snapdragons, dahlias, delphiniums, zinnias, and phlox bloomed in myr-iad varieties and colors for the cutting.

If there could be a place where you'd want to be in this heat, this was it. Chairs and tables from the center had now been put to use inside the garden. There had been a time when old car seats served as benches.

"Yeah, we going to have a black out. Sure thing." Tomato Man told them.

Dita conjured delicious thoughts of Randy and Arlen stuck in an elevator on some high floor with no air condi-tioning. She walked Albert back to Marge with a sack of tomatoes. Heeding Tomato man's warning, they avoided the elevator and took the stairs to Marge's fifth-floor apartment. Marge had made a pot of iced tea and was thrilled to see Dita with Albert.

ൟൟ

The rich voice of Violet had brought Dita back to her own apartment and the tasks facing them this July Sun-day. "Get someone to crawl inside and see what's there in that Dumpster," said Violet. "Who took the file cabinets? Were they emptied?"

"They might still be in the building," CJ had said.

Albert didn't say he'd helped Rex load the filing cabinets onto the pickup.

"Now that's a good question to ask," Dita said. "The reason they gave us so little time to retrieve our stuff is that they were afraid we'd find something that would incriminate them." "More than few people have already been there since we closed," she added. "Hauling out old furniture. The garden is completely furnished in folding chairs and tables, area rugs—you name it. It got salvaged."

"But no filing cabinets?" CJ said.

"I think I'll make a visit over there tomorrow, and tell them we are missing some things," Violet said. "I'll get cooperation."

"I'm sure anything we might want to take a look at hit the shredder."

"Maybe not. They think we are stupid and childlike and the center never had a shredder. They'd have to send out to rip into those files."

"I'll pay to store the records, Dita, Violet is right we need to have everything period," CJ said.

"I'm not going to move forward very fast if I have to keep so much of the past."

"There was a lot of good there, too," said Violet, ever the source of comfort. Dita envied that kind of faith.

The center's papers had been put in storage thanks to CJ. Dita and Dan were reduced to a few possessions, the piano, computer, the butcher-block dining room table, and its six odd chairs from different periods and in different styles, paintings, and their bed. Even the bookshelves went. They had donated most of their books to the library for its annual book sale. Dan's music had been deemed worthy of book boxes. The piano, a Steinway concert grand now occupied center stage in their living room. Dan had thought about trading it in for a Yamaha C7 and pocketing the difference in price. The Steinway would sell for over one hundred thousand dollars and a Yamaha C7 could be bought for seventy thousand. But Dita knew he would miss his wonderful Steinway. He always told her that he felt fortunate that his parents had bought it for him while he was a young piano student.

# CHAPTER 44

Dita was on her way to visit Dan at Rikers Island. She thought maybe she could give him some hope. She told him about the latest revelation about the extent of Arlen's fraud. She was hoping the latest nibbles would humor him.

"So what good does it do me?" was all he would say. Dan was in a foul mood. There was a bruise on his left temple—an ugly purple splotch that yellowed as it healed.

"How did you get that?"

"Trying to mind my own business."

"Do the guards know about it?"

"Get real, Dita. It's a very minor occurrence." Dan needed to avoid the other inmates, but he risked appearing aloof and superior. He tried to spend his time hearing music in his head and jotting down the notes. He could put his synesthesia to good use. *Beethoven was incarcerated by deafness*, he thought wryly. *I'm incarcerated.* Then he said, "I'm not sure I want you to come here anymore."

Dita began to cry. "You don't mean that, Dan."

"I do. If I can't get out of here, you have to go on

with your life. I mean that absolutely. I won't let them bring me into this room again. So don't bother coming here."

"Please, Dan, don't do that to me. It hurts painfully."

"I have to do it." He knocked on the door for the guard who cuffed him and led him out without a glance at Dita. Dita watched him disappear as if it was forever. The baby kicked in her belly.

She watched the closed doorway until the guard came to lead her out and make room for someone else's visitation. She could barely walk. She had never felt weakness in her legs. Her strength was being sapped. She'd be unable to care for her child. Her parents were no longer young.

*❧❧❧*

Dita told Duffy about their last visitation. "I fear for his life," she said, describing how his face was bruised.

"Yes, I saw that. He said it was a sort of accidentally on purpose thing with another inmate."

"Can't you do anything about it?"

"He'd be worse off in solitary. Trust me."

*❧❧❧*

Shortly after Dan's arrest, Duffy made the offer of an informal interview to Randy Smith Warren. He wanted to get her on the record. "You know that you are a witness to what transpired at the center."

"My function was to raise money," Randy told him.

"I understand you had a lot of say as to how it got spent."

"Not really. Dita was the one creating the day to day expenditures."

"We can talk about that. How's about you come to my office at two p.m.?"

"I have other plans."

"Trying to spare us both the expense and hassle of a subpoena. One way or the other Ms. Smith-Warren, we're going to chat."

Randy's ego deflated with an audible sigh. "We'll chat at my lawyer's office."

"Anywhere you say. Call him or her and get right back to me."

He then called Dita for more information about Randy. With a certain glee, Dita related one of her last conversations with Randy verbatim—replete with a brutal impersonation that made Duffy look forward to interviewing this witness. In one of her last encounters with Randy, Dita had said, "We should nail down some time for the two of us every week to go over things. CJ and I used to picnic in the backyard on Fridays. Fridays are the best time for me."

"I don't do sun." Randy was seated behind the desk in her office and Dita once again occupied the jacquard chair. She would have preferred the floor. Randy removed her headband and let her brown hair float down onto her shoulders. It was thick hair and enviably straight. Dita's own hair responded to the humidity and had become frizzy.

"The yard is fairly shady." Dita said.

"But that garden on the other side of the wall has a lot of ears."

"Suggest somewhere. I'm amenable."

"When I took this job, I made certain facets of my schedule very clear. On Fridays, I have a standing massage appointment at eleven a.m., then I pick up my daughter." Her daughter was a frosty little girl in a plaid uniform. Dita had only seen her from a distance. "There will be many evenings I have to devote to foundation people."

"So then let's be very clear about our standing appointments. I take an eleven-thirty ballet class at Steps on Broadway Tuesdays and Thursdays unless I absolutely can't get away. I make it my lunch hour." In reality, she hadn't taken this class in months. She just said this just to let the bitch know that her agenda was also tight.

"There's a cute little bistro on Ninety-Third and Madison. Say twelve-thirty Friday."

"'No problem. I'll hop the number four bus or, if it's nice, I'll cut a diagonal through the park," Dita said.

"No, maybe make that more like a quarter to one."

"I need to be back by three."

"Believe me, you will be."

Dita returned her thoughts to the reality of Duffy's law office. "You know, Duffy, there was no hint from Randy during that lunch that we were in terrible trouble. I'm very perplexed. If things were that bad, I should have been made aware of it."

"Maybe it means she wasn't in on it."

∽∾∽

Next Duffy, Dita, and Quirk paid a visit to St. James Church. Rex Turner was on a ladder by the entrance scraping away at peeling paint. He sported a brand new leather tool belt and the tools, suspended in its holders, glistened with the sheen of newness. Dita noticed it right away.

"Nice duds," she said, remembering the awl, scraper, and sewing kit she traveled with as a dancer. Had to get those point shoes perfect. She could have used a tool belt. "That's new, your tool belt and those tools? Looks almost like it's a toy-belt." Dita remembering the scuffed, darkened, and creased tool belt he'd worn at the center.

Rex grunted and froze. He did not look overjoyed to see them.

"Where can we find Reverend Teague?" Duffy asked.

"Where else?" Dita said, "How are you, Rex?"

Rex shrugged.

"Is the good reverend on the court?" Duffy asked.

Turner nodded.

"Through there," Dita said. Then she whispered, "That's Rex Turner."

Turner returned to his task. A pose? Turner's eyes followed them. Dita shuddered.

"Creepy," said Quirk.

They found Reverend John on the basketball court with his charges. The boys looked in great form bouncing and dribbling across the court. Reverend John was not in good form. His right ankle was wrapped in an ace bandage and he leaned on a cane. "Getting too old for this game," he told the company indicating his injured leg.

"Hoops are for the young," Duffy said, handing the reverend his business card. "I represent Dan Di Bello. Where can we talk?"

"I do pray for him," Reverend John said. His sun-drenched skin aged more every time Dita saw him. He'd stopped using red dye in his hair and had let it go to a yellowy white.

"Right now he needs more than prayers," Dita said. "We need your help."

Reverend John turned to his charges. "Guys, going to have to talk to these people. You know the drill. Do it on your own for a bit."

Reverend John led them into his office overlooking the basketball court, from where he continued to survey the boys. "Nice group! Nice group! They do me proud but I do ramble. You want to talk about something else."

"We do," Duffy said, getting right to the point. "I want you to reconstruct the real estate deals you did with Arlen Van Aiken."

"I already did that for the police."

"Do it again for me," Duffy said.

Reverend John focused on Dita. "Like I told Ms. Marx, I really wasn't involved. Arlen brought the papers for me to sign."

"How many times did you participate in Arlen's real estate transactions?" asked Quirk.

"Maybe thirty in all."

"And each time he was generous to you."

"No, to my boys. I took nothing for myself. My modest salary as pastor here is enough for me to live on. The real estate transactions with Arlen were an opportunity to fund the program."

"Are you familiar with Carecorp?" Duffy asked.

"Rings a bell," said Reverend John.

"It's the shell four doors down from the center. Did that belong to Arlen's group as well?"

"Yes, I signed the papers for that as well. Arlen gave me ten thousand dollars for the boys."

"Did you worry at all when you helped Arlen purchase that building and the building next door for the center?" Duffy asked.

"I assumed Dita was getting funded the same way?"

"For the record, she was not," Duffy said, exchanging a knowing glance with Dita.

"And what happens, they close her down."

"Your lousy real estate transactions closed us down," Dita said. "What you did was illegal. You didn't, by any chance, sprain that ankle jumping over any walls."

"No, I did it on the sidewalk."

Duffy put his hand over Dita's. "Arlen was defrauding HUD," Duffy explained. "He used the center's property as collateral and, somehow, the money for both properties disappeared. But I think you know this."

"Am I in bad trouble?"

"You are."

"Will I go to jail?"

"Maybe you should try to cut a deal with the US Attorney. I want names today. Let's start with who is on your board."

Reverend John reeled off, "Bennett Dawes, Mitchell Shepherd, Theodore Callahan, and Rex Turner."

"No surprise there," Duffy said. "Your board was comprised of the same members as the center's board."

Dita was astonished when she heard this. When they left, she said, "Okay, how can we use this to help Dan? Reverend John served as a straw man in the purchase of thirty properties."

"And they're probably all in default."

Dita dreaded passing Rex again but Rex was no longer there. "I want to talk to that man as well," Duffy said. "It's becoming clear he was more than a maintenance man."

"For sure, but Arlen really didn't inform Reverend John of the whole scheme. And I assume the same for Rex," said Quirk.

"They didn't want to know," Dita said.

"That shell down the street looked totally inaccessible. Every window bricked as well as every door. I looked at it from the street behind. No one went out that way. It would take a sledge hammer to knock out a way in or out," said Quirk.

He showed them pictures from the rear on his digital camera. The bricked up shell of a building seemed impenetrable.

"I'd say Arlen was feeling a bit of heat," Dita said.

"Was he planning to flee the country like Shepherd and Callahan, and let the other's take the rap?"

"Could be," Duffy said.

"What kind of punishment would Arlen have gotten if he had turned himself in?" she asked.

"He'd have gotten time. But they'd go easier on him if he cooperated with the US Attorney."

"What if that was what he was about to do? And what if someone didn't want him to do it. His intentions died with him."

"It opens a good line of questioning," Duffy said.

"That's all you ever say to me," Dita said. "It's a motive, right?"

"Yes, and we are still stuck with the twenty-minute timeframe. And his appointment book only shows an appointment with you and Dan."

"Let's hunt down Turner and have a talk. I think he left to avoid us."

"I believe we ought to. I'd prefer to visit him at home," Quirk said. "Right now he doesn't think he's on our radar. He's probably overheard Reverend John is about to go down and bounced out of there."

"I want to come along, too," Dita said.

"But we ask the questions."

ⅇↄⅇↄ

They visited the Turner apartment the next day. The caretaker Kathy had Becky Turner seated on the sofa when they arrived. Becky was a white woman with dirty blonde hair pulled back from her face. She was probably in her mid-forties but the illness made her look sallow and old. Rex wasn't at home. The television played CNN without volume. A wall air conditioner cooled the room. Everything seemed to be in a tidy order—new kitchen cabinets, newly scraped floors. It was clear that Rex provided well for his ill wife. Through the doorway to a bedroom, they could see a hospital bed and a bedside commode. Becky seemed pleased to have visitors. "I don't get out much anymore," she said in barely intelligible speech.

"When is your husband coming home," Duffy asked.

Becky looked at Kathy who said, "I leave at five o'clock, and Rex takes care of Becky for the evening. I come on again at seven a.m."

"You have a long day," Dita said, immediately realizing that what she said could be construed that Becky was trouble for Kathy.

Kathy took Becky's hand. "Becky's a great pleasure to be with. And tonight she has a date with her man. I got her all fixed up."

Dita sighed with relief and thought how lucky the Turners were to have such a devoted caretaker.

It was four-fifty, so they wouldn't have a long wait for Rex who was always punctual. Dita was seized by a visceral reaction to the idea of confronting Rex on his home turf. She knew him to be a very angry man. Could he be placed somehow in the center on the day of the murder? She chided herself that because she disliked this human being she wanted him to be the murderer. Yet he was a known entity. As Duffy said they lacked opportunity for him.

Rex entered on the dot of five. He was miffed to find visitors. "Don't I rate an appointment? You just show up here?"

Becky jetted him a pleading look. His tone immediately changed, and he went over and kissed her on the lips. "So you had a little company."

"They were admiring how you fixed up the apartment," Kathy said.

Rex swelled with a moment of pride.

"Is there somewhere we can talk privately?" Duffy said.

"Kathy needs to go. Her shift is finished. I was going to take Becky out for supper tonight."

"Rex, I can stay another half hour."

"There's a coffee shop across the street," Quirk said.

Rex glowered but followed his visitors out of the door and onto the sidewalk.

"I don't need a cup of coffee. Let's just get this over with right here. My van is parked at the hydrant, and I don't want no ticket." They saw a maroon van with a handicap sticker dangling from the rearview mirror idling in front of the hydrant. Quirk noted the license and snapped a picture of it with his camera when Rex wasn't looking.

"Okay," Duffy said. "Let's talk. First off, what was your business arrangement with Arlen?"

"I was his handy man on thirty properties. He paid me well, and I did good work. I'm owed money, a lot of money, and as you can see, my expenses are high."

"What else did he pay you well for?" Duffy asked. "We now know Reverend John facilitated their purchases. Did you do that also?"

"I might have on one occasion. I don't know. I worked hard."

"You were on the board," said Quirk. "What was said at the board meetings?"

"I attended one board meeting when I did some painting on Callahan's yacht. The center bylaws required two people from the community on the board."

"I see," Duffy said. "So you weren't a regular participant in board matters.

Turner nodded. "Can I go to my wife now? It's not easy to take her places."

"Yes," Duffy said. To Dita and Quirk he said when Rex left, "Not enough there to implicate him. He was involved in Arlen's scheme peripherally."

# CHAPTER 45

Dita paid a visit to Marge to tell her what Reverend John had admitted to.

"Oh, my," Marge said. "He's a crook pure and simple. What should I do? Pull Albert out of the program."

"I know you need to keep him occupied."

"But letting him stay in the care of a criminal. No, I can't do that. The ballet program will be enough, and we'll do some movies and go see some ballet on the other days."

Albert overheard their discussion and came into the living room. "Who's a crook, Grandma?"

"Well, you're old enough to know. How should I explain this, Dita?"

"Your grandma doesn't want you to return to the basketball program because Reverend John did illegal things with Arlen to get funding for it. He helped close down the center."

"I'm very angry at him," Marge said.

"Well, I didn't like it as much as ballet anyway," Albert said.

And Marge sighed with relief.

# CHAPTER 46

Reverend John gathered his group inside the church the following day. He had thought deeply about what he needed to do and resolved to come clean about his role in the demise of the art center. He needed to try to set a good example for the boys. He well understood that he had caused Harlem residents to suffer rat-infested shells in their community while Arlen Van Aiken and his minions enriched themselves. Why hadn't he reported it, rather than using it to enrich the program? It was to glorify him—the basketball program. He had sinned. He told the boys that he wanted to discuss a matter. The boys sat in the first two rows of pews, restlessly waiting to hear what he had to say.

Sunlight streamed through an Old Testament stained glass window depicting Moses parting the Red Sea. He wondered what Moses felt as the waters did his bidding and parted.

One boy was as of yet missing from the assemblage. "We'll wait until Marcus gets out of the bathroom," Reverend John told the boys.

"Maybe he fell in," suggested Terrence. "Why don't we get to play?"

"Because you are old enough to have a discussion with me about the future of the program."

The flush of a toilet echoed from somewhere in the vast church followed by footsteps on a staircase, and Marcus appeared in the doorway.

"Come and join us," said Reverend John. Then he got serious. "I need to tell you boys that we might have to discontinue the program. Some things happened that might make it difficult to continue."

"Because that guy got hisself killt?" Rashid asked.

"In part, but there are other issues," Reverend John said. "Some concern me and the way I found to fund this program."

"Why'd Albert leave?" Marcus asked.

"He said his grandma's mad at you," Terrance said.

"I want to share with you all that she has a right to be angry with me, I made a mistake. I took the easy way. But it was because I wanted this program so much for you that I didn't see that what I did could hurt another program."

"My mother said the man who got killt was a robber," Jose said.

"Your mother is right. He fooled us all. He was a greedy man. But I helped him get involved. And I'm not proud about that. And we might have to open the program bank account and give some of the money back which means we won't have money to run the program."

After the boys left, Rex joined Reverend John. "It's best you just leave things as they are. What's done is done and I don't want more questions."

"No, I think I need to make amends for my hand in this, Rex."

"It'll make it worse for Becky and me."

☙☙☙

Albert's dance program at Ballet Hispanico ended at four-thirty p.m. By then the dancers were usually so hungry that a group of them went for pizza to Zeppos' on Columbus Avenue and Ninety-First Street. There were only three boys in the program and the bonding was tight. The female dancers far outnumbered the boys and sat at their own table. The girls were not shy about boys and were titillated listening in to the boy's conversations. And the boys did their best to shock the girls. There was always a lot of giggling. Despite the six hours of various dance classes—classical ballet, African, modern, flamenco and hip-hop, the boys needed to work off the rest of their energy.

"Let's go to the waterfall," Albert suggested and the boys got up to leave. The girls looked a crestfallen as they exited the pizza parlor. The boys finished their slices and sodas walking up Central Park West and entered the park on a path north of where Ninety-Sixth Street crossed the park to the East Side. The waterfall was located in the northwest section of the park. A myriad of underground springs and streams fed it and it yielded treasures from time to time—condoms, broken toys, tennis balls. Albert once found a perfectly good Swatch watch there. He was still wearing it. The boys followed the twisting and turning paths and finally the waterfall came into view. It wasn't really a waterfall but a rocky cave the water issued from. There was room on the sides of the cave to just hang out. The boys crawled inside and sat on the dank earth leaning their backs against the rocky walls.

"I'll bet you can't kiss Anna Marie," a kid named Jorge taunted Albert.

"Now why would I want to anyway?"

"Because she's getting tits. They're showin' outta her leotard."

"She goes steady," said a small boy named David.

"Do you think they're doin' it?" asked Jorge.

Albert liked girls but he wasn't interested on the level of some of his friends, and he began to wander deeper into the cave. *This isn't really a waterfall,* Albert thought remembering the time Marge took him to the Canadian side of Niagara Falls by Greyhound Bus. It looked like a waterfall when it flowed over the rocks in its entrance but water from a fire hydrant had more thrust. It was a very timid waterfall. Niagara Falls, now that had been a sight. They rode the little boat under the falls and heard tales of people who went over the falls in barrels and survived. He savored memories of the swirly brew as it headed towards the precipice. Before the trip he'd gone to the Metropolitan Museum with Marge where they saw a painting of the falls before cars and busses. It was crowned with a rainbow. That was how Marge got the idea for the trip. Albert loved twirling the heads of the view masters on the walk overlooking the falls and Marge kept giving him quarters to feed the machines.

Albert could hear his friends continue to discuss the girl dancers. It wasn't flattering talk, and it made him uncomfortable, but he didn't want to leave and seem like a sissy so he stayed where he was. He'd gone far enough into the cave. There were tales of dogs and little kids lost down there. No one knew exactly where the water hole was. He'd like to know, but not if he got lost, too. Albert leaned back against the dank wall of stone to peer deeper into the gloom. A few feet beyond, he could make out a bundle of some sort. Maybe someone was sleeping in the cave and hiding their clothes. If it was a homeless person, maybe he could bring a slice the next time he visited. Marge said she'd rather give food than money to the homeless that begged near the subway. "They buy drugs with the money," she'd told him. He knew that's why his mother was in jail. He'd never do drugs. Hell, he'd never have to do drugs. He'd be a famous ballet dancer and rich. Sometimes, in the winter Marge carried a wooden-and-plastic-mesh box of tangerines to give out to beggars on the subway.

Albert inched toward the bundle until he could reach it with an outstretched hand. It was a rolled up white dungaree material and rolled up inside it was a leather belt and some rusting tools. A tool-belt. Something like Rex's tool belt. Albert tried it on. He was so slender it slid off his hips and clattered to the ground. There was a name stamped on the interior of the belt faded from the time it soaked in the water but Albert thought the tool belt belonged to Rex Turner. Maybe Rex would be happy that someone found it if it was lost or stolen. And if it wasn't his, maybe Rex could use it. On the overalls, a pair of work gloves were suspended from a loop. Albert gathered up the bundle and put it into his own backpack. He'd need to dry it out. Then he'd bring it to Rex's house.

# CHAPTER 47

Randy was already seated in her lawyer's office when Duffy and Dita arrived. It was the typical white glove law firm. Stunning views of the city and its waterways scintillating in the sunlight. A sleek blonde, well dressed, and fastidiously groomed reception- ist, a showpiece in and of herself, sat behind a massive marble reception desk and announced them. Right away, a graying, middle-aged secretary appeared and ushered them into a corner office with a view downtown and to the west. As they followed her down a corridor, Dita felt herself sink into the plush carpet. Peter Evers, Randy's lawyer, rose to shake their hands and offer them a seat. The secretary offered them coffee which they accepted. Duffy had told Dita that you get more out of people when you take them up on offers of hospitality.

Randy jetted Dita a hostile glance. "Why is she here?"

Peter covered her hand with his.

"No, why is she here?" Randy insisted.

Dita said nothing. Duffy took over. "She's here be- cause she has a right to be here and help defend her hus- band."

The present encounter with Randy reminded Dita of the uncomfortable lunch they'd shared at the Bistro Louise on Madison Avenue before the center closed. The Bistro was narrow with banquets and mirror lining the length of each side. The weather was warm and balmy and French door panels had been opened the entire width onto a sidewalk café. Dita had ordered a glass of pinot grigio from a waiter wearing black pants, tee shirt, and a white apron.

Randy had called to say she'd be late. The waiter had returned with Dita's wine. She perused the leather bound menu. A card insert told her that the soup du jour was carrot ginger. The Bistro also served the French onion soup, for which it claimed to be famous, every day of the week.

Dita doubted its authenticity. Probably made from Bouvril, instead of broth. She found her mind wandering as usual to food. Or had she been evoking food as a way of avoiding the impending meeting with Randy.

When Dita made French onion soup, it was a labor of love. She roasted marrowbones in the oven. Then she removed to bones to boiling water and added a clove-studded onion, a parsnip, carrot and a stock of celery with a bouquet garni. She boiled the bones until the gristle and fat melted. Her broth would jell if she'd let it get cold. She often chilled it to remove the fat. Her dancers' friends had been concerned about their bones, and called this "bone brew." Dita had consumed it often after her stress fracture. For her, French onion soup was the ultimate comfort food.

❦

"Let's begin," said Peter Evers. He had a craggy face and athletic build. His watchful eyes were deeply set and his hair a nondescript color of gray. "I might ask the two of you to leave the room from time to time."

"That would work," Duffy said. "This round is informal, but I might notice Ms. Smith Warren to a deposition down the road."

"Puleese," said Randy. "Let's get this over with."

"I have some questions I'd like to ask about the running of the center," Duffy said. "You were its executive director, were you not?"

"Yes."

"How would you describe your job?"

"My function was to oversee expenditures and keep up the level of funding we needed to meet those expenditures. I was in charge of developing an annual budget. But the board would have to approve it."

"How did you get along with the board?" Duffy asked.

"I felt sometimes that I wasn't in charge. Dita seemed to think I was the board's weapon, and that I didn't understand what the center was about. It was my job to balance the budget." She avoided Dita's eyes.

"Did you at any point feud with Arlen or other board members?"

"No, I felt the lack of support and was considering quitting. Now I'm sorry I didn't."

"Who is Bennett Dawes?"

"A board member," Randy replied.

"We are having trouble locating him," Duffy said. It was a test. "What do you know about him?"

Randy looked shocked. "Nothing. He's businessman of some sort. Has all kinds of amazing connections, I was told."

"You presented to the board monthly? Didn't you make his acquaintance then?"

"I always came in before the meeting started. Then I left. I didn't count heads if that's what you are asking. So it never occurred to me that the full board didn't meet."

"Do you own real estate in Harlem?" Duffy asked.

"I do not."

"Can you tell me about the purchase of the building next door?"

"Arlen thought it would be a good idea if the center had some revenue aside from donations. We didn't charge for classes. Post Nine/Eleven some of our funding dropped off. We had payroll taxes due. Even not-for-profits have to pay payroll taxes," Randy explained impatiently. "I'd like to get out of here."

"Okay, I'll come right to the point," Duffy said. "Where were you on the afternoon of August ninth?"

"Oh, so now I'm a murder suspect?" Randy asked.

"Just answer the question."

"I can tell you one thing. I was nowhere near the center."

"Can you give me a few moments with my client?" Randy's lawyer asked.

Dita and Duffy withdrew from the room. It gave Dita time to explain more about Randy to Duffy. She described the lunch in culinary detail. "All I could think about was food. I escaped from her through food. I always escape that way. I guess I'm pretty lucky I don't gain weight. Randy, laden with packages, had finally arrived but pursued a cell phone conversation on the sidewalk outside for another five minutes before making an entrance. *Randy was good at entrances*, I thought.

"'Would you mind if I put my bags next to you?' Randy asked.

"I had been sitting on the banquet side of the table. 'Do you want to switch?'

"'You're a dear,' she said.

"The food thoughts had tumbled out once again. The second component in my French Onion soup was the caramelized onions—three or four large, sweet Spanish onions, sliced thin and slow cooked in a sauté pan with olive oil until they wilted and browned. I then added a dash of Sherry.

"The onions and the broth, I assembled in individual oven proof bowls with handles and topped each off with crusty French bread and a slice of Gruyere cheese. I baked the soups in a three-hundred-fifty-degree oven until the broth was bubbly and the cheese molten and browned. This was a soup that had the power to cure. *Maybe I'll make French onion soup tonight*, I thought, getting up to rearrange our places.

"I had pushed the table out and picked up my wine and small plate containing a partially munched bread stick and a little butter tub. Randy ensconced herself between her packages, pulling the table toward herself.

"The waiter approached Randy to ask if she wanted a drink.

"'Perrier with a twist and I think we ought to order. I'll have the Niçoise," Randy had said impatiently. 'Hold the anchovies. You don't need to bring bread for me. You can hold the croutons as well.'

"'I'll take her anchovies. How is the ginger carrot soup?" I asked.

"'I recommend it. Anything else?'

"'The pâté de compagne. And I'd like bread with it. In fact, I'll take her croutons as well.'

"'Good choice," the waiter said. 'Your paté comes with a toasted baguette.'

"'I hope you'll have some of the paté,' I said to Randy.

"'I don't eat pork.'

"We both had sipped our drinks. Randy had spoken

first. 'Where do you see the center going in five years, Dita?'

"'I'm hoping it will be on more stable financial footing. You know our programs are highly successful, but we struggle too hard.'

"'What funding sources do you think are yet untapped?'

"The waiter had returned with Randy's Niçoise, and my soup and paté. He had set a white porcelain pedestal tureen in front of me, along with a small pâté platter arranged with cornichons and toasted bread slices. He also set down three anchovies on a tiny platter. The Niçoise, a grilled tuna affair plunked on a bed of romaine, he had set in front of Randy, then he had hovered over us with a humongous wooden pepper mill I had found incongruous with its three twist output.

"'You know the answer to that,' I said. 'Some of the bigger foundation money. Violet has been wonderful in making us inroads.'

"'But Violet is old. What happens to your connections when she is gone?'

"'That sounds...'

"'Realistic? I'm just playing devil's advocate here. I wish Violet many more years. Do we have her connections in our back pockets?'

"'They've been good to us for fifteen years.'

"'And the operating costs are ever on the rise.'

"'The teachers have all taken less in the past several years. They should be getting more.'

"'The teachers come and go.'

"'No, actually, we've built solid relationships with our staff and many of them have been with us since we opened. We are a major part of their incomes.'

"'And your husband is on staff also.'

"'He teaches a few hours of theory. But his contribution to the planning and contracting is free to us and invaluable.' I didn't think I would have to say that." Dita winced at this memory and wondered about what Randy and Peter Evers were discussing.

Dita used the ladies room and when she came out, Evers beckoned that they should return with him to his office. Randy seemed somewhat calmer.

"I believe on that afternoon I accompanied my daughter to Claremont Stables for a riding lesson. I, for some reason, neglected to write it into my book. But the stable will have a record," said Randy.

Dita whispered to Duffy and wrote on a pad, *I can't see her hanging around watching her kid's lesson. Opportunity?*

*You've got* killer *instincts*, Duffy wrote back, underscoring killer. He then asked Randy, "I assume your daughter's lesson is approximately an hour. Do you watch or do you go elsewhere?"

Randy seemed shocked at the turn the question had taken. "Sometimes, I shop."

"Did you shop on this particular day is what I want to know."

"I don't remember. I sometimes make phone calls from a Starbucks around the corner."

"And after the lesson did you return home with your daughter?"

"I probably took her to her hip-hop class."

"Probably or did?"

"Can I confer with my client again?" Evers asked.

Dita and Duffy left the room once again. "Does she have opportunity?" Dita asked.

"We'll see. She's very nervous about something."

"And she doesn't always fill in her appointment book. That surprised me."

"Me, too," Duffy said.

Evers beckoned them back in.

Okay," Duffy said. "Let's talk about the real estate."

"I really don't know anything about it," said Randy. "As I've already told you, it was presented to me as an opportunity to make some money for the organization."

"Were there other real estate deals you were aware of?"

"Yes, Arlen and Mitchell saw it as a way to capitalize the center. But the only purchase I have any knowledge of is the building next door."

"So where is that money? Two HUD mortgages for four hundred and fifty thousand dollars each were approved. HUD released funds into La Grange Trust Company. You're the executive director, and you can't account for that money. Two years prior to its closing, the center received a million and a half dollars from an empowerment zone grant. What happened to it?"

"Dita ignored my warnings and kept hiring. A million and a half dollars is not so significant an amount when you have a staff of fifteen on the payroll."

"Okay, let's return to the real estate. We talked to a couple that had a bid accepted at one hundred and ninety thousand with the rest of the four hundred and fifty allocated for repairs. Their deal went south when it became clear the title was clouded. Yet the center was allowed to buy the building next door in lousy shape for three hundred and ninety thousand, almost double, and with a cloudy title to boot. Did anybody attempt repairs? Or were you all waiting to make another flip?"

"I wasn't part of that, and I'm not saying anything else."

"I hate to ask, but can you wait outside again?" Evers said.

This time, the wait was almost an hour and when they returned, they found a chastened Randy. The view was more spectacular as the sun headed west. Evers, a tall man crossed the room with his long shadow to draw the blind with the push of a remote control. When he was again seated behind his desk, he said, "Ms. Smith-Warren has agreed to go to the US Attorney's office. She feels that she was had as well. She knows nothing about the bank. Apparently, she tried to call Ted Callahan and learned that he had disappeared from Arlen and Mitchell."

Dita was livid. "And you never came forward with that information, Randy. I left messages for you. You had knowledge we could have used."

"I was afraid of what I'd gotten into."

"A murder might not have taken place if you had come forward sooner," Duffy said.

"I realize that now." Randy began to sob.

*Another blank filled in*, Dita wrote on her tablet to Duffy.

"I have one other question," Duffy said. "Who all had keys to the center after it was closed?"

"Well, Arlen of course, but he had Rex Turner board up the windows and clean stuff out so he probably had to let himself in to get that work done."

"Do you have a set of keys?"

Randy gave a reluctant sigh. "Yes. I did. I'm not sure where they are."

# CHAPTER 48

When Dita and Duffy were out of the office, Dita said, "And if we reel off the names on the bank roster, none of them are going to be known to her? We need to check all of their connections, Duffy. Randy told me that her husband was an investment banker."

"Was her husband's name on the La Grange roster?"

"Not that I saw. But if there's a connection there, and if we can make it, she'll go down. Won't she?"

"Or someone close to her will go down," Duffy said.

"You know I almost had some sympathy for her in there," Dita said.

"Yes, she cut a more sympathetic figure to me, too."

"It's an abrasive personality," Dita said. "Where to now?"

"Let's ride uptown to that stable," Duffy said, hailing a cab and flipping open his cell phone. "I'll have Quirky meet us there. He had a meeting with Mindy Rothman Van Aiken."

The Claremont stable had its home on West Eighty-Ninth Street, a block away from the Central Park riding paths. The stable, a barnlike structure had multiple floors interconnected by ramps. In a small center ring instructors gave riding lessons. A girl of approximately ten years of age cantered around the ring led by an instructor. The lesson seemed to be coming to an end and Dita and Duffy watched. Quirk hadn't arrived as of yet. Dita noted that no parent was as of yet on hand for the end of the lesson. The instructor, a trim, athletic looking woman in her mid to late forties helped the child dismount. "Good work!" She then noticed Dita and Duffy. "Are you here to ride a horse?"

"No," Duffy said. "We need information about a lesson given on the afternoon of August ninth."

The woman looked perplexed.

"Do you keep an ongoing register of lessons? Can you turn back to that page?"

"There's no one in the office right now, but we instructors often fill in the book so I suppose I can."

They followed her into a little cubicle with a worn metal desk. The floor was strewn with riding boots and other gear. "We're looking for the name Smith-Warren," Dita told her. Quirk entered and quietly watched.

The riding instructor flipped back a number of pages to the date. "I'm not seeing a name like that."

"Can we see?" asked Quirk, flipping open his badge. "I'm a private investigator and it is important that we verify that someone was here when she said she was."

"Be my guest," said the instructor.

Quirk took out his digital camera and photographed the page. They thanked the still perplexed instructor and walked to a little Columbus Avenue restaurant that was between shifts. The kitchen was closed but an affable male waiter offered to get them coffee and they sat in the outdoor café area. Dita felt the deep craving for Dan as they seated themselves. They'd often sat in outside cafés happy after a performance or after seeing a show. She craved a glass of pinot grigio but didn't dare. The morning sickness had finally subsided. She'd developed an aversion to alcohol in the first trimester of her pregnancy. That had subsided, too. She conjured a vision of a prison yard where Dan would be pacing. She was pinning her hope on the interview with Randy opening new avenues of investigation that would cast more doubt on Dan's guilt.

Quirk fiddled with the camera and brought up the page of appointments for August ninth. He reeled off the list of names, their time slots, and the instructor. Dita and Duffy wrote on separate pads. Nine a.m., Jody Benson; ten a.m., Amanda Freihoffer; eleven a.m., Mark Shorr; twelve noon, Myra Katz; one p.m., Mike Thorne; two p.m., Amanda Knapp; three p.m., Tony Tracey; four p.m., Julie Glass; five p.m., Amanda Wainwright. There were two instructors on the day and the instructor for the two o'clock slot was Renee Thomas. The other instructor was a man named Jim Williams. Quirk had taken both of their phone numbers.

"No shortage of Amanda's in the horsey set," commented Dita. "Somehow I think I heard Randy call her daughter Mandy, but that doesn't jive with the last name."

"The little girl could be from another marriage," said Quirk.

"Did we receive a copy of La Grange's charter application?"

"I made a bunch of FOIA requests to HUD and other agencies, but it would be nice if we could get the US Attorney or Milton to cough up some of that stuff sooner."

# CHAPTER 49

It was clear to Dita that she couldn't put their apartment on the market. Murder tainted the place. No one would buy it. There had been a lull in the collection actions, but today bill collectors called all day long. She'd just hung up the phone when it rang again. She answered it to the sculptor Ricardo Montero. She hadn't spoken to him since the murder. "I'm back in New York, Dita. I've been very concerned about you and Dan. I feel somehow to blame for some of this. I'd like to take you to lunch," he said.

They met up at the Chinese Cuban restaurant Flor de Mayo on Broadway at 101st Street. It bustled as usual. The glass foyer was packed. They gave their names to the maitre d then waited for a table to be available. From the entrance they watched pollo la brass chicken turning on a spit. Waiters returned over and over again to make cafe con leche at an espresso station. The aromas of the two different cuisines and the rich espresso made Dita's mouth water. The place was about food and it was cheap as well. The Chinese dishes were served in metal pedestal bowls with lids. Dita received some stares as the waiter led them to a table for two against the long wall. She sat and hid her face behind the huge menu. "I suppose the police still have your sculpture," Dita said.

"I'm thinking to recast it altogether. I don't think I ever want it back. It was damaged, I understand. Arlen hated it. Some irony he was killed with it. How is Dan's case coming along?" Ricardo had doe eyes with a think fringe of lashes. Generous amounts of grey now twined in his curly black hair. He reminded her of a Cuban ballet dancer—an uncanny resemblance to José Manuel Careño.

"The issue is finding someone who could have been at the center before Dan arrived."

"And Rex never showed up that day?"

"Rex?"

"I asked him to help Arlen remove it from the niche."

"But he took his wife to a physical therapy appointment. He has a solid alibi according to the police." Dita began to incubate thoughts. In addition to the pickup truck, Rex had a van equipped to transport Becky. What if he made an extra stop on the way? She chided herself for thinking this way. "So, Rex knew we would be there? His work for Arlen was finished."

"I offered to pay him a hundred bucks. But he said no, he didn't want anything further to do with Arlen Van Aiken. So I let it pass. Was sure you and Dan could manage."

The waiter came over with pad and pencil ready to take their orders. "I'll have the pollo la brasa half chicken, yellow rice, black beans, and sweet plantains. Oh, and an avocado salad and a cafe con leche," Dita said.

Ricardo ordered the shrimp chopped suey and fried rice. Dita thought she'd call Kathy's caretaker and find out what physical therapist Kathy used. But the police probably did all that. But she could tell a little white lie about having a friend with a similar condition. Then

Quirk could check it out. Oh but, the physical therapist probably had confidentially issues. What did she expect to find anyway. She'd let it pass. No, the caretaker would know when Rex left with Kathy.

When she got home, she called Duffy and told him about her conversation with the sculptor and her thoughts about calling Kathy's caretaker. "That's interesting, Dita. So Rex did know about the appointment you had with Arlen. I'm going to put Quirk onto it. Don't make any calls to anyone. This is why we hired Quirk."

ও৩ও৩

Albert had taken the tool belt, gloves, and overalls to the laundry room in the basement of his apartment house. There were some stains on the things and, thinking he could get them out, he went upstairs for bleach and laundry soap from under the kitchen sink. In the basement laundry sink, he dumped a large portion of the bleach into the water along with the soap. He swirled the stuff around in it, then let it soak while he looked at a *Sports Illustrated* someone had left for the other tenants to read. His hand smelled from the bleach and he noticed he had gotten some on his own blue jeans. Marge wasn't going to be happy about that. She always told him, "Mind how you dress. The world is looking."

When he finished leafing through the magazine, he left it on the chair and went over to the sink. The garments looked cleaner. He hoped he hadn't ruined the leather tool belt. The tools were too rusty to bother with and that's probably how the stains got into everything. He pulled the plug and when the water drained, he turned on the faucet. The dirty sink looked clean and white as well. There were drying racks in addition to the driers, and Albert hung the tool belt and the overalls and gloves out to dry.

# CHAPTER 50

Dita still smarted from her visitation with Dan. He'd meant when he said not to visit him again. She tried to see him a few days later, and he'd refused to let the guards bring him into the visiting booth. She needed action to quell the panicky feeling in the pit of her stomach. It couldn't be healthy for the child growing inside her. On a whim, Dita went uptown to the center neighborhood. From the bus, she called Marge Bliss on her cell phone, "I'm coming uptown to talk to people in the stores. I can't keep sitting around, waiting. I know Duffy's going to be angry with me."

"Oh, honey, I'm joining you."

They met in front of the center and walked around to a bodega on Frederick Douglas Boulevard. The proprietor Ruben knew everyone well. His store was a snack stop for many of the center's children. Dita had convinced him to carry healthier snacks for the children, and he carried a line of packaged nuts, granola bars, carrot and celery sticks, as well as yoghurts. He had been pleased and surprised when the kids had chosen these.

"I was just hoping that maybe you remembered something unusual that day," Dita said.

"Well the police keep asking the same thing," Ruben told them. "The only thing I remember unusual was later on in the afternoon a kid came in for some soda for a guy he said fell and injured his ankle." Dita made a note to ask Reverend John if he'd injured his ankle the day of the murder. "But that was after five-thirty," Ruben continued. "Because my wife brought us our suppers. She's a nurse, and she brought El Presidente Pollo La Brasa when she got off her shift. She asked the kid if the man needed help and the kid said he was going to take him home in a livery."

"But you don't know who the man was?" Marge asked.

"No, I didn't see him."

"But do you know the kid?" Dita asked.

"I know him by sight. He comes in here all the time."

"If you see him again can you get his name and number, and maybe tell him to call me," Dita said.

Dita bought café con leche for both Marge and herself, and they drank it sitting on the center's abandoned stoop. Marge began to gather up the fliers and menus left there. "Albert is so happy at Ballet Hispanico. We were late for enrollment, you know, but they needed boys."

"All dance programs need boys. Well, that's a worry lifted."

"He misses you. He's so excited about starting American Ballet School."

"The two of you should come for dinner with Violet. It would do me good to cook." In this moment of conveying a simple invitation to a meal Dita felt the depth of her pain for Dan who couldn't join them, and might never be able to join Dita and friends again for a home cooked meal.

ာ၏ာ

The next day, Albert went to the basement for the tool belt and overalls. They were dry and good as new. He was on his way to Ballet Hispanico and thought he'd stop by Rex's apartment to give them to him. Rex had already gone to work. The nurse Kathy was bemused to see Albert standing there with his bundle. She invited him in. "I have ballet class in a half hour," Albert told her. "But I found these and thought Rex could use them."

"Well, I'll make sure Rex gets them."

"Thank you, ma'am." He waved at Rex's wife who was seated in her wheel chair. "Ya'all have a good day," he said, dancing out the doorway, through the lobby, and onto the street.

# CHAPTER 51

Duffy called Dita to say he'd scheduled an interview with Mort Rothman, his daughter Mindy and their attorney in his office the following day at eleven p.m. He had also had confirmation from the US Attorney that Ted Callahan had betrayed Arlen and Mitchell.

Apparently, he was laundering the funds from the enterprise over a long period of time. "It still amazes me how you worked out that bank account routing number. Too bad it doesn't do us any good," Duffy said. "In the end, there was nothing that either Arlen or Mitchell Shepherd could access. Callahan left the country on his yacht. There are a lot of agencies trying to trace him. He left his wife and family behind in Bronxville and without funds."

"Nice man," Dita said. "I'm nervous about meeting the Rothmans."

"Don't be."

"What do I say?" Dita asked, "I'm sorry for your loss but my husband didn't do it."

He laughed. "I think you can offer condolences without saying anything else."

"And what if they were somehow involved or looked the other way?"

"I've considered that possibility," Duffy said. "Nothing has come up that ties them into Arlen's activities. Mindy claims she was kept in the dark."

"But how do you live with someone and not know?"

"It might be the biggest river in Africa."

"De Nile!"

☙❧☙

The Rothmans arrived with their lawyer Scott Douglas on the dot of eleven. It turned out that Scott Douglas had matriculated at NYU law school the same years as Duffy, and that Mort Rothman had donated several new lecture halls to the institution. Duffy knew about the donation and openly thanked Rothman for it. When the conversation finally turned to the circumstances of Arlen's murder. Dita said, "I want you to know how sorry I am for your loss."

"I'm sorry for what you are being put through," Mindy said. "And I know how hard you worked to make that center succeed."

Dita simply said, "thank you."

Duffy cleared his throat. "I know you have been asked the same questions many times. I thank you for cooperation with my investigator Lumen Quirk. I'm trying to reconstruct what happened on the day of the murder. Arlen's book for that day only shows one appointment—the one with the Di Belloes. Did you get wind that he might have tried to meet with someone else as well?"

"I've been piecing together what I think I know," Mindy said. "If only to help myself understand. Arlen had liked to think of it as his secret empire. I'd overheard him on the phone using that term. He'd given himself a persona. He was the nice guy, the ne'er-do-well son in-law of developer Morton Rothman. Married to a scion of Rothman Real Estate. His wife Mindy Rothman Van Aiken, a wannabe socialite, sat at her pots of makeup—the ubiquitous samples from the benefit tables," she quipped bitterly.

Her father laid his hand over her hand.

Scott Douglas started to interrupt.

"No, let me. I need to get this off my chest," she said. "Cosmetic manufacturers were a presence at every event I hosted. Mine was the dressing table of a woman who could afford the best advice, who wore a different designer outfit to each and every event. But the advice I needed should have come from within myself. We had 'his and her' everything. And nothing!" It had taken a second apartment to accommodate their respective wardrobes. "This was my other life. On one of my last conversations with Arlen, I said, 'Where were you today?' Arlen absentmindedly helped with the zipper on my dress. I was repulsed by his touch."

"'I've been doing another small venture on my own,' he said."

"Oh?" Duffy said.

"I think this was several weeks after he closed the center," Mindy continued. "'I can't promise it will be successful,' he said.

"'Do you want me to talk to Daddy?'

"'No, I don't need him. I want this to be small.' He had neglected to tell me that Daddy had already disapproved of all of his ventures.

"'Good for you, Arlen' I said. I sighed with relief. He had seemed such a bundle of loose ends lately, and I had feared it would, once again, translate into a loss of fidelity. At this point, I don't know why I even cared. There was nothing left in our relationship. I suppose I just didn't want him flaunting some floozy in front of our kids. It was my pride reacting to everything he did at that point."

Mindy explained what she knew about Arlen's forays into Harlem real estate in the year before he became involved in the arts center. It had begun with a lecture he'd planned to give on the architecture of Harlem. He had driven his BMW up to 110th Street. He had an entire fleet of luxury cars. He parked his Beamer in an indoor lot and continued on foot north on Frederick Douglas Boulevard. A group of teenagers had accosted every passerby with candy for sale. Six of them had descended on Arlen. "Selling to fix our court," the childish voices proclaimed. "It's too cracked to play on."

"Who's your coach?"

"Reverend John. We play at St. James on One-Hundred-Eighteenth Street. We could win the state championship if it got fixed."

"What's it made of?"

"Cement!" said the smallest of the group with the accent on the first syllable.

"Is it nearby?"

Arlen had followed them around the corner to the church where he was introduced to the affable Reverend John Teague, a lanky tall white man in his mid-sixties with sun-damaged skin. Everyone was describing the reverend by the state of his skin, Dita thought. Arlen had learned the names of the six boys—Aaron, Jose, Rashid, Marcus, Terrance, and John who they called little John because he was the smallest, and to distinguish him from Big John, their coach. That's how he became acquainted with Reverend John. It made Arlen feel powerful.

They had taken Arlen through the church—once a synagogue with Old Testament characters rendered in its stained glass window, to the rear yard. The court had been fenced in cyclone and scraggly weeds had shot up through the cracked pavement. The court stencils had been worn off. "I worry one of the kids will get a foot twisted in there. But you can't just go over cement. It's all got to come up—bad planning by whoever did this. It didn't last eight years. Should have been asphalt to begin with," Reverend John had explained.

"I think I might be able to help you with that." Arlen told him. "You going to be here later?"

"I'm always here."

"Give me a few hours. I'm going to call in a favor."

There had been Arlen—and Arlen the continuous observer of himself as he had moved through life. They had been separable, like the optical illusion card found in the cereal box that you stared at until you could look away and project the image on the sky.

Mindy sighed. "He began to take his calls in secrecy. Like I said, I thought he was having an affair. It never occurred to me he was involved in a criminal enterprise that was going downhill. We have more money than anyone could ever need. He came from enough money. Why would he do that?"

After a moment of silence, Duffy said, "The police gave us a record of his phone calls, mainly from his cache of board members. And there were calls from St. James Church probably Reverend John. And Rex Turner."

"Several weeks before the murder, Arlen asked me if I could put Rex to work," Mort said.

"Because he couldn't pay him at that point," Dita said.

"Because the man was getting on his nerves," Mindy said. "I don't think Arlen could empathize with his plight."

"Sociopath," said Scott Douglas.

"He said that Reverend John was beginning to get on

his nerves as well. Calling too much. Wasn't grateful enough for what Arlen had done for the church. Referred to him as that goddamned preacher in front of our kids. Arlen was conducting business when he sat in a coffee shop with the kids. He couldn't get the man off the phone. He was panicked about something or other. Now we know what."

"Anyone else get on his nerves?" Duffy asked.

"The lawyer Mitch Shepherd. Now I understand why. At the time, I thought Arlen was preparing divorce papers with a demand for huge alimony."

Mort Rothman laughed.

"So, Mr. Rothman, can you tell us about your relationship with Arlen?"

"What's to tell? I tried to bring him into the business but he needed glory. He had credentials as an architect, but they were more on the academic side. Which is fine. I don't dislike academics. But he was arrogant. Arrogance is the flip side of ignorance. Arlen didn't want to be part of a team. We started avoiding each other. He did tell me he wanted to invest in property up in Harlem, and I told him how difficult it would be for some of the very reasons he got himself into trouble. Title problems, notice requirements to former tenants, you name it."

"Did Arlen buy properties the city had taken back?" Dita asked.

"Probably. We don't know much about his holdings," said Rothman. "Nothing seems to be in his name. He was taking the cash out of everything and gambling that the values would increase. He apparently had no intention of running anything on a day-to-day basis. What can I say?" Rothman's accent sometimes took on an Eastern European twinge. Dita guessed he had come to the United States as a young child.

"So, even if they acquired them legally from the city,

they would encumber them illegally. Shouldn't the city have oversight?" Dita asked.

Rothman laughed.

"In a perfect world," Duffy said. "What do you know about Bennett Dawes?"

"I don't know who that is? Do you, Dad?"

"No, who is he?"

It was an honest reaction Dita thought. "A board member who might be fictitious."

"Oh, my, it goes on and on doesn't it?" Mindy said.

Duffy's secretary knocked and offered them coffee. She poured from a carafe into stoneware mugs with the firm's logo with a four-leaf clover worked into his name. Duffy practiced solo.

"How did Arlen know Randy Smith-Warren?" Duffy asked.

"Actually, through me," Mindy said. "She bought a whole table every year to a charity event I chaired. How innocent is she?"

"She claims very," Duffy said.

"She called me, you know. Told me she had no idea what was going on. Cried and asked if we could meet. I said no. I was having trouble processing what happened, and I needed to address my children. They are hearing awful things about their father, and there is no way to prevent it. I removed them from school temporarily and hired a tutor."

"I'm so sorry about that," Dita said. A fleeting image of Dan sitting in his jail cell and refusing to see their child entered Dita's mind forcefully. It made her wince.

"Do you, by any chance, know the name of Randy's child?" Duffy asked.

"Mandy, Mandy Knapp."

"So she was at Claremont stables," Dita said.

"That's no surprise," Duffy said. "I have a call into Ms. Thomas, her instructor that day, to find out if Randy stayed and watched the lesson."

"Most parents today seem to dump their kids off," Mindy scoffed. "I guess you were dealing with parents who had no choice, Dita."

"True," Dita replied.

# CHAPTER 52

Doubt about Dan's guilt plagued Detective Milton. He was unable to make a connection with Arlen's murder to the murder of Shepherd, yet he sensed a strong connection. They still didn't have the coroner's results and couldn't pursue it as a murder. ADA Torres was beginning to get on Milton's nerves as well. "Let's go over the interviews with neighbors once again," Milton said to Sheila Nadler.

They took out the notes they had made. Milton had picked a six-block radius around the center and had his people going door to door. The backyards of the row of brownstones to which the center belonged backed up to the backyards of brownstones on the street south of the center.

Many of the buildings were vacant. But some were well occupied.

In one rooming house, an elderly man had called to say he saw a burglar on the roof. But that was early in the evening the day of the murder.

Dita had called to tell Milton about the injured man, but he had been abrupt with her. Gave her his usual spiel about not interfering. Now he wasn't so sure that they shouldn't look into the matter. "That woman has incredible gall," he told Sheila. "Let's go talk to our elderly gentleman."

Jessie Peters lived in a room to the rear of the building. It did have a clear view of the rooftops on the buildings behind. They asked him about his call to the police the day of the murder.

"Yeah, I seen Batman."

"As in a guy with a cape who flies?" Milton asked.

"He walked up the wall," Jessie Peter's insisted.

"Do you know what date it is today?" Detective Nadler asked.

"Is it Groundhog Day?"

"What's your address?" Milton asked.

He gave them an address on the Grand Concourse in the Bronx. He had been a doorman there they learned later.

"Short term memory seems to be failing him," Nadler commented as they took leave. "But still he might have seen something. No way to reach him."

"And if he did, maybe someone else did," Milton said.

They knocked on the door to another apartment. This time they were greeted by barking dogs. A thirty-something overweight black woman opened the door on its chain. Beyond, the detectives could see two pit bulls and a small boy child in a high chair. The place was filthy.

"We'd like to speak with you," Milton said. "Is there another room where you can put the dogs?"

"This is it."

"How's about the bathroom," Nadler suggested.

"I'm not in any kind of trouble, am I?"

"No."

The toddler began to cry. "Give me a minute.

S'okay, Sherrill." The dogs were obedient and followed her to the bathroom adjacent. She returned and undid the chain on the door. "Can I see your badges again?"

Both detectives held out their shields for her close scrutiny. When she seemed satisfied, she indicated a shabby sofa and went to take the toddler out of his high chair. He went immediately to the bowls of animal feed on the floor nearby.

"Won't the dogs mind his messing with their food?" Nadler asked.

"Nah! They good with kids."

Sheila nodded at Milton and continued, "Well, we didn't come here to ask about the dogs. One of your neighbors called to tell us he saw a burglar on the roof August ninth. We wondered if you might have seen something also. It was late in the afternoon or early evening."

"My dogs did get crazy the day that guy got kilt."

"How so?" Milton asked.

"Barking more than usual. Dogs know if someone bad is about. They sense it."

"But did you actually see anything?"

"Can't say that I did."

# CHAPTER 53

Dita finally went to her OB-GYN Martha Ineri. Dr. Ineri was sensitive to Dita's plight and had instructed her staff not to let Dita wait in the waiting room with the other patients. Dita was beginning to be recognized from news accounts of the murder and Dan's arrest and was very grateful to the doctor.

"I'm concerned about your stress level," Martha Ineri said. "I can only imagine what you are going through." She led her into the examining room where a nurse handed Dita a paper gown and instructed her to leave a urine sample in a bathroom adjacent to the exam room before getting undressed.

Dr. Ineri completed the pelvic exam and, as she pushed gently on Dita's lower abdomen, Dita explained how she had thought she wasn't pregnant because of the spotting. Dr. Ineri laughed. "I have no doubt that you are well into your fifth month. And I want you to have an ultra sound."

Dita had seen the black-and-white ultra sound images from friends' ultra sounds. "I hope I don't have to share the first photos of our baby with Dan in a letter to prison." She began to cry. "If there was anything I ever wanted to share with Dan, it was a child. We put it off, but we knew someday we would."

Dr. Ineri gave Dita her personal cell phone number. "Don't be shy. Call if you need something."

Dita thanked her and said she would. The doctor gave her a hug.

෴

Duffy had received the first response to his HUD FOIA request and the US Attorney sent copies of La Grange Trust's charter application. The name Arthur Knapp could be found throughout the documents, including on a sworn oath as bank director. The address was the defunct LaGrange trust office. A Google search produced copious Arthur Knapps.

Duffy called Peter Evers to confirm Arthur Knapp's relationship to Randy.

"Her husband's name is Michael. I will call Randy to find out if Arthur Knapp is any relation to them."

Evers called back a short while later to say that Arthur Knapp was not related to Michael Knapp, according to Randy.

"Okay, so we have a coincidentally common name appear in the documents."

The US Attorney said that she had not succeeded in tracking down Arthur Knapp.

# CHAPTER 54

Albert had an appointment with an orthodontist where he was supposed to meet Marge. He was excited about getting braces. As his adult teeth came in, his mouth began to crowd. Several teeth overlapped. The dancers were disappointed when Albert told them he couldn't join them for pizza. He was the class star, and all the kids were impressed that he was going to American Ballet School in the fall.

After the orthodontist, Marge had promised to buy him new ballet slippers and tights at the Capezio shop. Albert was more excited because Marge finally told him he could take the Broadway subway to the orthodontist's Fifty-Seventh Street office by himself where Marge would meet him.

Marge arrived at five p.m., for the five-fifteen appointment. The time came and went. No Albert. He wasn't picking up his cell phone either. Marge waited until six p.m., hoping he'd forgotten and had gone for pizza. But that wasn't like Albert, she thought. He was really looking forward to fixing his "goofy mouth." Marge was frantic and started to call everyone she knew but was reluctant to call Dita, not wanting to cause her extra worry.

She called Violet who said, "Don't wait. If he isn't at home, you go immediately to the police."

Then Marge called Dita who called Detective Milton.

"Wait a second," Milton said. "A kid doesn't show up for a dentist appointment and you call us?"

Dita and Violet waited with Marge in her apartment in Morningside Heights.

At eleven p.m., Dita called Milton again. "Look, Albert is mixed up in what happened to the center somehow. You have to know this kid to know he lived for dancing. He wouldn't go and disappear. His grandmother is frantic."

e⁄ɔe⁄ɔ

Marge brought out the most recent photos of Albert. He liked being in front of the camera. They chose a few of the best with Albert's brown eyes staring quizzically at the camera, typed up a missing person's notice and went to Kinkos. It was open twenty-four hours. In a jiffy, they had over a thousand copies. Armed with tape and thumbtacks, they posted the flyer onto lampposts, into stores, on boarded up construction sites. They began on West Eighty-Ninth near Ballet Hispanico. It seemed logical to start where Albert was last seen then work their way uptown.

e⁄ɔe⁄ɔ

Albert only perceived shadows. He was enclosed in total darkness. The shadows were in his mind. They took on different shapes—sometimes they were long filaments and then they would reduce and shrivel like cord being rewound. His mouth was dry, and he was trying to remember where he was.

*Maybe I'm no longer alive,* he thought, and tentatively moved his limbs. He stretched his legs until his feet reached solid wall. It was scratchy like cement, not smooth like marble if he had to describe what it felt like. He tried to raise himself up. On tiptoes, he could touch wooden rafters that ran low over his head but the ceiling between felt like the wall. Now he remembered the van with its tinted windows. His last memory was being ensconced in soft leather next to someone. Who?

Something hard dug into his hip—his cell phone. He'd turned it off for the ballet classes and had shoved it into the bottom of his baggy jeans pocket— covered with fistfuls of candy and ballet gear. He flipped it open. It still had juice and provided minimal light. He could see he was in some sort of windowless room. It had bunk beds, shelves with cans, and dehydrated food. He tried to call his grandmother, but there was no signal.

ᴄᴐᴄᴐ

Dita, Marge, and Violet worked their way uptown with the flyers. Daylight dawned and more stores were opening. They stopped in Tom's Restaurant on Broadway near Columbia for breakfast. Marge and Violet were showing signs of wear, and Dita suggested that they go home for a spell to try to sleep a few hours. But the two elderly women insisted on continuing the search for anything, anyone who might have seen Albert.

After several cups of coffee and hardly eaten bagels, they trudged on again, working their way further up Broadway and then farther east on Morningside Avenue which returned them back to 110th Street. They wanted to post the flyers near the center neighborhood where many people knew Albert and would be concerned enough to help.

⌾⌾⌾

Someone began to pound rhythmically overhead. Maybe it was best to just keep quiet. Albert was afraid to alert anyone. He tried the door. Apparently, it was locked from the outside.

He was beginning to understand that someone didn't want him to leave this space and that he had slept for a great long while. He remembered that he was supposed to meet his grandmother at the orthodontist and wondered if she was angry with him. No, she must be very worried about him. He remembered how the van was waiting by the fire hydrant outside of Ballet Hispanico. He was headed toward Broadway but was walking backward, waving at his friends who were headed toward Columbus Avenue.

Rex was waiting with the van that Reverend John took the kids in when they played against other teams. He'd offered him a ride to Fifty-Seventh Street and a drink and that's the last thing Albert remembered. Why would Rex want to keep him here? he wondered.

⌾⌾⌾

Ruben Soares, the owner of the bodega near the center, scrutinized Marge's flyer.

"That's your grandson?"

"Yes."

"Of course, I know him. He's a regular."

"Have you seen him in the last twenty-four hours?" Dita asked.

"No, but remember when you asked me about a kid who helped someone who fell? He's the kid."

"He never said a thing about it," Marge said.

At eight a.m., Dita called Duffy to tell him that Albert had disappeared and what they had learned from Ruben Soares. She had to leave a message. The three women trudged over to the Twenty-Fifth Precinct to tell Milton about this latest revelation. This time, he seemed thoughtful. "Okay, we're going to look for your grandson. I'll take a stack of those flyers, and we'll publish one of our own. I'm going to talk to Ruben. I want to hear his story, first hand."

"Can we come with you?" Dita asked.

"If I tell you no, you'll show up there."

"Probably."

Milton called Nadler into the room. Then they all piled into an unmarked car.

Ruben related once again how Albert had come to his store late in the afternoon on the day of the murder. "He said a man had twisted his ankle. I had the impression the man was sitting on a stoop around the corner waiting for him. He repeated how his wife had offered to go help but Albert seemed nervous. But you know teenagers."

"Did you get the impression he was helping someone he already knew or someone who was a stranger to him?" Milton asked.

"If I had to guess," Ruben said, "I'd say it was someone he already knew. Maybe even someone he wasn't allowed to hang with."

"But I've never told him to avoid anyone. I like his friends," Marge said. "And he never said anything to me about helping anybody."

"Maybe the person asked him to keep it a secret," suggested Dita.

"I'm worried it's related to his disappearing," Marge said. "I thought I was doing such a good job of raising a kid the second time around."

"You are," said Violet and Dita together.

Back at the Twenty-Fifth Precinct, Detectives Milton and Nadler pondered Albert's disappearance. They put in a request with Marge's cellular company to try to track the cell phone as well.

Marge and Violet went to Marge's apartment to soak their feet. Dita told them she would join them in a bit. She wanted to ponder the square city block that the center was part of.

On the street south of the center, she ran into community garden fixture Earline Wilson struggling with a shopping cart. She'd seen the flyer about Albert. "Can I help you get those groceries inside?" Dita asked.

"That's kind of you, yes!"

Earline mounted the steps slowly and pulled out her key. Her legs looked like they retained water.

"What floor are you on?" Dita asked.

"Back of the parlor."

"Can I help you up there?"

"Only if I can give you a cup of tea."

"That would certainly be welcome," Dita said.

Dita grabbed several bags and headed up the staircase then returned for two more. Earline grabbed onto the banister and began a slow climb.

When they were ensconced in Earline's little kitchen area, Earline began to set out teacups. She'd set her kettle onto a narrow stove and the water boiled rapidly. Earline turned it down and went to a closet for Lipton's loose tea.

"I like their tea," she commented. "Lemon or milk?"

"For me, lemon," Dita said.

Earline opened a box of Milano cookies and offered them to Dita.

"No thanks, Earline," Dita said.

"Of course not, you're a dancer. You need to stay skinny."

Dita let thoughts about being a pregnant dancer pass through her mind and exit. She was avoiding empty sugar and carbohydrates. But Earline was satisfied with her own interpretation. They sipped their tea. Earline was not shy about munching through a half box of cookies by herself, and Dita found the hot liquid soothing, despite the heat of the day.

"Such a shame for Marge," said Earline, "that Albert is such a nice kid."

"Albert's the joy and light of Marge's life. Yes, and a great kid, too."

"You think he took up with the wrong group? Sometimes things change with kids."

"He had everything to look forward to. He's going to one of the great ballet schools next month."

Earline looked thoughtful, "Always helped me just like you did getting the groceries up here. If I think back, I saw him helping a man with a bad ankle."

"You did?" Now Dita was excited but she tried to play it down. "Can you remember the day?"

"Easy because it was the afternoon after the murder."

"Would you recognize the man?"

"Tall white man, gray hair, maybe red once, early-sixties but in good shape. Bad skin from too much sun. Black don't crack, as we say, but white guys like that are a mess of freckles and moles."

Dita laughed at this. She realized that Earline was describing a person who spent a lot of time outdoors, possibly an athlete.

"Earline, can you show me where he was with Albert?"

Earline made her way carefully down the stairs once

more. Once out on the sidewalk again, she indicated that they should walk east. On the other side of a boarded up vacant lot was a well-renovated brownstone. "He sat on the steps there. I asked him if he needed help, but he told me that a friend went to get some water and a gypsy car to get him home. Said he sprained his ankle. Easy to do with the conditions of the sidewalks around here."

People had placed placards and flyers all over the plywood fronting the lot, including their missing persons flyer for Albert. Some of the boards were loose and Dita was able to enter the lot. Scrutinizing the center's back wall, something caught her attention. Her eye traveled up the back wall of the center. Something about the air conditioner wasn't right. Didn't air conditioners have to tilt down to keep water from accumulating? It was in its cover. There had been a big discussion about keeping the thing covered at one of the last staff meetings. But today the cover was off kilter. The cover seemed to pucker. Then she thought, if the air conditioner was not in its sleeve, a person could climb through there and onto the fire escape.

Then she remembered what seemed off kilter that day she toured the center with Duffy and Quirk. Light emitted from the grill of the air conditioner. Just enough to catch the dust moats but not enough to send light into the parlor. The air conditioner was missing. She knew at once that that was how someone could leave and not be seen. Then she remembered seeing a brand new Friedrich's air conditioner in Rex Turner's apartment. It had to have been him. He had access and probably motive. Anyone who had visited the Turner's new apartment might put it together if the center air conditioner wasn't in the place. She needed to get into the center to see if she was right, but there was no way.

She flipped her cell phone and dialed Duffy's number. It went to messaging. She then tried Milton. Again the phone went to messaging. "I think I know who Albert helped out. Reverend John. And the reason Albert didn't tell his grandma was that she pulled him from the basketball program when she learned about the real estate fraud." She explained about the air conditioner and one that matched in Rex Turner's apartment. "He removed it and left the sleeve covered up with the grill and the back covers in place but now it's not fitting tight. You can see it from the back of the center building. That's how he went onto the fire escape."

Dita thanked Earline for tea and the information and walked uptown. She had to be right, she thought. She wanted to talk to Reverend John about Albert, thinking that Albert wanted to continue his friendships with the boys in the basketball program and was afraid his grandmother would disapprove.

She stopped in the public library on the way because she needed to pee. On a whim she went over to a computer and googled Reverend John. She'd heard that he had been a star college basketball player. He played for the North Carolina State Wolf Pack in 1974. The other players called him "Knappy." His given name was Arthur Knapp Teague before he went into the ministry. A gambling scandal forced him out of basketball. "He must have wanted to leave the past behind," Dita told herself. "But some people can't."

On the sidewalk, she tried Duffy once more then remembered he had a visitation with Dan and the guards probably made him check his cell. She left Duffy the same message and added that she also knew whom Arthur Knapp the mystery banker was. She left the same message for Milton. Then she called Quirk. He answered on the first ring, and she explained what she knew.

"I'm on the Westside Highway just past Thirty-

Fourth Street. Tunnel traffic is backed up. You wait for me, Dita. Don't you dare do a goddamned thing!"

She needed to know if Albert had helped Reverend John on the day of the murder. Could it hurt to ask him about it? It would clarify things, and she was confident that Rex had murdered Arlen.

ぐろぐろ

Albert became alert enough to explore his cell. He found a light switch and a flickering tube fluorescent came to life. Albert had never seen bulbs like these. They were outdated way before he was born. There were packages of dehydrated foods the expiration dated 1959. It looked to Albert like someone had lived in here once. He was feeling thirsty but all he could find was a rusty can of tomato juice with a strange label. There was nothing to open it with. It didn't have a pull-off lid like the juices he was used to. He tested his cell again and found a vague signal if he stood on a box in one corner and held the cell phone as high as possible.

Marge noticed it right away. Albert's number was coming up, but they couldn't seem to get a connection. She called Milton who came for her cell phone. They were now connected to the cellular company who had begun a trace on Albert's cell.

ぐろぐろ

Dita entered St. James by a side door and found her way to Reverend John's office. Reverend John sat at his desk, sipping a large coke in a McDonald's cup and pulling chicken McNuggets to his mouth with long fingers. He looked directly at Dita. "I've been thinking what to do."

"And?"

Reverend John had a faraway look in his eyes. "I know it's best that I go to the US Attorney. But then more people get hurt. Rex depended on Arlen in order to take care of Becky."

"Rex took the air conditioner from the center and left the empty sleeve covered. I'm sure of it. I think he was in the center before Dan and confronted Arlen."

"No. Rex is a gentle person."

"A gentle person capable of murder when his back is pushed up against a wall. Was it you that Albert helped the day of the murder?"

"Yes. He's a good kid. I walked the block that day just thinking what could have happened and snagged my foot in a piece of sidewalk pushed up by a weed tree. I couldn't walk another step. Albert came along and saw me on the stoop. Got me a drink in the bodega and let me lean on him to get into a livery. Took me back here where I iced my ankle. I took a strong pain killer."

"I Googled you. You were a great college basketball player but your name was Knapp. Arthur Knapp."

"And you know the reason I needed to change my name."

She nodded. "But you used the name Arthur Knapp again to become Arlen's phony banker."

"I figured there were two of me. I let Arthur Knapp become a criminal again. But only for the boys."

"So you were a fucking Robin Hood?"

Reverend John's head began to nod. "I feel suddenly very tired. I think I need to put my head down." He slumped over onto the desk, trying to stay awake then collapsed into the chair.

Dita pulled out her cell phone.

Rex Turner emerged from behind the door. "I'll take that. I was waiting for you," he said simply.

"But we have to call for help."

"He's beyond help," Rex told her and pulled out a gun.

"He's breathing. You can't just leave him like that." *I'm going to die, I'm going to die with my baby*, was all Dita could think. What could she offer to defuse the situation? "You know this can stay between us," she told Rex. He laughed harshly. "What do you gain by more killing?" she asked. "I already informed the police and Dan's lawyer about the missing air conditioner."

That revelation seemed to take Rex by surprise. "You know, Ms. Marx, you are too smart for your own good."

"You went out through the air conditioner opening, didn't you?"

"How did you figure that out? Albert knew about the air conditioner because he helped me carry it."

"Didn't you think someone would eventually see that the air conditioner cover puckered and sagged on the back wall of the center? You still might be able to argue that Arlen toyed with you. He did that kind of thing— toyed with people. You killed him in a fit of rage. With your wife and all, you could get the charges reduced to manslaughter."

Rex laughed sardonically. "No more trying."

"But where is Albert? Have you seen him?"

"I'll take you to him," he said, waving the gun.

"So I was right. It was you!"

"That's right. And you had to go and ruin everything."

☙☙☙

Albert heard voices.

"Down there! Just go down to the bottom."

"What did you do with Albert?"

"He went gently."

"Where did you put him?"

"You are going to him now. I don't want to use the gun. I believe in gentle death."

"Is that why you struck Arlen over the head with the *Phoenix*?"

"I regret that mistake, but he was going to the US Attorney to make a deal for Arlen. Man could only think about himself. He had to be stopped. I kept trying to meet with him. It was about my wife and my ability to care for her."

"And you learned from the sculptor that Arlen was going to meet us at the center?"

"You're one smart lady. He thought you and Dan might need extra help. Always worried about that stupid piece of metal."

"You were there before Dan arrived and you hid in the dumbwaiter when he went looking for Arlen upstairs."

"I felt bad doing that to your husband. And I left Becky in the van, but I thought I could convince Arlen to cut a check to me. I was sorry to do that to her."

"You won't get away with this."

"Actually, my plan is very simple."

"Where are we going?"

"Your last surroundings are very comfortable. Don't make me use the gun."

"My compassionate murderer."

"Yes, I suppose I am."

Dita grasped the horror of the moment—Albert, her unborn child.

"The cover is dislodged. Someone would have figured it out. The air conditioner is supposed to tilt downward."

"I found a cardboard box to fit the space. My wife needed that air conditioner."

"And the rain softened the cardboard over time."

*Keep him talking*, Dita thought. *Isn't that what happens in the mystery books? Murderers like to brag. Rex is bragging.*

As if in answer to her thoughts, Rex said, "Enough chatting. I don't want to have to use the gun."

Albert heard the word gun. He recognized Dita's voice and realized the man was Rex. He realized that Rex had a gun pointed at Dita. Why would Rex want to harm Dita? The door would open any minute. Albert needed a plan. *Like in the movies*, he thought. In that short moment, Albert had to convince himself that Rex was now his enemy and not his friend. He needed to act. Old glass jugs of water occupied a corner of the space. He had thought about drinking some but noticed how cloudy it looked. He knew from Marge about the germs that could grow in bottled water. She'd always insisted he drink from the tap. He could hear her exclaim how New York's water came in from the Catskills and was the safest water supply in the world. He just wanted to get back to her. He loved her so much.

Albert positioned himself with a water jug behind the door, like he had seen many times in the movies and on TV. He waited for the door to open. *Any second now*, he thought, hardly daring to breathe.

ℰ୬ℰ୬

Rex told Dita to open the door.

"What if I refuse?"

"You'll force me to use the gun."

He was pressing it into the small of her back.

"I'm trying to open it," Dita said. "The key won't engage."

"Pull the door toward you and stop stalling."

Albert needed something else to distract Rex. He dragged his shoe through the dust, scrawling the word "devil" in big bold letters, and went back to his position behind the door. The door opened. Rex pushed Dita into the room. "Where's Albert?" she asked.

Rex then saw the word devil. It distracted him. Albert knocked the gun out of his hand with the water jug, and when Rex tried to retrieve it, he was struck in the face by a ballet foot. Albert had solid fouettés. Dita grabbed the gun and held it while Albert forced Rex to the floor and sat on him.

They heard the voice of Milton on the staircase. "You are surrounded. Put your hands in the air and come out."

"He can't. I'm sitting on him and Dita has his gun," Albert called.

They heard Milton command Quirk to remain where he was.

Milton, followed by Detective Nadler, entered the fallout shelter guns drawn. "We'll take over now."

"He left Albert for dead," Dita said. "He murdered Arlen and Reverend John."

"He also murdered his wife," Nadler said. "We sent someone over there as well, but it was too late."

Rex was led away in handcuffs. The police swarmed over the church. They found Tramadol in the reverend's desk drawer. Several of the tablets were crushed. Marge held Albert in a tight hug as Milton approached. "We don't have the toxicology yet but we think he administered a lethal dose of Tramadol to Reverend Teague and your grandson as well. But Albert somehow survived."

At St. Luke's Hospital, a team of doctors examined

Albert. As expected, they found Tramadol circulating through his bloodstream. One of the doctors insisted on a genetic test. "What saved Albert's life, I think, are his genes. He doesn't metabolize certain medications very well, I'd wager. He was administered a large dose of timed-release Tramadol. There's a warning on the medication that crushing it could release a fatal dose." The doctor turned to Albert. "Can you remember CYP four-fifty two-D-six? That's the gene for metabolizing medications by enzymes produced in the liver. It's very valuable information for you to have if you ever need medications. And I think, when we get the test results back, we will see that being a slow-metabolizer saved your life. It put you to sleep, and that was all."

Marge remembered having to give him a painkiller with codeine once after his appendix was removed at six years of age. It did no good.

# CHAPTER 55

Dan's release from prison was immediate. Duffy hired two limousines to bring them to Rikers for Dan. He even allowed Samantha Elder to come along with a photographer to cover Dan's release. Dita, along with Violet, Marge, Albert, Marla, and Brett applauded while Dan walked out a free man. Holding a property bag and clutching a stack of staff paper, Dan tumbled into Dita's arms as camcorders rolled.

Dita, holding onto Dan, looked Duffy in the eyes. "I'm inviting Samantha to the party."

"I'm all for that, but she's probably on a deadline."

Samantha promised to come after she got her story into the paper. "I wouldn't miss it."

Dita made a last glance at the Rikers entrance sporting rolls of barbed wire. She tried to banish thoughts of what could have been. After Dita, everyone tried to hug Dan at once.

The celebration took place in Dita and Dan's apartment. The center gardeners provided a feast—platters of grilled zucchini and eggplant, coleslaw and arugula salad. Violet had Amy Ruth's send over fried chicken and waffles, short ribs and salmon cakes. There were the famous layer cakes—the orange coconut and the rich devil's food. Albert brought in a watermelon, and Marge sliced it up on a platter along with fresh pineapple. Earline had made strawberry short cake slathered with fresh whipped cream. Violet had told her not to use the spray whipped cream.

"You don't know what it means to me to be free to eat this meal," Dan said as he helped himself to mozzarella cheese and heirloom tomatoes. "So I'm finally getting those heirlooms, Oliver." Tomato Man grinned from ear to ear.

Duffy supplied a case of champagne and some sparkling apple cider for Dita and Albert who couldn't drink alcohol. Quirk was there, as well, and that man could eat. Dita embraced him. Standing on her tiptoes she barely reached his shoulders. She thought about who she might introduce him too and chided herself for being a yente. Then Dan went over to the piano, raised the keyboard lid, and positioned the staff notebook on the music stand. "I've only heard this in my head," he told his friends. Everyone became very quiet and Dan played his own notes. "I'm calling it The Prison Rag," he said. "It contains the sounds I tried to block out—the clanging of metal, human pain, shuffling, shoving sounds. Sound is a constant companion in a prison. So I thought I'd end the piece in silence. And it isn't over until you listen to the silence." Samantha slipped in the door as Dan was playing.

When Dan finished playing, there was no applause but everyone stood in an ovation until Dan said, "Amen!" Then the laughter resumed.

The party went on until Dita found herself falling asleep. The guests began to gather their things and take leave. For the first time in many weeks, Dan and Dita were alone together.

"I almost lost you," Dan said to Dita. "Duffy filled me in on what you did. Just promise me you'll never do something like that again."

❧❧❧

Dita had begun to look pregnant. The coming baby occupied her thoughts. She took ballet class daily in a leotard stretched to the limits. Three orchestras, including the New York Philharmonic contacted Dan about playing his symphony. The notoriety had helped. He'd become well known. He was asked to score a major film as well.

Duffy called a few weeks later. After some banter, he said, "I had a call from Mort Rothman. He and Mindy wanted to get in touch with you and didn't know how. I suggested we meet up in my office. Are you both free tomorrow?"

Dita laughed. "Are we ever free?" She told Dan what Duffy proposed.

"I think I would like to meet them," Dan said.

The Rothmans were already waiting and sipping coffee when Dita and Dan arrived. When Dita and Dan were seated, Dita asked, "How are your children, Mindy?"

"Thank you for asking about them. They're much better. I simply told them that Arlen wasn't perfect. I know we will have to delve into it more. But for right now it was enough. I think the striving for perfection was what harmed Arlen, and I intend to spare my children any illusions that they need to be perfect, too. How's your pregnancy going?

"At least the morning sickness is done with."

"Do you know the baby's sex?"

"We opted not to know," Dan said.

"Well," Mindy continued. "My father and I have a proposal, that is if you want to go back to running the center again. I mean, I know you'll need to take a maternity leave. I assume you want to work."

"We need me to work," Dita said. "But the center's money is gone."

"Are you willing to work until the baby is born?" Mindy asked.

"Absolutely."

"My father is setting up an endowment for the center. HUD has been repaid for both buildings and the garden plot. So the title is now restored to the center."

"I don't know what to say," Dita said, tearing up. "I don't know how to thank you."

Mort grinned. "If I couldn't make something like this happen, then nothing I've done in my life counts. Money has to count for something higher than us. May God rest Arlen's soul."

Tears streamed down Dita's cheeks. "I'm so overwhelmed. I don't know what to say."

"Just say yes," Mort and Duffy said together.

"We have a commercial tenant for the garden level of the second building. What would you say to a coffee joint? A guy named Nick Alexander came to me for commercial space. Our buildings were too much a square foot," said Rothman. "He's calling his business the Coffee Exchange. It will bring a nice income to the center. And it will be a place to gather. He also intends to exhibit art."

"We have been over to the center a bunch of times now. I needed to see where Arlen died," Mindy said.

"I can understand that," Dan said.

"And I have only one more proposal," Mindy said.

Dita laughed. "We're liking your proposals so much."

"If you need an executive director, I'm yours for a dollar a year."

# CHAPTER 56

Rex made a statement to the police. He admitted killing Arlen, Reverend John, and his wife. He admitted the attempted murder of Albert and Dita. He denied killing Mitchell Shepherd. The coroner found Shepherd's heart to be enlarged and was calling his death one of natural causes. Probably from the stress of finding his money gone.

Rex had confronted Arlen and demanded what he was owed. He'd participated in turning the center windows and fixtures into salvage and was owed a promised cut of that. The pianos had been sold to a dealer in the Bronx for far less than their true value. The dealer was notified that they were stolen property.

Rex went on to relate what happened in his last encounter with Arlen. "He asked me to help him remove the statue. I refused. 'You owe me, man,' I told him. 'It's each man for his own self now,' Arlen said and went down into the basement. He came back with some tools. He barely knew how to use a screwdriver. Some architect! Then he said, 'You made a lot of money through me and all good things come to an end. Tell me you could have made it some other way.' He laughed at me. He'd gotten the statue loose and went back to the basement to put the tools away. I picked up the statue and followed him down the stairs. I was going to keep him from taking the statue unless he cut a check to me. He kept his back to me. He was holding a flashlight on the tool table trying to figure out where things went.

"I asked him again but he said to forget it, he was going to the US Attorney to cut a deal for himself. He said he should have gone fugitive like Callahan, but he shrugged and said his wife would never support him as a fugitive, and he was broke. 'You'd be best to do that, too. Otherwise, you're looking at time, too,' he told me. I brought the statue down on Arlen's head. He never saw it coming. I removed my tool belt, my work shirt, and overalls. They were bloody. I went to the subbasement and opened the grate. I threw the tool belt into the stream with all my tools and my work shirt and closed the gate.

"Then I heard Di Bello calling for Arlen. I had left Becky waiting in the van, and it could get hot in there. I didn't expect to be there so long. It sounded like Di Bello left again. I went upstairs again and prepared to go through the air conditioner opening but then Di Bello returned with a flashlight and began to climb up to the parlor level, and so I tiptoed over to the dumb waiter and waited. He never checked the dumb waiter or I would have had to kill him, too. When Di Bello went to the basement, I went out of the air conditioner hole. I'd done such a good job installing the grate so no one could tell it was gone. I couldn't screw it back in from the outside but it didn't matter. I was out. I went up the fire escape and onto the roof. I waited a while on the building next to that other shell and watched the action on the street. No one was looking up in my direction so I walked back over the roof. I had keys for the skylight to the building next door to the center. I walked out the front door right as the police came and went into the center. No one ever looked my way."

ℰ᷉ℰ᷉

The whirring sound that Dan had heard, Dita surmised was wind coming through the opening when Rex removed the grate. When they returned to the center after she solved the crime, they'd heard it again—wind blowing through the open hole in the outside wall.

The center reopened in time to serve the neighborhood for the fall semester. Mort Rothman had the building fully restored in a matter of weeks. The Exchange opened several days after lessons began. Marge was back on the payroll and the teachers gladly returned to work. Marla called and offered to volunteer three days a week. She was pregnant as well and had taken a leave of absence from her job teaching special education.

Dita was alone in her office. Someone knocked on the doorframe. Randy stood there, "I hope you don't mind my stopping by."

"Come take a seat, Randy," Dita said.

"I wanted to apologize to you."

"There's no need. We were both blind to what was going on."

"No, not about that. I want to apologize for not understanding what the center was and how it needed to operate. I'd like to make it up by learning as a volunteer."

"Welcome aboard," Dita said, shaking her hand.

"I think this would be a good place for my daughter to take lessons, and we can afford to pay for them. Oh, and I don't wear tea roses anymore."

Dita looked a bit sheepish.

Dita and Dan became parents in January and they named their baby girl Violet Marjorie. A good spring name, they thought as they watched the falling snow from the window of the maternity ward.

# About the Author

Sarah Levine Simon enjoyed a dual career as a musician (opera singer) and writer. She appeared as a soloist throughout the United States and Europe, singing difficult soprano repertory, such as Bach Cantata No. 51, Lukas Foss's "Time Cycle," and the lyric soprano operatic repertory. Writing began for the soprano as a way to access the literary texts she sang, and it led to her creating her own narratives. Writing credits include: *Bernardo's Farewell* and *Mouse Music,* stories for actors and orchestra, produced with a grant from The National Endowment for the Arts and narrated by actress Tovah Feldshuh, among others. She wrote two plays on commission for Plays for Living. *The Portrait,* written as a radio play for National Public Radio in 1983, finally received a full production by the Ad Lib Theater Company at Theater 54 in New York City in 2014, to critical acclaim. She wrote, produced, and sang as the "gourmet diva" five musical videos to introduce classical music and have a little fun with it, as well.

In February of 2017, *The Dressmaker's Secret*, a play co-written by Mihai Grunfeld received a full production at Theater 59 in New York City. With *Winged Victory*, she made her debut as a novelist.